A BOND OF DESTINY AND DRAGONS

THE GODDESS AND THE GUARDIANS PREQUEL

KAREN TOMLINSON

Copyright © Karen Tomlinson 2018

It is the right of Karen Tomlinson to be identified as the author of this work.

All rights reserved. With the exception of quotes used in reviews, no part of this publication may be reproduced, stored in a retrieval system, or transmitted, in any form, or by any means (electronic, photocopying, recording, mechanical or otherwise) without prior written permission of the author.

This book is a work of fiction. Names, characters, places, organizations and incidents are either products of the author's imagination or used fictitiously.

Any resemblance to actual events, places, organizations or persons, living or dead, is entirely coincidental.

Cover art by Deranged Doctor Designs https://www.derrangeddoctordesigns.com

Map by Gregory Shipp
https://www.facebook.com/gregoryshippmapmaking/?fref=ts#

Map illustration by Kevin Heasman at
https://www.facebook.com/dynamodoodles/?fref=ts#

Edited by Monica Wanat

for Jenny—
THANK YOU for being an ear to bend,
a shoulder to cry on and the best friend anyone could ask for.

KAREN TOMLINSON

A BOND OF DESTINY AND DRAGONS

THE GODDESS AND THE GUARDIANS
PREQUEL

*When kings and gods fall, a queen will rise.
The game of war is changing, and the destiny of two friends will alter the world forever.*

PROLOGUE

The connection with his sire snapped. Agonising silence echoed where there had once been a bond of love and pride between father and son.

Vaalor released a roar that reverberated through the layers of the Eight Kingdoms. His green and gold-faceted eyes narrowed on the distant peak of the snow-capped volcano. Anger and grief seared his soul; fire burned in his belly, clamouring for release.

Harder he pushed, his powerful wings thudding against the air.

The green and gold of his scales glinted in the unrelenting light of the sun, but for once he did not rejoice in the orb's fierce touch.

Higher and higher he pushed into the blue sky, riding the airstreams until he could peer down upon the entrance to the guardian's lair.

The outline of his brother's black-scaled bulk appeared on the ledge. Red eyes of pure fire and hatred fixed upon Vaalor, burning brightly as the black dragon spewed forth an immense arc of fire.

Vaalor back-winged, holding his position high above. Even so, his brother's flame scorched his scales.

Vaalor snarled, showing rows of razor sharp teeth. He had not fed from the lava for weeks. The fire burning in his belly was only embers, too weak to best his brother's flame.

Sulphurious's voice grated through Vaalor's mind.

Come, brother. Our mother is calling for you. Are you going to fail her as you failed Father? Are you going to leave her to suffer the agony of her wounds before I decide whether to kill her?

Vaalor's blood boiled, but not at his brother's cruel taunts. Narrowing his eyes, he honed in on the devastation of the mountainside.

His father, Zulad, had fought hard. The rocky entrance to the lair had been blown away and scorched by fire. Rubble littered the rocky slope of the volcano beneath the ledge.

Grief ripped through Vaalor as he focused on the outline of his father's crumpled body. His long neck was broken, his head twisted grotesquely at an impossible angle. Eyes that had once been so warm and wise now stared unseeingly at the beautiful land below.

A jagged wound gaped in his father's forehead. Dark streams of blood had congealed on his scales, dull and colourless in death, and stained the ground under his head.

No! The key!

Vaalor's thoughts stumbled, disgust turning his stomach. Sulphurious had fed on the blood of humans. It was the only explanation for his strength, his defeat of the mighty Zulad.

Sulphurious shifted his bulk. Debris skittered from under his talons, tumbling down the steep mountainside to lay against Zulad's body. Sulphurious bared his black teeth.

If it's any consolation, brother, he fought hard. But he always was too soft-hearted. He thought I meant it when I said he could save Mother by sacrificing himself. He was wrong! Sulphurious grinned, drooling acidic saliva from his maw.

With acute hearing, Vaalor heard the saliva sizzle as it hit the ground.

Black scales glinted, reflecting the sunlight as Sulphurious turned and reached his front talons into the dim cave.

Vaalor almost unleashed his fire as he beheld his mother hanging limply in his brother's claws. Blood covered her beautiful purple and gold body.

Vaalor's heart cracked. His mother had never wanted to believe her oldest son capable of the darkness that consumed him. She would have listened to her son's lies, wanting to believe him—both his parents would have.

Sulphurious chuckled, dangling his mother's body over the lip of the lair. More rubble skittered down the slope, the lip of the lair crumbling further under his weight.

Sulphurious, hearing Vaalor's thoughts, agreed. *Oh, she didn't believe in my darkness. She believed I was there to crawl back to them and rescind my allegiance to Erebos. Father was feeding, you see, and she was alone. It was too late when she realised my true intentions. She begged for Father's life. He came quickly enough when I made her scream.*

Nareen lifted her inner lids, exposing her gold-flecked, purple eyes. *Destroy him,* she urged, her voice like a light breeze touching Vaalor's mind. Then it was gone. Vaalor felt her energy fade, drifting from his soul just as his father's had done.

Anger exploded from his heart.

Arching his long neck, Vaalor reared back and fully unfurled his wings, beating them up and down against the invisible force of the wind. Plunging his head down, he dived. He closed his inner lid to protect his eyes, collapsed his wings flat against his now armoured back and pulled his fire up from his belly. It burned his throat, begging for release.

Sulphurious screeched, tossed Nareen's body down the steep slope of the volcano and hurled himself off the ledge.

The two dragons shot towards each other.

Though physically smaller than his brother, Vaalor moved at a far greater speed. Not only was gravity on his side, but his powerful body formed into an arrow—his wings tight against his back and his head, neck and tail in alignment.

Both dragons summoned their fire. Sulphur saturated the air seconds before a ball of flame ignited from their open maws. Orange and red flame engulfed them, but it was the impact of their bodies that shook the Fire Mountains and sent a wave of hot gas and flame exploding outward.

Too close now for fire, Sulphurious flipped over and sunk his teeth into the back of Vaalor's neck.

In turn, Vaalor clamped his jaws down on his brother's front claw. Blood washed over his tongue, running down his throat in metallic streams. He bit down, severing the limb clean off.

Sulphurious yanked his teeth from Vaalor's neck. Screeching in pain, blood splattering Vaalor's scales. The black dragon fell away.

A bank of thick, white clouds hugged the snow-capped summit of the volcano. Without looking back, Sulphurious dived, his black-mirrored bulk heading straight for the cone.

Blood gushed from Vaalor's multiple wounds. Ignoring them, he rolled and headed after his brother. Rage fuelled his movements, his desire for revenge.

You will die for what you did to them, he promised Sulphurious.

A dark chuckle was his brother's only reply.

Vaalor bared his teeth through his scaled lips. Despite that evil chuckle, he could feel his brother's pain. Determination fuelled him, propelling power into his flesh, healing his wounds.

You have learned a new trick, brother, Sulphurious grated.

Vaalor snarled, his brother's blood dripping from his teeth. *You have no idea what I am capable of now,* he hissed.

Sulphurious chuckled darkly, his bulk disappearing into the thick cloud.

Vaalor followed. Close now.

Oh, I don't need to. I was strong enough to kill Father, so I can easily kill you. Together with my lord, we will rule every soul, living or dead. Eter-

nity will be ours. You, brother, are only fit to join our parents. You deserve to die. You are weak, just as your goddess is weak.

Vaalor let his brother rant. It allowed him to sense his brother's presence in the cloud. He did not dwell on the danger he had put his goddess in by coming here. But she was strong and had powerful allies to fight alongside her. *She will be fine*, he told himself.

Steeling his nerve, he let his huge body delve farther into the cloud, bracing his body. When his brother's tail slammed into his side, he was ready. Sulphurious' barbed tail sank deeply into Vaalor's flesh. Agony tore through him, and he roared as Sulphurious ripped it out and swung again, embedding it into Vaalor's side again.

Quickly, the black dragon curved his body around, reaching to gouge out a hole in Vaalor's wings, unaware his vicious move left the base of his tail vulnerable.

Vaalor silently thanked his brother for his ignorance, growling as Sulphurious managed to rip a wound in his left wing before Vaalor could twist it from his brother's reach.

Vaalor swiftly struck. His jaws latched onto his brother, clamping down, biting through those mirror-black scales.

No matter what, he would not let go. But Sulphurious would have to be distracted for this to work.

The black dragon screeched, clawing at Vaalor's back.

Vaalor pushed out more power, his armour simmering under his scales. Keeping his teeth embedded in his brother's flesh, Vaalor allowed his brother to gouge ridges down his body.

Wind and mist rushed by as they spiralled downwards, falling out of the cloud. As they plummeted, a lush valley came into view.

Fighting the wind, Vaalor slashed out, clawing his razor sharp talons along Sulphurious's wing, ripping it to shreds. The damage sent them into a gut-churning spin. Vaalor did not let go. He pushed more power into his jaws and ground his teeth—hard.

Below them a jungle rushed closer.

Sulphurious clawed and bit Vaalor's now-bleeding body, tearing chunks from Vaalor's flesh. His brother was becoming desperate. As agony burned through his flesh, Vaalor made no sound. He could not release his brother's body. The only thing he could do was grind his jaws harder. His brother's blood gushed between his teeth and over his tongue. Vaalor blocked the pain as his flesh was ripped again and again, thinking only of his mother's last command.

Destroy him.

Hoping his judgment was correct, Vaalor looked down. Forcing his power to obey, he pushed. Blood loss made him weak, but he ignored that weakness and commanded his body.

Armour clattered across his scales, and the tough membranes of his wings instantly healed. Vaalor flipped them over, ripped his jaws from Sulphurious's tail and then, in two calculated swipes, shredded Sulphurious's other wing completely.

The black dragon rolled his eyes towards his brother in horror as he spun into an uncontrolled fall, the weight of his body dragging him toward the earth.

Vaalor dived and slammed his claws into his brother's orange belly, digging in through scales and leathery flesh. The satisfaction of his brother's agonised roar was like balm to his broken heart.

I will avenge you, he promised his parents, digging his claws in harder and curling his talons.

Blood from Sulphurious's wounds sprayed into the wind. Vaalor snarled, blinking and snorting it from his eyes and nostrils.

Beating his wings with more force than he had ever used before, Vaalor drove them downwards. His mind was consumed with hate as he stabbed his talons in and out, over and over again, making it impossible for his brother to heal himself.

The impact of the two guardians into the ground was colossal.

Energy exploded outwards, sending a wall of debris, earth and rock to decimate the lush valley.

Vaalor slammed into his brother's body.

Bone cracked and snapped.

Flesh ripped and burst.

Vaalor's talons were wrenched from his brother's flesh. Giving himself no time to recover, for he knew even this impact would not stop the black dragon, he latched his jaws to the underside of his brother's neck. With a muffled roar, he clamped down. Sulphurious slashed with claws and tail, recovering more quickly than Vaalor had thought possible.

Rivers of blood spilled from them both, turning the scorched ground red.

Sulphurious spewed fire from his jaws, trying to blind Vaalor.

Vaalor snarled and clamped down, sending his power into his jaws as he had learned to do.

The fire abruptly stopped.

Sulphurious squealed in agony.

With one mighty swing of his golden-horned head, Vaalor wrenched his jaws backwards.

Blood spewed from his brother's severed neck in a gruesome fountain.

Vaalor's body shuddered at the taste and feel of his brother's flesh and bone. He tossed his grisly prize aside.

The horned head thudded against the ground, rolled, then stilled.

Vaalor did not hear it or see it. His roar of grief and anger shook the very foundations of the great fire mountain, drowning out all other sound.

I have destroyed him, Mother. Be at peace, Father. May our brethren guide your spirits home, he prayed.

The sun glared down upon the distraught green and gold dragon. He hung his head for a moment, allowing the sun's warmth to bathe his weakened body. Shaking himself, Vaalor made to step away from the evil that was his brother when something snagged his attention. Sucking his armour into his body, Vaalor stomped toward the tightly clamped claw of his brother's hind leg. Hooking it with a talon he pulled it open.

The keys!

Then his heart sank. His mother's key lay in two pieces, glinting back at him with the malevolence of Sulphurious's eyes.

Reaching out, he scooped them up. Power rippled through his body as he touched them. Gripping the keys tightly, he stepped back, out of his brother's blood.

Elongated pupils flickered as he beheld the remains of the black dragon. He would not leave this evil here to contaminate the land. Vaalor forced a bubble of gas up from his belly. As it mixed with his saliva, heat rushed up his throat.

Opening his jaws, the last guardian of the goddess unleashed his flames upon his brother's ravaged corpse.

I hope you suffer in the darkness and ice of Chaos for all you have done, he cursed, then watched with satisfaction as the black dragon burned.

CHAPTER 1

GRIANA

Griana unlocked her fangs from her soldier's throat and released him back into battle.

The clash of steel and the clatter of armoured wings proclaimed the collision of the two armies. The air rattled and magic exploded—the thunderous bursts drowned out the roar of battle between the warrior fae and the monsters of the Chaos realm.

Ruby red blood stained the snow. The new General of King Arjuno's army inhaled the metallic stench. It filled Griana's nostrils but, unlike many fae, she relished it.

At twenty-five, she was not old in fae terms. However, Griana had spent years orchestrating this moment—ever since the Goddess of Creation had taken an interest in the heir to the Avalonian throne. Griana was determined to prove her strength and fighting prowess, especially now she had inherited her new position from her father. This was the beginning of her destiny.

With a sword in each hand, she ducked and spun underneath the clumsy attack of a rotting Dust Devil. With a swift strike, she embedded one blade in its abdomen before decapitating it with the other. As its body exploded into a cloud of black dust, she spun and sank one blade into the belly of the nearest fae warrior. Blood sprayed, his screams lost to the din of war.

Sacrificing her own kind was a small price to pay for earning her chance at immortality.

Around her more fae fell to the swords of their brethren.

Once this battle was won, Griana would become a valuable ally of Erebos, the Lord of Souls and creator of the Chaos realm. No longer would he be her enemy but her sole deity—a power worthy of her devotion.

Erebos had amassed his army of the dead in the depths of the Endless Forests, uncharted lands believed to be thick with monstrous creatures and vicious faerie. No Avalonian ventured there for fear of what they might find.

It had been nearly seventeen years since Erebos had last launched a major offensive against any of the Eight Kingdoms. He had all but disappeared after being defeated by his sister, Lunaria, the Goddess of Creation. No one really knew where, but tales of entire forest villages being wiped out, of having no remains of the dead, had been surfacing for years. There were sightings of Erebos in the frozen north where he was said to be abetting the Ice Witches; in the Barren Lands in the south, where tales raged of him trying to free his incarcerated wraith commander. Others said the dark god had returned to Chaos and that these attacks had nothing to do with him.

Griana smiled. She knew it was Erebos. He planned his attacks carefully, sometimes leaving years or sometimes only days in between them.

For months now, Erebos had been regularly attacking the bigger Avalonian towns, orchestrating the attacks to draw the king northward. She knew that her lord did not seek to triumph over the Avalonian army in this current battle, but rather acquire the dead to reinforce his army and take their souls to strengthen himself.

Indeed, Griana knew the true numbers of rotting corpses and

monstrous creatures in Erebos's army far outweighed the ranks of fae warriors she had brought with her to this battle. Her men would triumph today, for only a fraction of the dark god's forces had been sent to this battle.

Breathing hard, Griana glanced around at the carnage of slain fae and the ash-like remains of the Dust Devils. *This is just the beginning of the end for Lunaria.* A grin twisted her perfect features. *Soon she will lose her war with her brother—and everything she holds dear.*

Lunaria was expecting her child in less than a month, which gave Griana over a week to fly the remains of her army back to Valentia and convince Lunaria and Noan of the need to fight Erebos without waiting for reinforcements from the other kingdoms to arrive.

They would believe her—or at least Noan would.

In truth, Erebos was clamouring to bring war back to his sister and the fae kingdom that harboured her. This battle on the northern borders of the Ancient Forest was far enough away from the city of Valentia to begin Griana's plans.

A satisfied smirk curled her lips. This battle was not about reinforcing Erebos's army—and definitely not about saving this pathetic excuse for a market town. No, the slice of her blade across the throat of yet another fae was about something far greater.

Power.

Revenge.

Hate.

They all had a place in her immortal future.

Besides, she thought, smug in her own self-belief, *every great shift of power throughout history started somewhere; this time it starts with betrayal.*

With a malicious glint in her green eyes, Griana watched the King of Avalonia fighting his own men. No sun, no heat had made the red fae vulnerable, but even this experienced king had listened to her advice about fighting the Lord of Souls before he got too close to Valentia.

Gathering her magic, she sent an onslaught barrelling into her red-winged king. Totally unprepared to defend himself from such a close magical attack, it propelled him sideways just as she bid one of his attackers to slice his wing where it met his body.

A scream rent the air.

Before her king could recover, Griana attacked again, this time sending him stumbling. With one wing hanging half-cleaved from his back, he was unbalanced and vulnerable. Seizing her chance, she thrust her power into his flesh and bones, finding that special place in his soul where his magic existed. Fighting past his weakening defences, she wrapped her own magic around that centre. She mercilessly ripped it from him and propelled it inward, fusing it with her own power.

Her face tipped to the sky, her lungs expanding as she felt that new power course through her own flesh and bones. Her eyes snapped open, watching King Arjuno fall to his knees, wounded and bleeding. As a smirk curled her shapely lips, particles of foul black dust blew into her mouth.

She grimaced.

Urgh! Why do my lord's soldiers have to make such a mess when they die? she thought with distaste.

Piles of black dust, remnants of the soulless creatures, littered the forest floor. She felt no sorrow for the Dust Devils. Whether once fae, human or monster, they were now the fodder of nightmares, their flesh reduced to a rotting shell. But in a twist even Erebos had not foreseen, when he devoured their souls, it gave them the ability to use the dirt under their feet to turn into columns of swirling dust. The dry earth made them fast and deadly.

Griana snorted. The damp and snow-covered ground of a forest, however, was of no use to them. The Dust Devils were only rotting, soulless corpses in this forest.

My lord Erebos will forgive me for destroying a few of his soldiers when I eventually lure his sister to his trap.

Unable to stomach their dusty remains near her mouth, she swiped the back of her gloved hand over her lips, then wished she hadn't bothered. Such a move only smeared the blood of her own people over her mouth. It wasn't that she disliked it; quite the opposite, in fact. Her tongue flicked out to savour the metallic sweetness, sending a shudder of pleasure vibrating through the fibres of her rejuvenated body. Fae blood—or rather, the magic that laced it—was her salvation. It would always heal her and always keep her young.

She didn't bother to hide her satisfaction. Immortality. A gift from her lord in return for his sister and access to the souls of the Eight Kingdoms.

Her attention returned to the guards as they pulled back to form a ring around her and the fallen king.

Griana stalked forwards.

Time was hers now. A laugh bubbled up her throat, exhilarated by being immortal and planning the demise of her enemies.

She rested her attention upon the dirt and blood that streaked the face of the male in front of her. Her monarch. On his knees —before her.

Horror and fear bloomed, his brown eyes widening as he recognised her glee.

Griana cocked her head, her eyes glittering in contempt. *Why do Avalonian males all look so similar?* she wondered. *Handsome, as fae males mostly are, but so boring; brown hair, brown eyes...only their wings and markings differ. Of course, Noan and Lexon are beautiful exceptions, their eyes being such a deep sapphire blue and their hair so dark.* Griana snarled. Even so, they were not pure Avalonians. Their looks were courtesy of their dead mother, who had been a princess of some far off land across the Rough Sea.

"How could you do this, Griana? Kill your own kind? You are

sworn to protect the monarchy and the people of this land," the Avalonian king croaked.

"Oh please, I *am* protecting the monarchy—my monarchy," she drawled in reply.

"Please. Please don't hurt my sons. They trust you..." he pleaded, the whites of his eyes visible.

A snake's smile curled Griana's lips. She cocked her head, listening to the sound of the ongoing battle. It raged somewhere through the trees, but it was not visible. The forest here was thick with firs and red-leafed Lyca trees. This was the perfect spot, especially as the canopy made it hard for aerial troops to see the battle below. Indeed, it was going to be easy to hide the demise of this king from any of his loyal warriors.

"Oh, I know they do, your majesty. But don't worry your royal head about them. At least one of them will survive. After all, I will need a king by my side—or at least in my bed," she shrugged, "for a time."

She prowled around the fallen monarch. Under her feet, her boots squelched through the thick, mud-like mixture of the remains of Dust Devils and the blood of the slain fae. Griana paid it no mind, focused entirely on the pleasure of this moment. Power surged through her blood, and she welcomed her magic.

Around her, most of the fae warriors looked on in horror, but some were utterly still, their eyes dark and stormy. There was nothing any of these powerful warriors could do to defy her. Whether she had recently bitten them to inject them with her venom or enslaved them months ago, they were all equally her slaves. Her will was theirs.

Griana completed circling her prey. Once again standing before her king, she made sure to remain out of his reach even though he was on his knees with bleeding wounds. The fae king was an experienced and vicious fighter, and he knew he was about to die.

Which always makes people desperate, she reflected.

"Be pleased your bloodline will continue, my king. I will make sure that my child, your grandchild, will rule Avalonia long after you and your sons are gone," she told him.

Using her mind, she bade two of the king's guard to come forward. They obeyed. With fear and confusion in their eyes, they reached his side. One kicked the king's wounded wing as the other pulled the king's sword from his weak fingers.

Through the venom bond, Griana bid that warrior to discard the king's blade, then both grasped their monarch's arms, holding him in place.

Sheathing her own blade, Griana bent down and wrapped her gloved hands around the pommel of a rusty, blood-covered sword. Lifting it from the ground, she cocked her head and smiled.

Iron. A fitting blade for this task.

"You know, my father did not beg for his life. He did beg for yours, though. Of course, I told him that was completely pointless. But he insisted. It was fun to hear him plead, to see him on his knees before me after all those years of being made to feel so inadequate for being born a female, instead of being the son he always desired." Her beautiful features twisted into an ugly mask. "He thought me weak. Pearl-winged fae are always kind and gentle, he often told me as a child," she scoffed. "All except me. Unfortunately for my father, he only realised that too late. But I am a pearl wing no more. Look, I can armour my wings, thanks to your magic." She extended her once gauzy wings behind her, enjoying the feeling as she stretched the feather-covered membranes. Pushing magic into them, they became armoured gold.

The king's general adjusted her stance to better grip the rusty pommel of the sword.

The fallen king's eyes glistened, his face pallid and etched with pain.

"My lord grows impatient for revenge on his sister, and I want the kingdom that should be mine. I deserve to have it for all the effort I have put into serving you, for all the battles I helped you and my father win, for keeping your son and heir safe, when all you have done is bring that silver-haired whore here to take my love and this throne away from me." Griana's eyes flashed malevolently. "But I will have this city and I will have one of your sons. If Noan fights me, if he refuses me, Lexon will give me what I want. His red magic will soon be far stronger than his brother's. A child from him will do well as an heir, don't you agree? Oh, don't looked so horrified, Majesty. You love your sons, and I'm sure you agree one of them deserves to live and even rule by my side, and neither can do that whilst your immortal self is still around. So you have to go," she smiled and shrugged.

"You're mad," panted the king. "My sons will see through you. They will work out what you have done and strike you down—"

"Mad?" interrupted Griana. She chuckled coldly. "Maybe I am, but with the magic that the goddess bestowed upon the fae of this world, I can live forever; and I will kill every red and green-winged fae in this kingdom—and every other fae too, if I have to —to do it."

The king growled and thrashed against his captors. "You cannot do this. Those fae are innocent! My sons are innocent; they have never harmed you or ridiculed you!"

"Oh, I know. But all those innocents will soon be my people, so I can do as I please," she sneered, her eyes glinting with excitement for the dreams of her future.

"Help me!" the king yelled to his warriors. None of them moved. He tried again. "Help me. Do not follow this mad female. She will lead you to death! The only thing she offers is an eternity of shadow and pain!" Nothing. No defence came from his personal guard, his most trusted warriors. "You traitors!" he bellowed. "My sons will avenge me, and they will not be merciful. You will all die!"

They only stared at him, some blankly as if lifeless, while others were rooted to the spot, their eyes wide with panic.

Griana laughed, hinting at the reason for their compliance.

"You've bitten them," the king whispered, sweat trickling from his brow into his horrified eyes. "But no one has that trait anymore."

"And that is why you do not deserve to be king. You are a fool for believing such rumours. *I* hold this unique fae gift. I was born with it. And these warriors are now mine. When you are nothing but a rotting corpse and serve in my lord's army, whilst you kill your own people, I will find Noan and I will make him mine too. He will serve *me*, not this land or that simpering goddess. Once I have your son's seed growing in my belly, he will die. Soon all the pieces will be in place and my Lord Erebos will strike his sister down. And once Erebos is by my side and darkness reigns, we will raze Valentia to the ground and rebuild it with the strength and darkness of his magic. This whole world will quake at his name, and the Eight Kingdoms will be ours to rule."

"Erebos will not rule with you. He will take what he wants, use you and crush you. He will destroy this whole world with you in it, before he moves on to the next," the king whispered.

Griana, his young and trusted general, just laughed. "I don't care, because I will not be in this world when that happens. Goodbye, your majesty," she purred, then as fast as a serpent, she struck.

CHAPTER 2

ERZION

"No, Mother, I will not leave him. He is my friend. Besides, she is not here, so..."

"So what, Erzion? Griana is wicked, and she will control Noan, or even Lexon, in the end. Females like that will not be spurned and forgotten. She is planning something evil, mark my words," Erzion's mother predicted.

"All the more reason to stay here with Noan—to protect him and Lexon," he answered patiently.

"Erzion, you are my son. I love you, and I will not stand by whilst she drives a dagger into your back. You and young Lexon are in her way, almost as much as Lunaria is—may Vaalor protect her," she added quickly, and dipped her head in a gesture of respect to the goddess and the great dragon who was her guardian.

Erzion smirked at his mother. "Griana can hardly believe we are competition for Lunaria, Mother," he said, waggling his eyebrows. "Noan has always preferred females to males."

Despite her worry for her son, Mariel Riddeon chuckled.

Fae were not bound to love or mate with a specific gender. They went where their heart and their feral nature took them.

"You know what I mean, you wicked child," she scolded, her golden eyes twinkling.

Erzion took his mother's hand. Her skin was soft under his calloused, warrior's fingers. Becoming serious once again, he replied, "I do know, Mother. It's true—Griana wants Noan, and it has nothing to do with love. I can't leave my friends just because she may try and harm me. Besides, what else would I do? I am a warrior. I serve Prince Lexon and his brother, just as his father ordered me to. I will not betray that vow and leave because of one spoilt female."

Mariel sighed and looked at her son with a mixture of pride and anxiety. The beautiful rainbow colours of her fae wings shimmered as they trembled.

Erzion frowned at this obvious sign of his mother's distress. Pearlescent-winged fae were the most emotional of their race, often feeling extremes that were difficult to hide.

"Mother, I am not a child anymore. Do not fear for me. I can look after myself," he tried to reassure her. His heart constricted; he hated to see his mother upset.

"I know that, Erzion, but she is clever and cunning—"

"So am I. But more than that, we both know Noan's heart belongs completely to the goddess. There is no way Griana will win him now."

"That is what worries me. When she realises that she does not stand a chance of ever winning his heart or this kingdom, Griana is going to kill you all in vengeance. And she will happily destroy this city along with you."

"No, Mother, she won't. She will try, but I will be ready for her. Lexon and I have both been training our magic. We are young but still stronger than she—or even Noan—realises."

Mariel pushed up from her stool, the skirts of her gown rustling as she went to look out of the leaded tower window. Sunlight illuminated the russet highlights of her chestnut hair, making it seem more red than brown.

"Lexon is but an awkward boy," she murmured, her breath steaming up the diamond panes of glass. "He is not strong enough to fight her, even if you are."

Erzion inhaled, managing to stop his sigh. He loved the flowery scent of his mother's room. It always calmed him, just as it had as a child. Even as winter approached, she always had a vase of colourful blooms somewhere, filling the air with their perfume. Absentmindedly, he glanced around Mariel's chambers. As befitted a companion to the goddess, they were spacious and luxurious. He brushed his fingers over the silken threads of one of the beautiful tapestries. He loved the works of art, depicting the forest and sea, that hung over the walls of her sitting room.

Erzion glanced over his mother's head and out of the window to view the city slopes, a large ornate bridge and the valley beyond. He was still in awe of this huge tower—was still frightened, even after living in it all of his life, that it may just crumble to the ground.

The goddess had constructed this tower from stone and magic nearly a hundred years earlier, and she always returned here, no matter where in the Eight Kingdoms she fought her brother. The tower was the tallest structure in this kingdom or the next; only the great marble wall that protected the Rift Valley was comparable. The wall sat upon the sheer cliff edge, protecting the forest valley from invasion by land, while this tower stood as the pinnacle of the island city.

Erzion, Noan and Lexon had been children when the goddess had returned to Valentia seventeen years ago at the side of King Arjuno. Noan had been seven, Erzion four and Lexon a babe in arms.

Erzion's memory was somewhat hazy of that time, but he remembered Lunaria had called a gathering. She had bade all the rulers of all the disparate kingdoms to travel to Valentia. As crown prince, Noan had been expected to be by his father's side, to observe and to learn.

Until that meeting, many of the kingdoms, especially those across the rough seas, had fought among themselves—for land or power or both.

He had learned from Noan after the meeting that Lunaria had called for peace among the kingdoms, and that she had threatened to take away the gift of immortality from any ruler who did not agree to honour the treaty to keep the recently imprisoned Wraith Lord, Ragor, in the Barren Lands in the far south.

Mariel glanced over her shoulder at Erzion, her arms crossed over her chest. She folded her wings tight to her back. "You know, Vaalor will keep both Lunaria and Prince Noan safe. You could still leave. Go far from here and find your father."

Erzion snorted. "To what end? He has never acknowledged me —or you. I don't need him. I have never needed him. And like I said before, I am not leaving my friends, my responsibilities to my homeland—or you." With a shove of his broad shoulders, Erzion pushed off the wall and strode forward. He gently grasped his mother's arms. She was so small—small and gentle and intuitive. Deep down he knew she was right. Griana would raze this city to the ground before she let Lunaria push her from her goal of becoming queen. Her vindictiveness knew no bounds.

He wrapped his arms carefully around Mariel, not wanting to crush her delicate wings. Erzion had always envied pearlescent-winged fae their peaceful and kind ways. That is, all pearls except Griana.

Erzion frowned. The former Primary General, Griana's father, had died in battle only weeks ago, and Griana had not seemed to mourn his loss at all. If anything, she was revelling in her newfound position of power.

The majority of warrior fae were male, not for any other reason than most female fae were born as pearls and could not armour. Red-winged fae, even half-breeds like him, were by far the most powerful, harnessing the heat from the sun and the energy of light to boost their power.

Being half wizard, Erzion was even more powerful than most reds. He hadn't thought that part of his heritage would make much difference to him, but the old wizard who had become his mentor had taught him to think differently. Master Yagus had been living in Valentia for years. He had been the only one who understood Erzion's power.

A smile curled Erzion's lips.

Master Yagus was a kind, if somewhat wily, old man who just wanted to be left in peace by the rest of the world.

Erzion had never met any other wizards. However, if they were all as powerful as Master Yagus, he was glad his king was in negotiations with the High Wizard of the Southern Hotlands to form an alliance between the wizards and the fae.

A frown creased his brow. Lunaria had fought alongside the wizards before, but their alliance was currently weak. After the last vicious battle with her brother, she had declined the High Wizard's proposal to take him as her mate. "Besides, if negotiations go well with the wizards, the other kingdoms, even Houria, may ally their forces with Avalonia too. That will mean both kingdoms sending a force over very soon. And if King Oden agrees to bring the Combined Army to fight with us too, this war will be over before it starts."

The army that had defeated Erebos seventeen years ago had been a collaborative force of all the Eight Kingdoms. When Erebos had turned Sulphurious against his parents, it had resulted in a long and bloody war. Battles had raged across the kingdom of Gar Anon, leaving its interior a barren desert. It had been the wizards and the red-winged fae who had made the difference in the last battle.

They could defeat Erebos once again—Erzion was sure of it—but the king hadn't yet returned from this latest battle. It could be weeks, months even, before treaties were signed and armies mobilised.

Erzion swallowed hard, dread squeezing his heart.

"Let's hope it won't be too late for us all, by then," his mother said, echoing his own thoughts.

"Even if we have to fight alone, I will not run. I will harness the power and the heat of the sun, just like other red fae. And I am learning to combine my spells with my red magic, just like the reds and the wizards did to defeat Erebos in Gar Anon. I can turn Erebos's monsters to dust, just like they did."

"I know you are powerful, Erzion. But as much as you are, you are still young. We need numbers, not just powerful individuals," his mother sighed. "I, for one, do not want to end up thrown into the dark and frozen world of Chaos."

A shudder rippled through Erzion. Like many red fae, Erzion hated the darkness and the cold. He was suddenly glad of having a wizard for his mentor. The wizard was teaching him how to become as powerful as the red fae and the wizards combined, and Erzion was well aware of the powerful spells Master Yagus could wield. The years Erzion and Lexon had spent training with the wizard in the subterranean tunnels of this island city had proven that, but it was not just his power but his complete control that Erzion envied.

"Erzion, your wings," his mother whispered.

Erzion gave a start and snorted, berating his lapse in concentration that caused his wings to glow a hazy red.

He quickly forced his magic into obedience, and his wings soon shimmered gold again. Disguising his wings came naturally, unless he was totally relaxed and in the company of those he trusted—or he became very distracted.

His mother looked back out over the distant valley.

Erzion smiled at her lovely silhouette and wondered why his young and beautiful mother had never taken a mate. She had been a girl of fourteen when the High Wizard's emissary had forced his attentions upon her. Erzion knew King Arjuno had sent the emissary away as soon as Mariel had confided about her ordeal to a senior maid. The maid had been outraged enough to tell the queen.

Like the fae, wizards were sometimes unable to control their more feral urges—particularly fae males who were reaching the mating urge. At around eighteen years old, the time when their magic surged, they made the transition from adolescence to maturity. That transition was when most fae had to learn to control themselves and their bodies. Some managed it better than others.

Erzion was still fighting his more feral urges. Every time he was attracted to another, male or female, and they did not reciprocate, he had to force himself to walk away. He would never behave like his father. He would never force another to lay with him, let alone abandon a female pregnant with his child.

Avalonian society was accepting of the need to mate physically outside the constraints of any bonds or mating vows. All males experienced the same thing; females did as well, but to a much lesser extent. The mating urge lasted anywhere from a few months up to a few years. Some fae found a lifemate in that time, others just used it as an excuse to bed as many partners as they could.

Unfortunately, there were those fae who became feral with need and had to be subdued or locked away for everyone safety, including their own. Sometimes the inherent wild nature of their ancestors, the forest fae, took over. It had been thousands of years since the forest fae had begun living in cities, but their wildness was still in Avalonian blood, and sometimes it won.

Erzion leaned forward and kissed the top of his mother's head. A few errant strands of her wavy hair tickled his nose. He pulled away, rubbing at his face. It hurt his heart to see his mother so anxious for him. He had hoped she would find a mate, someone not only to love her but who she could love too; this hope had increased as his responsibilities took him farther afield.

Being sworn to serve as Prince Lexon's personal guard was

not a chore. Erzion loved his friend and would gladly die for him, but he knew his mother would not allow herself to mate unless she let him go.

Erzion stared out over his mother's petite form. In the distance, the wall shone like a gleaming snake, its long form winding gracefully round the distant cliff about thirty miles away. The forest-covered the valley like an emerald carpet, broken only by the small areas that had been cleared for farming.

"Erzion? If you are going to stay in this city and be the honourable fool, when are you going to find a mate and give me more children to love?" his mother asked, a smile in her eyes now.

"Mother, if you want more children to love, have your own. I could do with some brothers and sisters to bully."

"Ha! No one wants an old lady like me."

"Rubbish! You are not old. Besides, Garnald wants you, and he does not bother to hide it either," Erzion joked, laughing as his mother flushed crimson.

"That green-winged oaf needs to work harder to win me then," she returned haughtily, sticking her nose in the air.

"Mother, what do you want him to do? He already jumps to do your bidding. You run the poor sap ragged. Short of sweeping you off your feet and claiming you as his mate, I'm not sure what else he can do to win your favour."

Mariel just looked at her son then looked at the floor slightly sheepishly.

Erzion barked a laugh. "Oh, I see. Mother, if that's what you want, you need to tell him, or at least be more obvious about it. He's filled this room with flowers. He worships the ground you walk on. It's obvious how much he wants you, but he would never push you because he knows what my father did to you. He is waiting for you to show him you want him—"

"I will," interrupted Mariel. Her throat bobbed and her eyes turned bright with tears. "But what if he rejects me? I am older than him, and I am...used."

"Oh, Mother, stop it! You are only two years older than him. And never talk like that about yourself. My father was a bastard, and he left you with me. That was not your fault, and Garnald does not care. Do you think any other fae male cares if his chosen mate is not untouched? Love is unconditional, Mother; you taught me that—so practise what you preach and give him a chance. He has loved you for years. Besides, I told him I would break his jaw if he hurt you."

Erzion grinned at his mother's wide-eyed expression.

A heavy knock sounded at the door, and his mother flushed as Garnald's voice carried through the thick oak. "Mariel? Are you ready?"

Erzion cocked a brow at his mother, who smiled. "Well, I am a wise teacher," she agreed, then looked mischievously at Erzion, her cheeks rosy. "Don't call on me for a few days...I might just be a little busy."

Erzion grinned and placed his mother's cloak around her shoulders.

"Coming, Garnald!" she called.

Erzion held her close for a moment.

"Life is too short to spend it alone, Mother, and he is a good male. He will take care of you if anything happens to me."

"I know," she said softly and hugged him back. "Gods, when did you become older and wiser than me?" she questioned ruefully. "I love you," she said and sniffed, hiding her face as she walked for the door. She yanked it open. "Don't let her destroy you," she warned with a parting smile and stepped out, closing it softly behind her.

"I won't, Mother," he whispered to the empty room. *I have far more patience than that evil female does. Griana will make her move. If I cannot stop her, and the king or Noan—or even Lexon—fall to her cunning and wrath, I will avenge them, no matter how long it takes.*

CHAPTER 3

LEXON

"When did the news arrive?" Noan asked, grief etching the contours of his face.

Lexon loved his older brother dearly, and right now it crushed him to see Noan so broken. Lexon swallowed the lump in his throat. His brother was king now. Their father, the ruler of the fae lands, had perished.

Nausea rolled in Lexon's belly. He grieved too, but he hadn't known their father, not like Noan had. Being first in line to the throne had meant Noan went everywhere with their father. Lexon had princely responsibilities, but not like his brother's.

Duty. Power. Authority.

He shuddered. Right now, he was glad of being second in line.

Noan is king. Noan is king.

Saying it again and again, even in his head, made it more real. Lexon shook off the sense of foreboding that filled him, making his chest heavy. Being king, and the fact that he was Lunaria's mate, meant Noan was the next target for the approaching Lord of Souls.

Taking a shaky breath, Lexon tried to control his voice. "Only a few moments ago," he replied to Noan's question. "Griana sent a messenger with the news. She is on her way back and will be here by dawn tomorrow."

Noan puffed out his cheeks. "Good," he exhaled. "At least Griana still lives. Who is this messenger?" he added suspiciously, narrowing his green eyes.

Lexon understood Noan's hidden question, wondering if the messenger could be trusted, yet hoping he could be mistaken. Lexon chose to remain quiet, unsure how to answer his brother's question. He didn't know.

"He is a red, part of the king's guard, Majesty. I would suggest he is trustworthy, if only because of that," Erzion replied.

Of course, why couldn't I see that too? Lexon looked at the floor, his inadequacy burning across his cheeks before he could meet his friend's eyes.

"So there is no doubt then?" questioned Noan, his attention shifting briefly to Erzion before returning to Lexon.

At nearly eighteen, Lexon was still lanky and under-confident. It was true his temper was as fiery as any other red-wing, but it scared him. His father had wielded his own red magic and temper often enough, and Lexon had no desire to be as volatile as his father had been. He hid his temper from everyone except Erzion and their red-winged warriors.

Noan, however, was a green-wing. He wasn't weak by any means, but Lexon knew his brother well. The paleness of his skin, the slight shake of his hand—they gave his brother away. Noan had never wanted to be king. He had secretly confided in Lexon when they were both still young boys. Gods, Noan was never happier than when he created, rather than destroyed. A desire he shared with the beautiful goddess, who now stood silently by his side.

"No," Lexon answered firmly with a shake of his head.

"So it's true. But how could Father fall? Nothing—no one could ever get close to him in battle. He was too strong—too powerful, and his guards were always with him." Noan's face fell, his eyes glistening with tears, his throat bobbing.

Lexon frowned, his own breath catching in his throat. He knew his brother did not want this, but he *had* to pull himself together, he *had* to lead them—someone did. And it couldn't be Lexon. He would be useless as a king. The thought of what could happen—not just to the kingdom but to his own life—if Noan fell apart knotted Lexon's stomach, though he pushed those fears aside and squared his shoulders.

"I don't know, brother, but he is gone. You are now king. You must lead us, both your army and your people, against the Lord of Souls. Only then can we defeat him," said Lexon, his voice stronger than he had thought he could manage. From the corner of his eye he caught the approving look Erzion sent him.

The brothers locked eyes. Grief and fear made Noan's normally sapphire eyes turn a bright vivid green as his magic responded to his mood.

Noan swallowed hard, his shoulders squaring, if only a little.

They knew each other well. Lexon gave Noan an encouraging smile.

Noan took a breath, nodded in what could have been thanks or understanding, and turned to Lunaria.

Lunaria gazed back at him, her bright blue eyes steady and her head tilted to one side. It was as if she could read Noan's tumultuous thoughts as she interlaced her slim fingers with her mate's. The tension in Noan seemed to dissolve immediately.

"I will be by your side," she said gently. "We will fight Erebos together, and we will beat him—together," she told Noan, her voice soft but laced with such belief and resolve that even Lexon straightened.

As if in answer to her words, an ear-splitting roar resounded into the sky. The palace tower shook. Heat poured in through the open balcony windows, bathing them all.

Despite being red and not fearing flame or heat, Lexon did his best not to cringe. The mighty green and gold dragon never failed to unnerve him. Such power—and teeth—in one beast was frightening. Not to mention the way his eyes always seemed to look right through to one's very soul, as if he could see someone's worst weakness, no matter how one tried to hide it.

Though...

Licking his lips, Lexon caught Erzion's eye. Vaalor's fire was not as fierce as it should be. He had delayed his return to the Fire Mountains, wanting to wait until the king returned. It was clear now that Vaalor needed to feed from the rivers of molten rock to replenish his flame, but he would not leave his goddess.

Biting his lip, Lexon lowered his eyes. He did not want to voice his thoughts about Vaalor and cause more problems for his brother, but he didn't want to put their people at more risk either by ignoring the guardian's weakness.

Noan straightened his shoulders, frowned and looked out of the balcony doors into the sky beyond.

Lexon willed Noan to voice those very same thoughts. Surely he would have noticed. Lexon hoped Erzion or one of the others would say it instead. Lunaria was a goddess. She might be honour bound to send Vaalor to feed on the lava flow if it meant his weakness put so many innocents at risk.

Their father had refused to use Vaalor, Lunaria's last guardian, in this battle. He had been determined to preserve what he called *'the last hope of Lunaria.'* His father believed if the unthinkable happened and they lost Avalonia to Erebos, Vaalor was Lunaria's only hope of escape. Perhaps the late king had been right. Vaalor may be the only way to get the goddess far enough away from danger to fight again with new allies, should Valentia fall.

Lexon looked at Lunaria's swollen belly, then shuddered, unable to help himself.

Surely the baby can't grow much more? There isn't any room left, he thought with genuine concern.

How females didn't burst during pregnancy was a mystery to

him. He really didn't understand why they would want to put themselves through such an ordeal, especially when the baby stole its mother's magic towards the end.

Lexon scowled at Lunaria's belly.

Like with Vaalor, no one had voiced their thoughts, but they all knew Erebos was attacking now because Lunaria was weak.

If that child wasn't about to be born, our people wouldn't be in such danger, Lexon thought bitterly, even though he knew he was being unfair.

Lunaria raised a hand and placed her palm on Noan's cheek. He turned his face into her touch. "I am not leaving here, and I am not leaving you—no matter what," she said, then turned her cerulean gaze upon Lexon.

Lexon bowed his head before raising his eyes. He worked hard at holding that immortal gaze. He did not lower his eyes and neither did Erzion, who stood strong and watchful at Lexon's side.

The goddess was a powerful but benevolent presence. Lexon adored her, as the deity she was, and the female who had chosen to give her heart to his brother.

Vaalor gave a high pitched screech of agreement at his goddess's words. Lexon flinched. Beside him, Erzion snorted.

Lexon glared at his friend, trying to stop the flush that now heated his cheeks. Erzion would tease him relentlessly later. He knew how much Lexon hated being near the dragon. He found it hilarious. Lexon didn't understand his fear either. As far as he knew, Vaalor had never harmed a fae, which made his irrational feelings all the more embarrassing.

"Perhaps now would be a good time to reconsider my offer, my love," Lunaria asked her mate, her face hopeful.

Unconsciously, Lexon fisted his hands, his spine stiffening; not at her words but at the anxiety, the pleading in them. He swallowed hard, turning his head to where a sweet breeze blew in, cooling his hot face. The scent of roses tickled his nose.

He considered leaving and letting them discuss this subject in private. He shuffled from one foot to the other, unsure whether his new king and queen remembered he and Erzion were still in the room. Sometimes their focus on each other was unerring. His boot heel scraped the wooden floor as he turned and raised his brows in question at Erzion.

"Please stay, Lexon?" asked the goddess immediately.

Lexon snapped his head back to look at her.

"I will not change my mind," began Noan; clearly he knew what this conversation was to be about. "Not even if you get Lexon to try and persuade me."

Lexon dropped his eyes to the ground, hating that he was part of this. He should have walked out whilst they were focused on each other; now he would have to get involved. He really didn't want to. He hated that his brother didn't want to live forever, even if he understood why. But Noan was stubborn, and this discussion had been going on for months.

Lexon looked to the lush valley that lay beyond the island city. He thought of all the people at risk in the beautiful forest towns and villages of their kingdom. Lunaria was right. Noan needed to live—for so many reasons. And as a mortal, his brother was too vulnerable to survive an attack by Erebos.

Lexon wiped his sweaty palms down the softness of his wool leggings. The air around him suddenly seemed too thick. His chest was tight as he fought to pull up his courage and speak his thoughts. He didn't want to upset his brother even more, but his brother was his king now and had responsibilities.

Lexon forced air into his lungs, determined to keep his nerve. "Brother," he said, his voice shaking slightly. "Please, consider your queen's offer." He felt his face heat again as he glanced at Lunaria, who regarded him with kind, bright eyes. She smiled encouragingly when he hesitated. Despite his dry mouth, Lexon continued. "Most of us would be honoured to find someone as beautiful as your mate to love and to share our mortal lives with.

But to be given the chance of an immortal life with them? That is a gift you should not refuse."

Lexon's eyes drifted to the portrait of his mother. It hung above the carved marble fireplace, the sunlight illuminating its beauty. Tears burned his eyes.

It was his fault she had died. He had killed his own mother when she had birthed him. Erzion and Noan had told him a hundred times or more those thoughts were wrong and useless, but he still believed it to be true, even as an adult.

He blinked his tears aside so he could see her properly. He loved this picture of her standing underneath the branches of a Lyca tree. Some of the large red leaves were falling around her, others floating away on the invisible breeze the artist had created with the cleverness of their paints and brushes—maybe even their magic too. Tu Lanah, the large ice moon, shimmered behind her, illuminating her beauty.

"We are all but leaves on the winds of time, waiting to be carried away," he whispered, almost to himself as he studied his mother's dark hair and olive skin. Her sapphire blue eyes regarded him a little sadly. Not giving in to the urge to wipe his eyes, he turned back to his brother.

Noan's wide-eyed expression almost made Lexon smile. He seemed utterly surprise at Lexon's rhetoric.

"But you, Noan, you can be immortal. Take what your love offers; be here for your people, just like Father has been for hundreds of years. Protect them, and protect your descendants for as long as you are able," he said holding Noan's gaze, willing him to take Lunaria's gift.

Erzion tore his golden eyes away from Lexon and nodded wholeheartedly.

Silence fell as Noan and Lunaria stared at each other.

Noan cracked his neck and stretched his wings.

Lexon hid a grimace, but only because he wanted to do exactly the same thing to relieve his tense muscles.

Lexon and Erzion exchanged a glance as the new king sent small tendrils of green magic to caress Lunaria and her swollen belly.

Lexon's face heated again at being witness to such intimacy. He tried to look unaffected by it, but knew his friend would see through him, so he looked out of the window and avoided Erzion's attention.

Noan barked a laugh, clearly noticing his brother's discomfort. "It's alright, Lexon. You and Erzion may go now."

Lexon turned back to his brother, who was already staring deeply into the eyes of the goddess.

"Me and my queen have much to discuss," Noan murmured, looking adoringly into her face, his green eyes dark.

Lexon rolled his eyes at Erzion, who grinned broadly and gestured to the door with his head. Lexon nodded, not bothering to hide his relief.

The king and queen didn't even notice when they left.

Lexon sighed as the cool air in the antechamber caressed his face. "Thank the gods," he muttered.

Erzion chuckled and slapped Lexon's shoulder. "You'll end up like that soon."

"Like what? A mate, a father and a king? Not bloody likely," declared Lexon. Such responsibility didn't bear thinking about.

"Why not? Well, maybe not the king part, but you must be ready to start your urge soon. And you are a prince, even though you *are* a damned ugly one. You'll be fighting off males and females in their droves very soon," quipped Erzion. "Then I'll *never* get any peace from babysitting you. All these horny fae following you around. How am I supposed to keep you safe?" Erzion's grin grew wider as he spoke.

Lexon grinned back even though his gut clenched at the thought of submitting completely to his body's needs. "It already has started," he confided to his friend. "And just like you, I intend to have fun, lots of it. But I am not going to be hunting for a mate, especially if we will be at war soon," he told his friend firmly. "There is no point. Oh, and just so we're clear, you are *not* coming with me when I'm bedding anyone."

"You sure?" Erzion responded, waggling his eyebrows. "I could give you some pointers."

"Find your own fun, you prick. I don't need pointers—or *babysitting*. I'm capable of taking care of myself," he laughed.

The wave of red magic Lexon slammed forward warmed his entire body.

Erzion grinned widely as he shielded. "Still too slow," he quipped, and slapped Lexon on his back good-naturedly.

Air exploded from Lexon's lungs making him cough.

"Well, *prince*," Erzion drawled, heading to the stairs. "Let's head for the docks. I know a nice little inn where plenty of females are looking for fun with handsome males such as us."

Lexon rolled his eyes as his friend's banter lightened his heart. Following Erzion down the stairs and out into the sweet, rose-scented, sunlit evening, he grinned and hoped his friend was right.

CHAPTER 4

LEXON

Shards of rock flew into the air, catching Lexon's cheek.
"Ouch!" he hissed, curving his spine backwards and twisting away. Instinct guided his magic-swathed hand. He unleashed a red wave that deflected the other razor-sharp splinters over his head—just.

Still too slow, he grumbled to himself.

The heat from Erzion's magic singed Lexon's eyebrows, sparking the smell of scorched hair.

"Arse!" muttered Lexon.

Erzion chuckled. "Too slow again, my prince."

Lexon growled, releasing his counter attack as he snapped upright.

Red wings flashed with gold as his opponent moved. Swift for such a big warrior, Erzion ducked, twirled and released more red-hot magic back at Lexon.

Lexon did not relent. His attacks were controlled and swift, driving back his friend and his team of red warriors. From behind, his own squad attacked Erzion's.

The red prince grinned inwardly. Submitting to his urge had been fun in many ways, but his biggest surprise had been the extra control it gave him over his magic. It was no longer as wild and difficult to master as it had been six weeks ago.

Erzion skipped sideways and launched himself up into the air. His wings thudded against the air, the domed roof of this subterranean cavern amplifying the sound.

High above the warriors, the roof hung with stalactites. To Lexon, the slimy-looking growths resembled the overgrown teeth of a guardian. The crystals that lined the walls, however, were amazing feats of nature. Lexon wondered if Lunaria had created them or if it had been the work of one of her sisters—the goddesses who had abandoned this world.

The glittering growths soaked up any unused energy and magic that bounced freely through the air. The more unwanted power they pulled in, the more they glowed with their bright, purplish light.

Lexon's sapphire eyes glowed red as he summoned his magic. Grinning, he followed his friend upward, though he knew he would likely regret it.

The other warriors stayed on the ground, watching and egging on their commanders.

Erzion was fast and powerful, far more powerful than Lexon.

Lexon huffed. *Wizard blood!* "Show off," he grumbled in mock disgust as a grinning Erzion laid his hand on a big stalactite and whispered a spell. Just like that, it loosened and fell into his outstretched hand. The half-wizard grabbed it.

Lexon readied himself, noting the devious glint in Erzion's red gaze.

A tapping sound echoed around the cave, stilling all the warriors instantly.

Master Yagus.

"Get you later," Lexon mumbled.

"Likewise, *prince*," rejoined the half-wizard.

With matching grins, they looked down.

The small, wizened wizard continued to tap his stick impatiently. His white, wispy beard floated freely around his face. "Enough!" Master Yagus blustered, holding his staff in one hand. "Come down here, you two," he ordered.

"What are you going to do with that?" asked Lexon suspiciously as he landed next to Erzion, who still gripped the stalactite.

Erzion raised one brow and smirked. He weighed the stalactite in his big hand then looked at Lexon's groin.

"Like to see you try," said Lexon with a challenging grin.

"Wouldn't dare, my prince," Erzion retorted. "You might need that part of yourself if you are to entice a female worthy of your royal oats, though you do seem to be enjoying sowing them these last weeks," he mocked. "Perhaps if you rested more you might actually be able to beat me."

Lexon couldn't help but flush a little, though he held his friend's gaze and raised his brows. "Ha! That's rich coming from you! You're the one who's dragged me to every different inn in the city," he pointed out. "And I *will* beat you eventually, you arrogant prick," he muttered from the corner of his mouth.

"Of course you will—eventually," Erzion smirked.

The stalactite was suddenly gone, leaving only the warmth of magic floating in the air, and dust running through Erzion's fingers.

"Smooth," Lexon said, impressed as always by Erzion's magical abilities.

"I know," his friend said smugly.

Lexon huffed and rolled his eyes. "By the goddess, you seriously need your arse kicked."

Erzion just chuckled and dropped the rest of the dust at their feet before wiping his hand down his leather-covered thighs.

Master Yagus shuffled closer.

No one, including the two childhood friends, had a clear idea of how old the wizard was, but Lexon knew the wizard was probably far older than he looked, and he looked ancient. Lexon smiled as he studied the old wizard's features. His face was a map of tiny lines. His eyes crinkled tightly at the corners, and his spine was stooped.

Yep, definitely old.

Erzion glamoured into a gold-winged fae.

Lexon pulled a face, then tried. He had never been able to glamour, much to his disgruntlement. Casting his gaze around their chosen warriors, he saw that most of them had controlled their magic enough to form gold wings too. A few were stuck somewhere in between the two, and about ten were full reds, just like Lexon.

"Do not worry, my prince. Hiding your magic is not necessary," advised Erzion, serious for once.

"No. I suppose it is a bit late for that," agreed Lexon. "Griana knows what I am. Still, keeping these red guards away from her clutches may prove wise. I don't trust her. Not one bit," he said fervently.

"Has Noan voiced any suspicions about your father's death?" Erzion asked quietly, laying a supportive hand on Lexon's shoulder.

The weight of Lexon's suspicions dragged his shoulders into a slump. Noan was loyal to the point of blindness, especially to those he loved. He would not even consider removing Griana from her position, not based on suspicion alone and not when the warriors of the king's guard corroborated the new general's story.

Five king's guard were slain by Battle Imps before the king fell to the monsters and the remainder of his guard could not save him. Or so those questioned had reported. But something about their story did not sit well with Lexon. Not when Griana's own father had been killed in similar circumstances only months before.

"No, my brother is too blinkered where that female is concerned. He always has been," Lexon sighed. "He'll never believe Griana is anything but loyal, let alone that she had anything to do with Father's death."

"What about the goddess? Does she believe you?"

Lexon rubbed his face, feeling a mite foolish. "I—I haven't seen her. She...er...I didn't want to worry her. She's been in her rooms..."

Erzion sighed. "You mean you weren't brave enough to go and tell her."

"No. It's not that. Not really. I—just," he groaned. "I didn't want to go to her with just suspicion and no evidence. There's no more reason for her to believe me than Noan. Especially when she has other things on her mind."

"Then maybe we should take matters into our own hands," suggested Erzion.

"And do what? We still have no proof Griana killed my father," pointed out Lexon. In his agitation his wings cramped. Snarling at the discomfort, he extended them. They vibrated, setting his unique swirling markings glowing with fire. Such a display showed the extent of his frustrations.

The group of warriors watched him, some with more disdain than others.

Lexon's stomach lurched. He quickly controlled himself. *I am no longer a child,* he chided himself. *I am their prince. War will be upon us soon enough, and these warriors deserve a strong leader. It is my role, just as being king is Noan's.*

Flames flickered in the floating sconces sending shadows dancing upon the walls.

Lexon deliberately held the eyes of each male in turn, willing himself to be strong. He was far younger than many of them and nowhere near as heavily muscled, but he knew his magic could out-match theirs. He may not be immortal, but he did have his father's blood in his veins—and it was becoming obvious that his magic fed from it.

He gritted his teeth and buried the nervous flush that wanted to creep up his face. He had to assert his authority over these powerful warriors or they would never fully respect him.

Boots scraped on the rock as the warriors began to shuffle uncomfortably at his continued red glare.

Out of Lexon's eye line, Erzion smiled as each warrior submitted and lowered their eyes from their prince.

When the last one lowered his eyes and bowed his head, Lexon's shoulders squared further and his chin lifted. For the first time in his life he did not feel uncomfortable at this unanimous show of respect. It was needed.

This secret legion of red warrior fae—the First Legion—was his alone. Pride washed through him at that thought, fuelling his determination to lead them.

Lexon's boot crunched on dust. He faced his friend. "Lunaria is close to giving birth now, and Erebos is on our doorstep. I will talk to Noan again tonight. Perhaps he will be more inclined to listen to my concerns."

"Let's hope so. Once Erebos unleashes his army on this city, we may be too late to protect Noan from Griana."

"It is already too late," said Master Yagus, his strange nasally voice echoing into the shadowed reaches of the cave.

By Lexon's judgement, this large cave was under the ocean floor, heading toward the mainland. Lexon had a strong suspicion if these caves were explored farther, they may even lead as far as the Rift Valley itself.

"What do you mean, Master Wizard?" he asked respectfully, even as his stomach coiled into knots.

"Noan's path is set. His fate is planned by the powers that control our lives, but that of his descendants and, therefore this world, is not."

Lexon caught Erzion's eye.

Erzion swallowed hard, his face tightening.

Ice spread through Lexon's insides at that look.

Master Yagus often talked of the future as if he had seen it;

what he foretold often came to fruition. He had recently talked of Eternity—the homeland of the goddess, a place protected by the mighty guardians. Every person in the Eight Kingdoms knew Eternity was where the souls of the dead were guided to.

Lexon suppressed a shudder. At least, that's what they hoped. There were rumours of the dark kingdom of Chaos, ruled by Erebos...

"My brother can still be saved," Lexon stated, swallowing hard.

Master Yagus's green eyes softened, pity softening his wizened features. "There may be a chance, prince. But only if you can stop Griana from luring him into battle."

"Erebos is still over a week away," Lexon said. "I will stop her."

"Is he, young prince?" replied Master Yagus. His eyes narrowed. "And who told you that?"

"The watch soldiers from the forest. They report in every few days..." Lexon's voice petered out as realisation hit. Griana's warriors.

"Shit," Erzion breathed. "How could we have been so stupid?"

Lexon's sweat-soaked skin turned cold, dread filling his soul.

"Surely Noan would not leave Lunaria now? Not if Erebos is already so close. He would have the sense to stay behind the wall and use it as it was intended. To keep the enemy's army out," argued Lexon.

"No. If Noan believes the only way to keep Lunaria and his baby safe is to stop Erebos from attacking the wall and entering this city, he will take the battle to Erebos in an instant," said Erzion quietly.

Master Yagus nodded his head sadly. "Exactly, my young apprentice. And that is precisely what the general is going to make him believe."

"Wait! You have seen this?"

"Yes, indeed I have," replied Master Yagus.

"Then we have to stop him," said Lexon, determination driving his voice.

"Maybe you do, prince, or maybe your path lies in a different direction altogether."

"Oh, by the goddess, your rhetoric is extremely annoying at times, Master Wizard. We do not have time for this."

"Indeed you do not, and if you wish to help the future of the kingdoms, you must go now, for Erebos is marching on this city as we speak."

Swearing loudly, the red prince and the now golden-winged, half-wizard turned on their heels, gathered their legion of warriors and ran.

CHAPTER 5

ERZION

The cold autumn air stung Erzion's cheeks, his boots thudding against the dry ground. In front of him, Lexon sprinted ahead before bending his knees and snapping out his wings, launching skyward. Red armour instantly coated his prince's wings, his markings flowing across them, burning with fire.

Erzion's stomach lurched with jealousy. He missed such freedom. But his deception was necessary. He pushed aside his petty thoughts and allowed only gold armour to clatter across his own feathered membranes.

The air rattled as the other warriors armoured, powering their wings against the sky. Goosebumps lifted on Erzion's skin. It was a sound he would never tire of.

They flew up the steep cityscape, over the roof tops and twisted chimneys that covered the island's slopes.

Taking the steepest route, the First Legion passed over a newly built temple, dedicated to worshipping Lunaria. Its white domed roof dwarfed all other structures nearby. But Erzion did not have time to admire it. Breathing hard, he soared next to Lexon.

Together they sped above the city, reaching the palace walls in minutes. They passed right over the few warriors who still manned the wall. None opposed them, though all watched them, confusion on their faces.

Even with the wind in his ears, Erzion heard Lexon's curse.

There were so few left on guard, all of whom seemed bewildered and unsure.

His stomach dropped. Swallowing hard, he gulped down a mouthful of air. He hoped they weren't too late.

Urgency lent them speed. Magic heated the air as Lexon summoned his power. His wings moved in a blur of speed, eddies of warm air propelling him on.

Erzion gritted his teeth, wishing he could use his full magic too. Not wanting to let his friend pull ahead, the half-wizard muttered a spell and felt his magic surge.

Below them, the palace grounds were eerily empty. Erzion's stomach clenched.

This was so wrong. There was no reason for Griana to leave the palace and the city so vulnerable.

Together, the two friends landed outside the king's tower. Lexon sprinted inside. He was gone when the legion landed moments later.

"Captain!" bellowed Erzion to a stoic-faced warrior. "I don't like this. It's too quiet. Leave ten warriors to guard this door and get the rest of these men out of here. Go back to the cave and wait for us there."

"Yes, sir," the captain said, clearly unhappy to leave them. He looked to the door Lexon had already disappeared inside.

Erzion cut the captain off. He had no time to explain, but he could not risk the lives of all these warriors, not until he knew what was truly at stake. "Go. I will find you again, my friend," he said to the male, giving him a curt nod before sprinting after Lexon, not checking to see if his orders were followed. He knew they would be.

Inside was in chaos. Servants hurried through the rooms to who-knew-where, their eyes wide, their faces pale.

Warriors guarded the base of the stairs. They eyed him nervously as he shot by them, leaping and taking the stairs three at a time.

Up and up he ran, his lungs burning. He muttered vicious curses.

The tower stairwell was purposefully narrow. A security measure, much the same as the small tower windows. The king's balcony was its only weakness, though the doors were iron-clad, impenetrable to fae.

Above him, Lexon's footsteps had ceased, and Erzion could hear raised voices. Pushing his aching thighs, he bounded up the last flight of stone steps and rounded the corner.

Down the small dimly lit hallway, four king's guards were stubbornly refusing the prince entry to the royal quarters.

Erzion snarled.

Lexon clearly did not wish to harm them and, although the prince's red wings were still armoured, his magic was tightly under control. Noan had given orders for no one to enter this chamber other than him.

Hope bloomed that Noan was finally realising the enemy was at his back, not protecting it.

Erzion skidded to a halt just as a scream of agony rent the air. Without hesitation, the red wizard summoned enough magic to knock two of the guards across the hall.

Lexon blasted the remaining two sideways, deliberately knocking their heads into the wall. They all lay still.

Not caring about them, Erzion banged on the locked chamber door.

"I'll blast this door in if it isn't opened right now!" bellowed Lexon, his face pale and his voice shaking.

The door immediately cracked open.

Erzion sucked in a breath. "Mother?"

Her face was streaked with tears.

Relief coursed through him at the sight of her, but the devastation on her face had him pulling her into his arms.

"What is it, Mother? What's happened?"

"Oh, Erzion. She's done it! Griana has pulled our king away from the goddess. H-he flew into a rage when he learned Erebos is near the city."

"Oh gods. Why? Why did he listen to her?" asked Lexon, anguish twisting his face.

Another scream rent the air.

"That's why," sobbed Mariel. "The baby is coming. I have never seen him in such a way. H-he's lost. He would not listen—even to his mate. Griana convinced him the only way to keep them safe was to defeat Erebos before he reaches the city."

Lexon's eyes widened, a frown furrowing between his brows.

Holding his mother close, Erzion watched his friend.

"Mother, I'm sorry, but we have to go. We will find him. Lock this door and go back to our queen and the baby. We will leave our guards outside. Trust only our warriors. Do not open this door to any of Griana's men."

He pulled back and looked into her tear-lined eyes. Using the pad of his thumbs, he wiped away her tears and gave what he hoped was an encouraging smile.

Mariel nodded.

Not allowing his anxiety to show, he kissed her forehead and pushed her gently back into the room.

The door closed and the iron lock snapped shut.

"W-what do we do?" Lexon stuttered, his armour coming and going in his distress.

Erzion squared his shoulders, his heart breaking as he watched his friend's world collapse. Grief swamped Lexon's face as he realised they were likely too late to save his brother.

"We gather our men, and we find Noan. Even if we have to fight Griana to get him back."

Lexon swallowed and nodded, not giving in to the tears that rimmed his eyes.

Erzion could only hope his prince would hold it together under the pressure of a real battle, especially as the chances of getting Noan back were low. If Griana was indeed in servitude to Erebos, there was no way one legion, even of red fae, could beat two armies.

He and Lexon raced down the stairs and out into the bright sunlight. Barging out through the heavy oak doors, it took but a fraction of a second to lose any chance at saving their king and city.

Before Erzion could react to the realisation that all his men lay dead on the ground, a tidal wave of magic knocked them both off their feet. It was powerful. And wrong. It sent ice skittering along his bones and screams of agony into his mind.

The turmoil of red and green and gold magic skittered alongside his own. Disgust ripped through him, horror freezing his heart. She had stolen the magic of her own kind!

The moment he hit the ground, a bitter liquid was splashed in his face.

Monksweet!

He felt the foul tincture burn his eyes. Then rough hands were holding his head, the poison forced into his mouth. Coughing and choking, he tried to fight, knocking two of his assailants away. Before he could force his body to move, more of that disgusting magic held him down. Soon the bitter essence of Monksweet was running down his throat, leaking from his nostrils and burning through his blood, smothering his magic as he choked.

A hard blow to his temple. Then darkness.

∽

Erzion groaned, the stink of damp earth, iron and blood swamping his nostrils. Bile rushed his throat.

Hogs balls! What is that gods damned hammering? he thought, even as he realised it was his own pulse banging inside his skull.

Awareness of his body returned in a tidal wave of pain across his back and shoulders. Mud squashed between his fingers as he clawed the ground and growled.

He made himself lie still, even as a bone-chilling cold seeped through his clothes and into every cell of his body. He was on his belly, his cheek flat against the slimy soil. Sluggish thoughts tried to form, but they drifted away before he could grasp them. Erzion tried again to clear his mind—to remember.

It was a huge mistake to shake his head, it only made the thumping pain more vicious.

"Shit," he mumbled, his throat and voice scratchy. His tongue stuck to the roof of his mouth, perfume and bitterness coating his tongue as he tried to swallow.

Monksweet!

The bitch had drugged him, using the herb to neutralise his magic.

Erzion calmed his anger, forcing himself to lay still and concentrate on his surroundings. Griana's men could be watching him right now.

Overcoming his desire to force himself up and fight for his life, Erzion ignored the slimy feel of the ground under his cheek and the wetness soaking through his shirt; instead he absorbed the sounds and feel of the space around him. His acute fae hearing soon picked up quiet breaths nearby.

His body stiffened causing a wave of pain to crash through his muscles. Clenching his teeth, he swallowed his cry, hoping those breaths didn't belong to one of his enemy.

Nothing changed; the breaths remained soft and regular, and there was no hint of anyone else nearby.

He forced opened his burning, dry eyes. Blackness greeted him.

Erzion had never been afraid of the dark, not like most red fae, who loved the light. Then again, he had never been surrounded by such an oppressive lack of light either. It was disorienting.

Wincing, and cursing Griana's soul, he forced himself up onto his knees, his wings dragging through the filth of the ground, too heavy and painful to expand.

Bolts! Iron bolts!

Erzion swore as he leaned forward over his knees, his hands in the dirt. The noxious metal burned with every tiny movement he made.

We should have stopped her when we first thought she'd killed the king, he berated himself.

After a moment, his nausea settled. He slowly expanded the muscles in his back, then gritted his teeth and tried to shift his wings. Pain shot through his muscles and bones, flooding instantly up into his shoulders and down his back. A scream rose in his throat but he bit it down, still not sure whether the sleeping being was friend or foe.

Sweat beading on his brow, Erzion stopped moving, letting the agony subside.

He inhaled. And gagged. Away from the foul ground, the tang of iron burned his mouth and nostrils. It seemed at least some of his prison was made out of the poisonous ore. If he had been pure fae, that knowledge would have filled him with horror. But he wasn't. A fact Griana had clearly forgotten when she dumped him in this place.

He took a deep breath. All he needed was some time to recover from the Monksweet suppressing his magic. In the meantime he could use spells to melt the iron piercing his wings, and maybe even the iron bars of his cell.

They had to be bars, he reasoned, otherwise the steady breathing he could hear would be muffled or non-existent.

A slight shift of air brought a welcome sweetness into the dank confines of the black prison. Erzion lifted his nose to the breeze and inhaled gratefully. Hope bloomed in his chest. If he could scent fresh air, that meant they were near the surface. That meant a way out.

It was tempting to reach for his magic, to use what little had recovered, but Erzion could almost hear Master Yagus telling him to control his emotions. He needed to be calm, to work a spell first and conserve his magic to fight for freedom. So he remained still, ignored the pain in his wings and forced himself to be patient.

∼

Erzion took a deep steadying breath. He could not believe he had been so stupid, so unaware. Of course Griana would not have left Lexon out of her grand plan. At least the prince had an excuse for running headlong into a trap; he was thinking about saving his brother.

I wasn't. I should have been concentrating on saving the prince. Erzion squeezed his eyes shut at the memory, sick at the thought of Lexon's fate.

Master Yagus had been right. Noan's time in this realm was over, perhaps even Lunaria's.

Erzion swallowed his sorrow for his king and queen. All he could do was pray to the guardians to save their souls and guide them to Eternity.

As he lay in the darkness, recovering his magic, Erzion grieved. But grief didn't mean he should give up. Clenching his jaw, he forced his brain to focus through the devastation in his heart.

Magic sputtered inside him. Only an ember, but enough to bring the faintest outline of bars into view.

A pain-filled groan echoed down the corridor, followed by the rustle of clothing as someone moved. The timbre of the voice was instantly recognisable. Erzion bit down on his shout of relief.

Lexon!

That gentle breathing had been his friend, though his breaths were now uneven and loudly rasping.

The moaning turned to retching. Erzion grimaced, his muscles tensing; that sound wasn't due to the aftereffects of Monksweet.

Lexon vomited, then followed it up with numerous deep belly heaves.

Still not sure if they had gaolers nearby, Erzion silently inched forward, giving his wings room. Trying to ignore the pain in his back, he whispered a weak spell, one that didn't tax his wizard blood too much.

Controlling small fingers of air, he probed the iron bolts that pierced his wings. The muscles in his jaw clenched, his teeth grinding as he worked at the noxious metal rods.

After a few minutes of agony, he had only succeeded in shifting the bolts through his flesh by a mere fingerbreadth. By now, sweat ran freely down his forehead into his eyes.

He needed to stop.

This method of incapacitating a winged fae was something Erzion had seldom seen. It was an effective but evil way to suppress magic and render a fae useless. It could damage wings permanently if the bolts were left for too long and scar tissue formed.

Taking a steadying breath, he concentrated on the noxious metal of the cell bars. Shuffling forward on his knees until he was close enough, he ran a finger down one bar, then gripped it tightly and rattled. The calloused skin of his palms and fingers hissed as they burned, but the half-wizard did not let go, grinding and shaking the bar until he couldn't stand it anymore.

Breathing heavily, he listened intently for any signs of a nearby guard. Nothing. No other breathing or moving or swearing, except Lexon, who was cursing over and over, but mumbling in such a distressed state Erzion could not understand him. Only occasional words were clear.

"Wings."

"Bitch."

"Kill her."

"No. No. No."

Erzion could not suppress the dread in his heart.

"Lexon!" he whispered harshly, then listened, feeling for any change in the air that might suggest a hidden presence nearby. Nothing.

He risked raising his voice. "Lexon?" he almost yelled. The sound of his voice seemed to break through to the red prince.

"Erzion? Oh, gods. She took them. She took them," he mumbled over and over in a voice that sounded like it came from the next cell.

"Thank the goddess, you're alive," uttered Erzion, then raised his voice again. "I thought Griana might have killed you. The goddess only knows why we both still live."

"I don't want to live!" his friend cried out. "She has ruined me…" A harsh broken sob echoed into the darkness.

"What? Lexon!! Tell me what she has done!" Erzion begged, nausea churning in his stomach.

"She has taken my wings. I am no longer a warrior…" Lexon's voice broke again, grief and pain making his voice thick.

For a moment Erzion couldn't form any words. His friend's beautiful red wings—gone. Over and over he swallowed down the bile that burned his throat. "Lexon! I am so sorry, but you have to pull yourself together." There was no time for false platitudes and reassurance. If Lexon's wings had been hacked off, nothing could bring them back. "You need to concentrate on finding your magic. You have to fight your way out of this city."

"How?!" yelled Lexon, "Even if we get out of these cells, I can't fly anymore. I will be stuck at her mercy."

"No! You will not! You are not helpless, Lexon! You can still fight, and your magic *will* return. We will gather the First Legion and leave the city. Any of us can carry you."

"I don't want to be carried!" Lexon bellowed, despair raging in his voice. "I want to die!" He panted, banging the bars ferociously and making them rattle in the darkness.

Knowing he would feel the same if their fates were reversed, Erzion held his tongue. But he could not let Lexon die or leave him at Griana's mercy. Both thoughts filled him with horror. "I will not let you die," he growled to Lexon.

"Why?" sobbed Lexon. "I cannot live like this. Stuck on the ground forever, only half a warrior. Who would listen to a mutilated warrior like me! *I am nothing!* My brother is gone, my home is gone. Please kill me. Don't let me become her slave."

"Never," uttered Erzion and began weaving more spells as the devastated prince fell to his knees in the darkness.

CHAPTER 6

GRIANA

Wind whipped at Griana's braided golden hair, but she had deliberately styled it for battle. It was so tightly secured that not even the smallest strand came free.

She huffed derisively.

Every move, every death and every manipulation leading to this day had been deliberate.

This is it. This is where all my plans begin to take shape. Erebos will destroy the goddess whore, and I will get my vengeance on this weak-willed warrior.

Griana snarled at the king's back as he flew just ahead of her, his green wings armoured and gleaming.

To think I ever wanted to be his queen! Lexon is a far better warrior. He is young, but he will soon be far more powerful than Noan. And without his wings, he can never leave me.

She ran her tongue over her teeth. A frisson of excitement shuddered through her at the thought of biting the young prince and controlling him. Lexon would give her a strong son, an heir she could mould into the perfect king for this world.

Around her, thousands of wings thrummed through the air, the turbulence churning the trees and grass below into a frenzy.

The noise was incredible, demanding that she concentrate on leading her army, not just her own agenda.

King's guards surrounded her and Noan, the sun reflecting a kaleidoscope of colour off their red, green and gold wings.

This plan would not fail. Her lord had promised her this world to rule, along with an eternal life—as long as she had enough ice in her heart to take it.

Around her, the vigilant warriors scanned the ground, lifting their eyes to search the clear blue skies, both near and far. Little did they realise *they* were her greatest weapon. *They* were the ones who would secure her crown today. The venom running through their veins made them her greatest asset, and the king's greatest danger.

It was hard to conceal her glee as a huge swell of shadow appeared on the horizon. What looked like a flock of birds, preceded it. Sparse and erratic they flew, but soon dark thunderous clouds formed, obscuring not only the blue sky, but whatever those writhing airborne creatures were. It hung over the forest, swallowing the trees in darkness and blocking the light of the low autumn sun.

The king's face was hidden, but Griana knew him well. He was determined to win this battle and return to his whore and their new-born. Despite that, he would soon be quaking inside once he realised the hopelessness of his solitary quest for victory against a god.

Griana didn't know exactly what those aerial monsters were, but she knew they would be vicious and hard to kill.

A spiteful smile curled her ruby lips.

Behind her the valley and the city were now vulnerable. She had left only the bare minimum of warriors at the palace. Mainly for show, but she did need at least some males to survive if she was to breed more souls for her Lord. It also left Lunaria vulnerable and alone. Especially now Lexon and Erzion were incarcerated.

Soon the goddess would feel Noan's pain, and she would come running. With her magic depleted from childbirth and her guardian weak, she would be at her brother's mercy.

Griana snarled. And the child would be dead. Her warriors were already in place, waiting to end its short life.

The din of Erebos's army marching through the trees sent a shudder of anticipation travelling down Griana's spine.

Noan stopped, his focus on his enemy.

Griana's fist flew up into the air. Her unspoken order to halt rippled through the ranks of armoured fae. The grassy knoll she now hovered above was an ideal place for the demise of a king, she decided gleefully.

Ranks of dead soldiers came into view, their lifeless, milky eyes staring forward. It seemed Erebos had fed on the souls of Avalonia as he marched. Some of the more recently deceased still walked upright; they had not even begun to rot. The long-dead corpses shuffled between the trees. It didn't matter if they were whole or missing limbs, each hideous one swirled with shadow and was capable of fighting and killing without mercy.

Monstrous Battle Imps strode among the ranks of the dead, their bald, misshapen, blue heads standing a foot or more higher than the dead soldiers, their small beady eyes fixed on the enemy in the skies.

Griana snarled in disgust as they roared, revealing wide mouths full of yellowed, pointed teeth.

The clamouring—caused by the clash of the dead army's weapons and mixed with the swish and thud of the thousands of armoured wings from her own army—hurt Griana's ears. She wanted to cover them but would never show such weakness.

Griana schooled her features into a mask of concentration and respect as Noan turned and nodded, his signal to take control. Griana almost laughed out loud at the effortlessness of his demise.

She raised her hand again. The wind produced by the hovering army whipped at the hair and clothes of the ranks of warrior fae, but none faltered. All were trained for this.

"Hold the lines! Archers forward!" Griana yelled, trying to hold in her excitement.

Great swirling clouds of ice-flecked shadow moved closer.

Gold and green-winged warriors shifted uneasily and looked toward the more powerful in their ranks. The red fae, their wings swirling with markings of fire, seemed intent on facing down the shadow that closed in. Little did they realised it was ready to devour them as it had done the sunlight.

Griana held her nerve and delved inside herself, dragging up the power she had been harnessing for months. This was such a powerful gift Erebos had given her: to devour and store magic. A shudder rippled down her spine.

She flicked her braid down her back, her emerald eyes flashing in the dwindling light. Warmth seeped through the fingers of her glove as she reached down and curled them around the handle of the specially made weapon and withdrew it from its sheath.

She held her breathing steady, though her body trembled.

The newly forged blade was iron, and iron was not to be trifled with. Tipping her head back slightly, Griana welcomed the cold air that fanned her hot cheeks.

She reached for the venom bond to her newly claimed warriors.

It had been overwhelming at first to take control of so many strong minds, but Griana had never been one to back down from a challenge. Mastering them had taken time and patience, but she had done it. Her link to them was like a spider's web—delicate but intricately connected—and infinitely strong.

King Noan Arjuno failed to notice his guards drop back to leave him utterly exposed.

Soon a tight wall of muscle and magic formed between her and the king, and the other nearby warriors.

A dark chuckle echoed in her mind. Erebos.

Do it now. My army is ready to attack.

Griana sent back her agreement to her lord, though she deliberately hesitated, wanting to savour this moment. Hate spiked through her as she eyed the male who had spurned her for another. Then, silent as the darkest shadow, she lunged.

The king screamed.

Iron burned through his skin and bone. Griana grunted and shoved the blade forward, burying it to the hilt between his wings.

Warriors yelled in panic.

Griana laughed—and laughed, as her line of guards cut down any who tried to help.

King Noan Arjuno lost the green armour from his wings, spinning like a falling leaf as he dropped to the grassy knoll.

He thudded face first into the ground.

Above them, warriors fought desperately to reach their king.

Noan groaned and struggled to his feet. His bloodied lips worked, but no sound came out. He swayed violently on his feet.

Griana cackled as he tried to use his magic—and failed.

Iron.

It had weakened his magic; it could only sputter up towards her, never really a threat.

Noan's pain-filled eyes drifted to the forest. As a green, he could summon nature to help him.

Griana leered. It did not matter. He was too far away from the forest. His ability to summon plants would not help him now. Even the grass beneath his feet withered.

Noan staggered in a circle, his eyes widened enough to see the whites, his face pale in the ever dimming light.

A shield of ice and shadow slammed into place.

Erebos!

Desperately, warriors began diving from above, slamming themselves against the shield, intent on rescuing their king. Their bodies froze before dropping lifeless through the shield to the ground. Erebos, though invisible, made short work of them. Their souls were yanked from their bodies, leaving them to emerge from the shadow moments later as vacant-eyed, slack-winged husks.

My Lord is certainly feeding well, reflected Griana, before turning her full attention to her enemy.

"Why?" Noan rasped as she landed.

A cruel, bitter smile thinned her lips. "Are you really so blind? So ignorant of my wants and feelings?" she hissed. "I have put up with being your lowly companion since I was barely old enough to walk. All my life I have protected and served you because I knew that one day you would make me your queen, that you would give me a kingdom and a child of royal blood. I worked hard every day of my life—for you. You should have respected me, Noan. None of this would be happening if you hadn't rejected my love and my loyalty. You gave my crown to that silver-haired whore and planted your seed in her belly."

She spat in Noan's face as his legs buckled, and he fell to his knees.

"Love?" hissed the dying king. "You know nothing of love—or loyalty! Only greed and ambition."

Griana laughed.

Noan watched, wide-eyed as a figure materialised from the shadows. At the same time an almighty roar went up from outside the shield.

Noan raised his gaze. His throat bobbed, and his jaw became slack.

Hideous monsters graced the skies, bigger than even Battle Imps. These creatures had large bat-like wings tipped with razor sharp talons. Their bodies were protected by a thick exoskeleton that looked as though it were made from ice and stone. The deftly-aimed arrows of the fae bounced uselessly off their bodies.

Such natural armour was not a match for the red fae.

Heat and flame seared through the air.

Noan gulped as, one after another, the flying demons turned to dust. Bones turned to ash, which floated down like snow, shimmering as it hit the shield.

Recognising their most powerful foe, the demons honed in on the red fae, their large black eyes showing neither fear nor anger. They attacked in droves; their high pitched screeches filling the sky.

The green and gold warriors began to panic as their brothers fell, their lines breaking. Such disarray allowed the creatures to separate and weaken the fae army even further.

Dipping and swirling, the demons picked off the red-winged warriors by the hundreds, their long pointed fangs ripping through flesh and raining blood and bodies down upon the forest below.

"No," Noan whispered, tears running down his ashen cheeks.

Erebos, the Lord of Souls and the ruler of the Chaos realm, eyed his prey—and smiled.

The sound of crunching bones and the crack of magical warfare did not distract the dark god from his purpose.

"It is truly a pleasure to meet you in the flesh, young king," he greeted smoothly, his voice as dark as night. "Do you like my new warriors? They are magnificent, aren't they?"

Erebos moved alongside Griana and trailed icy fingers down her neck. Shuddering with pleasure, she stretched her neck to one side to allow him access.

"I call them Ashmea. They are forged from the stone and ice of Chaos. I gift them the pain and suffering of the souls who must die to allow them entry to this realm," Erebos crooned, looking down upon the fallen king.

Noan shrank back with a whimper.

Griana could not suppress a satisfied smile. It was a horrific sight to see the souls and eyes of the dead staring back at one from such darkness.

"They are a special gift for my sister—your mate." Erebos

took Noan's chin in his long fingers, digging his curled, yellowed fingernails into the mortal's soft skin.

Blood welled.

"I have to say, I cannot understand what lures my sister." A quick glance back at Griana. "Or indeed, why you would give up such a prize as Griana, a mortal you could have grown old with, who has far greater potential to conquer and rule than my sister. No. I cannot quite understand. But no matter, Griana will become my mortal queen on this world. She will harvest souls to feed me. In return, she will have all the power and immortality she wishes for."

The Lord of Souls reached around the fallen king's back and twisted the iron blade.

Noan screamed.

Griana smiled.

Noan's waxy skin glistened with a heavy sheen of sweat.

Griana glanced back towards the city. It was gratifying to know the magical bond Noan and Lunaria shared would amplify their ability to sense each other's emotions. That it meant the goddess would feel every bit of pain and suffering of the fallen king.

Pulling Noan's sword from his scabbard so he could not reach for it, she thrust it aside, then kneeled to look into his eyes.

"Know this, my king. Your queen and your child will both die this day. Giving your heart and my kingdom to another was the worst decision of your very short life. I will live forever. I will rule this city and all these lands." She smiled cruelly. "With your brother as my consort and Erebos as my Lord, your people will accept me as their queen, or they will die and their souls will feed the darkness."

Griana leaned in as Noan swayed on his knees. His cheek was icy cold against hers. She curled her fingers carefully around the handle of the blade in Noan's back. Slowly, savouring every second, she pulled her head back until her lips touched his, and she could look into his eyes.

A storm of raw emotion swirled in their depths.

She shivered enjoying the pleasure of this moment.

"You were never cut out to be a king, Noan. See this as a mercy," she breathed onto his bloodless lips—then yanked the blade out.

CHAPTER 7

LEXON

"Lexon? Answer me!" ordered Erzion, his voice harsher than Lexon had ever heard.

After an internal battle, Lexon capitulated. "What?" he replied, his voice hoarse and lacking in strength. All his new found confidence had vanished. He was nothing. Less than nothing. Not a warrior, not a prince, not a brother or a son.

He gulped, trying to swallow the tightness in his throat.

The pain in his back and shoulders burned with every slight movement he made. He inhaled slowly, deeply, and tried to regain his equilibrium. The loss of his wings had unbalanced him, in body and soul.

Another wave of grief assailed him. No. He was alive. He could survive this.

"Have you any magic yet?" whispered Erzion in a gravelly voice.

"No. The Monksweet—it's still in my system. I can even taste it," Lexon panted, then hawked and spat into the darkness.

Erzion chuckled darkly. "That's because they poured it down our throats," he reminded Lexon.

Lexon grunted. "Well, at least I was unconscious when she

hacked off my wings," he stated bitterly, then took a breath. "So, half-wizard, do you have a plan to get us out of here before *she* decides to return?"

A faint glow lit the darkness.

"Working on it, your highness," panted Erzion from the next cell.

Lexon forced his heavy limbs to move, although he avoided touching the iron bars again. His hands were burned and blistered from where he had smashed his fists into them and rattled them in his anger and grief. Using the wall instead, he pulled himself on his feet. Keeping his hands against the slimy, cold surface, he steadied himself. It took a while for the pain in his back to recede enough to even think straight, let alone move. "Can I do anything to help?" he grated into the darkness.

Erzion only grunted before chanting in a language Lexon had never been able to understand. It was a language Erzion had spent hours learning from Master Yagus. Lexon had tried not to feel left out during those training sessions, had quietly practiced his magic in a corner as his friend learned to become a wizard as well as a warrior.

"I guess not," Lexon muttered to himself.

Then again, he was no longer a warrior.

Lexon reached over his shoulder to touch the stumps of his wings. He retched at the foreign feel of his body, but made himself explore them. The stumps were jagged and rough, but dry. It seemed Griana did not want him to bleed to death. The stench of burned flesh came from his fingers when he pulled his hand back. She had cauterised the stumps.

Dried blood was caked across the surface of his skin, making his naked back and stomach itchy. He rubbed at it gingerly, not really wanting to move. It helped though, to move his muscles more. The stiffness and pain settled to a more bearable level. That, or he just got more used to it.

Red light flared as Erzion's chants became stronger.

Lexon's heart sped up. Maybe they really could escape. His eyes closed as he swallowed hard. He wasn't stupid. He knew why Griana had kept him alive—and becoming her plaything was something he could not stomach; he would rather die.

His insides tensed as the cell was plunged into darkness once again. He hated the dark. "Are you alright?" he barked after a moment when Erzion remained quiet.

"Yes," came the breathless reply. "I'm almost done with this lock. Another few goes and we'll be out."

Lexon squeezed his eyes shut. Despite his fear of becoming a slave to Griana, he huffed loudly at Erzion and forced himself to speak. "That many tries, hmm?" he said dryly.

"Yep."

A pause.

Water dripped, its rhythm a staccato beat that grated on Lexon's nerves. Other than their harsh breaths, that was the only sound.

"Do you think he's already dead?" asked Lexon, not really wanting to hear the reply.

Erzion let out a long heavy sigh. "Not unless Lunaria has joined the battle. Griana will wait for Erebos to be in position, and Erebos will use Noan's pain to call his sister to him."

"Do you think Vaalor can save them?" Lexon asked quietly, his head drooping, chin to chest, his shoulders sagging inward.

Erzion was quiet for a moment. "I...err...don't know," he said on a sigh. "At full strength—yes, but he is already weak; he has not fed from the Fire Mountain for months. Griana knows that. And I suspect so does Erebos."

Lexon nodded even though his friend couldn't see him. He blinked the burning tears from his eyes, then cricked his neck and squared his shoulders.

The baby.

Even if he could not save his brother and the goddess, their heir needed a protector.

Just as he opened his mouth to speak, a bright light flashed, temporarily blinding him.

As if summoned by his thoughts, Lunaria stood before him. Her blue eyes glowed as she stared at Lexon, then Erzion.

Her silver hair floated around her shoulders, alight with magic. White, impenetrable dragon scales hugged her figure. Over the places she needed more flexibility, a white fluid covering moved with her body and shimmered like liquid silk.

Her brow furrowed, then she lifted her chin. "I will let you out from this prison, Lexon, but first I need your word and bond to do as I ask," she said.

Steel honed her words, but Lexon could hear the slight shake in her voice. He peered closely at her. The goddess appeared unchanged—unless you knew her well, which Lexon did. He had spent hours studying her, and that was before she was constantly by his brother's side.

A slight sheen of sweat covered her top lip, and her skin had a waxy appearance.

With a knot in his stomach, Lexon realised Lunaria was not immune to the hardship of childbirth, goddess or not. She was weaker than he had ever seen, both physically and magically.

Lexon stared, dread tightening his chest. Then he lifted his own chin and clenched his teeth. It did not matter what she asked of him, he knew he would follow her every order. He didn't care if he died. She was his goddess and queen, and he would fight until he died for her and his brother.

"Of course, my queen," he answered, dipping his head and shoulders before raising his eyes again.

Lunaria swallowed but held his sapphire gaze steadily as she spoke. "I want your word that if I release you, you will protect my daughter. That you will guard her forever. I will make you immortal, but you must take her far away from this city."

Lexon stared at his queen.

Immortal?

Lexon suddenly understood Noan's reluctance to live forever. Living without the ones you loved was not living at all. He didn't even want to live now, let alone forever.

Lunaria narrowed her eyes. "Accept my terms for your freedom, Lexon. My daughter needs you."

"I can't," he whispered, regret making his voice shake. The thought of living forever without his wings was abhorrent.

"So be it," she replied, her blue eyes sad. "I'm sorry you will not accept my gift of immortality, but you will not die today. Your bloodline, your destiny, will shape our future."

Lexon slowly lifted his eyes to hers. "Erzion. If I am to do this, he must come with me. I will not leave him here to die."

Lunaria shook her head sadly. "No, Lexon. I am afraid Erzion's path is to be a different one than yours."

Lexon's heart squeezed at those words, and he could only watch as the goddess turned and approached his friend's cell. He could not see Erzion, but he could hear clearly.

"Erzion? Your task will be a grave one and will take much courage and fortitude."

"Yes, my queen," Erzion replied steadily.

Lexon's throat tightened.

"You will remain here in this city. You will find a way to ingratiate yourself with the false queen. You will get her to trust you, and you will serve her as a loyal subject."

Silence.

"I need someone I can trust. Someone who can protect this city and its people from deep within."

"I don't understand," croaked Erzion. "You want me to *serve* her? H-how do I do that? I can't. I am loyal to my prince —to you."

"Erzion," Lunaria interrupted gently. "I know. That is why it has to be you." Her voice hardened, power seeping into it, despite her weakened state. "Agree to my request or I will leave Lexon in this cell for Griana."

"No!" Erzion gasped. "You need him. You can't!"

"I have no time left for discussion. Your mother has my daughter; she has Tanelle. She has an escape planned. If Lexon has to remain here, Tanelle will still stand a chance of survival," Lunaria answered. "But I would rather not leave him here as a chattel to that monstrous female, or for his soul to become sustenance for my brother. Do you accept my terms, Erzion?"

"Of course," Erzion answered.

Light flared, suffocating power filling the air.

Erzion roared. Long, agonising seconds passed before he became silent. Lunaria's magic faded, leaving them both panting hard in its aftermath.

"You...are...now...immortal," Lunaria said, taking deep, heaving breaths until she could speak again. "I have no misconceptions about my fate, but this city and the power beneath it must be kept hidden and safe until an heir of my bloodline or—if destiny decrees it—Lexon's returns. Promise me. Promise me you will do everything Griana requires, that you will become indispensable to her. You must protect the people in this land as best you can until the time is right to fight for Valentia again. Even if it takes a thousand years, promise me you will honour my wishes as your goddess and your queen."

"I promise," replied Erzion, though his voice was laced with unhappiness.

Lexon inhaled as the metallic odour of blood hit his nostrils.

A blood seal.

He didn't know whether to be horrified or not. Only Lunaria could break that seal. Even death was not powerful enough to unlock it. Erzion's body and soul were stuck here until his pledge was complete or the goddess released him.

Metal clattered as the lock on Erzion's cell opened.

Lexon held his breath as Lunaria returned to him.

"Well, prince? Do you wish to remain here as Griana's plaything or will you guard my daughter with your life?"

"My queen," Erzion protested. "You said you would release him if I agreed to your pledge."

Lunaria silenced him with a look before sending out a small burst of magic.

Lexon hissed.

A small, deep cut had appeared on his inner forearm.

"I know what I said, red wizard. But I will promise much to keep my daughter safe. Lexon still has to make a choice," she said, gesturing to the blood running freely down his arm.

"Do it, Lexon. You cannot want to refuse to care for your own niece. Surely?" Erzion asked desperately.

"Of course not!" bit out Lexon. "I just do not want to live forever—or I didn't. Now you are immortal and would be around to annoy, it wouldn't be so bad," he tried to sound positive. Then he felt the cold air brush his naked back. His stumps burned at its touch. He didn't know if he could live forever as a wingless warrior. He hung his head, ashamed of his mutilated body.

"Lexon, the gift of immortality is only offered once. You refused it. I can no longer grant you long life, but if you agree to care for my daughter, you will be released and I will gift you far greater magic than you possess now." Her eyes rested upon the stumps of his wings. "Remember, you do not need wings to wield magic," she reminded him gently, looking at him with such sympathy that his throat ached.

"Falter now and Griana will become your very personal nightmare," she whispered.

Lexon did not hesitate this time.

He walked forward and stuck his arm through the bars, ignoring the burning pain as the iron touched his skin.

He needed a purpose. He needed his niece.

Lunaria did not hide her sigh of relief. She immediately bent forward, sealing her lips around the wound she had inflicted. She sucked once and released him.

"Your bond to my request is sealed. But by refusing my gift of immortality, you have ensured it will pass to your heirs. They shall remain protectors of my bloodline until this city is retaken, whether that be in ten years or one thousand. My daughter is in the tower with Mariel. Take her and run from this place. Return only when the time is right for my descendants to reclaim this throne."

Wide-eyed, Lexon didn't know what to do when Lunaria held out her own arm. A cut similar to his oozed blood. "Take my blood. To protect my descendants, you and yours need stronger magic."

Uncomfortable with the intimacy of taking her blood, Lexon gulped. She gave him an understanding smile. "Do not worry, this is not the beginning of a mating bond. My blood is a conduit for my magic, that is all."

Feeling slightly better, Lexon held her arm. Placing his lips on her cut, he drew long and hard. He swallowed, but was forced to release her. His magic flared. Heat, ancient and powerful, crashed through his body. For a few seconds he could do nothing but lean his shoulder against the damp wall. A pained grunt escaped his lips as his blood burned, their magic fusing. His mind, his very soul, felt it.

Panting, he closed his eyes. Vaguely he registered the cell lock clattering to the ground. By the time he opened his eyes, the goddess had disappeared, leaving them in darkness once again.

Erzion jerked Lexon out of the cells, and they stumbled away from the noxious iron. Once the effects of the iron waned, Erzion muttered some words and his wings began to glow.

Lexon swallowed the sick feeling in his stomach and staggered behind his friend down the dark, dank corridors. They soon found themselves at the base of a set of old stone steps that spiralled upward.

They ascended as quickly as they could. Meeting no resistance, they ran through a heavily armoured door hanging off its hinges and out into the late evening light.

Temporarily blinded and disoriented by the low sun, they staggered. Erzion pulled Lexon down, and they crouched against the nearest wall. Lexon blinked until his vision sharpened.

Above them towered the palace temple, its large stained glass windows illuminated beautifully. Lexon frowned; he hadn't even know these old cells existed under the temple. Nearby, steps led up to the manicured grounds of the rose garden.

Raised voices rang out. Both Lexon and Erzion stiffened.

"How's your magic?" asked Erzion, keeping his eyes on the steps.

Lexon dug deep. Without warning, power slammed through him, setting his eyes on fire. It sought out the damage to his back, instantly healing him and taking away his pain.

"G-great," he stammered in surprise.

Erzion gaped.

Lexon's body now glowed with spiral markings, much as his wings once had.

Erzion visibly pulled himself together, closing his mouth. "Good. Let's go and get the child." Already he was beginning to edge up the steps. "I will help you get out of this place before I think of...*her*."

Lexon reached out, grasping Erzion's tunic, effectively stopping his friend from going any farther. "No. I will go and get Tanelle. You have to find a way to get into Griana's good graces if you are to—serve her," he said through gritted teeth as he forced out the hateful words out.

Erzion filled his lungs and snarled. Then his eyes filled with sorrow. "Lexon? When you go—wherever you go—please keep in touch; don't leave me to suffer her alone. I..." he gulped, tears glistening in his now golden eyes. "I never wanted to live forever. I-I don't know if I can. To see you age... To live on without you—without my mother." His voice ground to a harsh, agonised whisper. "I don't know how to do it," he said, a tear escaping his eyes. He squeezed them closed.

When he opened them, they swam with such sorrow and raw grief that Lexon felt his own eyes burn.

They were both losing their way of life and the friendship that meant more to them than anything else.

Lexon swallowed past the grief tightening his throat and hugged his friend tightly, perhaps for the last time. Erzion would live, maybe not forever, but Lexon would soon grow old and die. They both knew it. "You do as you promised, my friend. You keep this city and this throne intact for a descendant to return and claim it. I will keep my part of our pledge. I will bring Lunaria's daughter up to fight, and I will teach my descendants of my oath, one that is theirs to keep. We shall be protectors of Lunaria's bloodline as surely as we are also heirs to this throne. One day we will return, but until that day, know that I love you as my brother. And please, forgive me."

Erzion only had time to blink before Lexon slammed a wave of red magic against his friend. The half-wizard was thrown back into the wall, his head bouncing off the stone. His body sagged to the ground before he lay still.

Lexon warily approached his friend. Erzion was a formidable force, especially when he was angry. After satisfying himself that Erzion was indeed breathing, Lexon rolled him onto his side.

Hoping his friend would understand his motives, Lexon crept up the steps and into the rose garden without a backward glance.

CHAPTER 8

LEXON

Lexon spun on his heel, swinging the sword he had pulled off a fallen guard. It seemed Griana hadn't tamed all the Avalonian warriors, and some were still fighting for their city and their king.

He ignored the pain in his heart at the knowledge that by now his brother would have fallen prey to Griana's trap. He could only hope that Lunaria and Vaalor would have time to save Noan's soul from being devoured by Erebos.

He fought a shudder and focused on his enemy as one of Griana's men approached. The warrior showed no fear or remorse as he refused Lexon entry to the king's tower. Knowing he would soon be out of time, Lexon adjusted his weight to change his balance. Pushing magic into his sword arm, he overpowered the male in two strikes, then gutted him with one powerful swipe. Blood spilled, and the warrior collapsed face first.

Killing another Avalonian sickened him.

No. I am no longer Avalonian or a warrior prince. I am a protector for my niece. I will find a safe place for her to grow. Then I will build her an army, as Erzion will do here.

Jaw clenched, nausea roiling in his belly at the thought of

leaving everything he loved, he ran into the tower.

Inside, more guards cut him off from the stairs. It was clear Griana did not want the princess to be rescued. Lexon swallowed, his mouth suddenly dry—or Griana had sent these warriors to kill the child.

Lexon's belly tightened with fear. He had never fought so many without Erzion by his side. Stealing his courage, he snarled at the fae, noting their threatening stances and the stormy darkness of their eyes.

She was controlling all of them.

He had no idea how that was even possible.

Lexon pushed that thought aside. Magic boiled through his blood; he had no idea how long his new power would last, and he needed to escape the city. He would fight with a blade and rely on magic only as a last resort.

Calling on all his training, Lexon took a deep breath. Before he had time to expel it, the nearest warriors attacked. Lexon stumbled when both their blades connected with his. They were heavily built and strong; he was not. Without his wings, his balance was off. Nevertheless, he kicked one away with a foot to the warrior's belly and punched the other in his gut. Then Lexon was fighting for his life. He had no wings to protect him, but he still had the skills Master Yagus had taught him.

In minutes, only corpses lay at his feet.

The distant high pitched cry of a baby drove him towards the stairs. He took them at a sprint, pulling on a little magic to propel himself onward. The magic tattoos on his chest and back glowed.

Each floor he sprinted past seemed deserted. No warriors. No servants. No courtiers. Warning bells clanged in his head but he continued on, ignoring his burning muscles and heaving lungs.

Lexon eventually reached the stairs below the royal quarters. His niece was screaming loudly. Lexon slowed, though that sound had his neck and shoulders bunching in anxiety.

His palms were sweaty, inhibiting his grip on his sword. Taking a deep breath, he carefully stepped onto the landing.

The door to the royal quarters hung in splinters, the door guards dead.

Lexon swallowed his dread.

Stalking forward, he stepped around the broken door and into the main chamber.

Bodies of fallen king's guards littered the ground. The air was thick with the metallic stench of blood. It coated his mouth and nose.

His chest heaved as he recovered his breath.

Splatters of red covered the walls, and blood ran in viscous rivulets across the wooden floor.

Clearly someone had fought hard to protect the princess. Mouth set in a thin, tight line, Lexon tried to control his trembling body. Silently, he stepped around the fallen. Holding his sword out ready, he crossed the room. He peered into the antechamber.

Empty.

Alert, Lexon took a steadying breath and tried not to let his niece's distressed cry steal his concentration.

A door stood wide open—the room where Lunaria had been giving birth only hours earlier.

Rasping breaths echoed from that doorway.

Lexon's heart jumped into his throat. *Please, don't let it be Mariel,* he prayed to the guardians.

Steeling his courage, he stepped inside—and cursed.

Mariel looked at him, tears streaming down her cheeks. Blood covered her face, but it was Garnald who lay propped against the wall, the wound in his chest oozing steadily. At the sight of Lexon, the male's brown eyes grew wide, and the sword he had been clutching, fell from his fingers.

"Mariel?" Lexon whispered hoarsely.

"Please. Help him," she begged, grief etched in every line of her face.

Lexon knelt beside the injured green-winged fae. "What happened?" he asked, quickly and firmly pressing his hand against Garnald's wound. Sticky blood oozed between his fingers.

His heart sank. Garnald would die, unless...

Lexon took a breath and pulled gently on the flame that burned inside him. Nervously, he tugged it up and channelled it into his hand.

Lexon was red, he was made for destruction and fire. With the addition of Lunaria's magic, he could feel a vast, destructive power simmering inside his soul. With difficulty, Lexon controlled the fear he would burn or incinerate Garnald.

Sweat beaded on his brow. He knew Garnald would ultimately do a better job of healing himself. As a green wing, he would know about herblore and healing. But that knowledge was only any good if he survived this blood loss.

"Garnald? This is going to hurt. I have to stop the bleeding," he told the green wing, his voice shaking.

"Do it," growled Garnald between clenched teeth, meeting Lexon's trepid gaze with belief and determination.

Lexon nodded. Praying this would work, he sent a rush of heat down through the hand he lay over Garnald's wound.

Garnald did not scream, only gritted his teeth harder, until they creaked like they might shatter, and snorted his agony out through his bloodied nose.

Lexon was concentrating so hard, he missed the horror on Mariel's face as she saw the stumps on his back.

His niece screamed harder, almost as if she felt the sorrow and agony in the air.

"The. Baby," Garnald ground out, his eyes darting to Mariel.

Mariel nodded and ran to the crib. Reaching in, she pulled the tiny squalling bundle into her arms. "Shhh." She tried to sooth the child, rocking her gently.

An acrid smell of singed flesh polluted the air. Panting, Lexon surveyed his work. The wound was cauterised, even if some of the skin around it was blistered.

"Thank you, prince," Garnald whispered, squeezing his eyes shut for a moment.

Lexon looked around the destroyed room in awe. This green wing had wreaked destruction on these dead warriors. Garnald was not a warrior, he did not know how to armour his wings, but he had managed all this—alone.

"You protected the princess with your life," he stated. "Why?"

Garnald huffed and smiled a little guiltily before looking at Mariel. "No offense, prince, but it wasn't the princess I was thinking of when I fought my way up here."

Lexon looked at Mariel, whose eyes widened at Garnald's words.

"Oh, I see," Lexon responded, wondering if he would ever love anyone enough to do such a foolhardy thing.

Mariel tore her gaze from Garnald's. "Where is Erzion?" she asked, her face paling, her eyes resting on the doorway.

Lexon rubbed his face with his hands, unsure how to reply.

"And what happened to your wings, you poor boy?" she asked before he could answer her first question.

The pity in her face made him feel sick. He didn't want pity—not from anyone. He could still use magic, he could still fight, he had just proven that to himself. Still, he owed this female an explanation. Mariel had been the one constant adult in his life. A surrogate mother. She had been the one to pick him up when he fell, to wipe his tears and hold him when he was sad, to care for him when he was ill. He loved her.

"Don't worry, Mariel. Erzion is alive and well, but he is no longer bound to serve me. He has a greater purpose."

Quickly, Lexon told them about the imprisonment, about waking up with his amputated wings and the pledge they had both taken to Lunaria.

Mariel listened, her face tight, her lips pressed together. When he had done, Mariel handed the princess over. "Here. Take good care of Tanelle, Lexon. I know you are young, but you will be a good father to her. You have courage, and much love to give her. Please, treat her as you would your own child."

Lexon held his sword in one hand, and the bundle of swaddling in the other. Tanelle had calmed and was taking rapid, hiccoughing breaths now that she had stopped crying. Her blankets were soft and warm against his skin where she lay in the crook of his arm. Lexon gulped at how tiny and vulnerable she felt.

"Go to the Fire Mountains. Lunaria said that was where I should take her. It is unclaimed land. You are a warrior and a prince; now you must become a king. Use the gift Lunaria gave you. Take that land and hold it. Build Tanelle an army—and your descendants, a kingdom."

Lexon nodded, feeling strangely calm about his fate. His voice was thoughtful now. "You are right. Perhaps the mountains themselves will give me a safe place to raise Tanelle."

"Send word when you are settled," said Mariel. "There are many Avalonians who would follow you there rather than serve a false queen—or become Erebos's next slave." Mariel cupped his cheek with one cold hand. "And no matter who he serves, Erzion will never go against you or this little one. He will always be loyal to you. He will always love you. As do I." She met Lexon's red gaze with determination, and then she told him what she wanted him to do.

Lexon listened, his heart breaking as she laid out her plan for her son. When she had explained, her eyes filled with tears.

Garnald took her hand in his and kissed her cheek. Mariel smiled at him, love shining in her eyes.

"Lunaria has done a cruel thing to my son," she whispered to Lexon, her wings shivering in distress. "But it is done, and now he needs a reason to change his allegiance from you to Griana. Please, do not worry if he does not understand straight away.

Someday I will make sure he knows what really happened here. And when he has her trust, he will do everything he can to protect this city from her cruelty."

Lexon swallowed the lump in his throat. "I know, which is why I will do as you ask." He stared down at the tiny creature in his arms. Huge blue eyes looked at him. "We will be fine, little one," he whispered, kissing her soft forehead before he passed her back to Mariel.

"Let's get you up," he said to Garnald.

Gritting his teeth, Garnald grabbed onto Lexon. Once on his feet, he took the sword Lexon proffered.

"We will go to the east harbour. There are boats taking people away from the city. I know someone who can get you out and take you to Houria," he told Lexon.

Lexon sighed in relief. "Thank the goddess, that's far enough away that it will be impractical for Griana to send an army for us."

Mariel laid a hand on his arm as she tried to comfort Tanelle. "She won't need an army, only an assassin," she warned.

"I know. Don't worry. I will learn how to use my magic to protect us. When we reach the Fire Mountains, I will grow this little lady an army—one strong enough to protect her and her children. We will be ready when the time comes to retake Avalonia, no matter if it is in my life time or not," he answered quietly.

"I know," replied Mariel. "And my son will build an army here for that purpose too." Then she looked him in the eye and swallowed hard. "Don't forget, if Griana eventually finds Tanelle, your descendants are entitled to this throne as well."

Lexon nodded once. *What descendants? Who would fall in love with a mutilated and deposed fae prince?* But he kept his bitter thoughts to himself. "Ready?" he asked Mariel, his heart banging wildly inside his chest. He did not want to do this next task. It sickened him to his core—but it was the only way.

Mariel nodded and looked at Garnald. "Remember, my love,

this is my choice. Erzion has to have a reason to betray his prince."

Garnald leaned in and kissed her hard on the lips. "I know. I will find you again soon," he promised and took Tanelle from Lexon. He limped out without a backward glance.

Lexon steeled his courage and bunched his fist.

Mariel smiled bravely at him. "Lexon, it's alright. You can do this," she reassured him.

Lexon shook his head, not sure he could.

Mariel frowned. "Prince Arjuno, if you love my son and value his life, you *will* do this. We both know Erzion will not be able to fabricate a reason for Griana to trust him in such a short space of time! Now do it!" she hissed at him.

Hating himself and the circumstances that put him in this position, Lexon slammed his fist into her jaw.

CHAPTER 9

ERZION

Erzion groaned. His tongue stuck to the roof of his mouth when he tried to swallow, the lingering taste of the Monksweet making him want to throw up.

He pulled himself upright.

Lexon! You stupid bastard!

Erzion knew his friend had done this to help him. They both knew it would be hard for him to have a reason to remain behind, especially if he was seen fighting alongside his supposed enemy.

He groaned as he pushed up. It took only a moment for his magic to recover and become accessible again. Erzion glamoured his wings back to gold.

The sounds of heavy fighting came from the lower echelons of the city, blown towards his ears on the sea wind. His king and prince were gone, quite possibly along with the goddess who had created this world, and Avalonians were now being forced to fight each other.

It made Erzion sick to his soul. Pushing those thoughts aside, the red wizard carefully ascended the stone steps. He peered up from the stairwell.

The gardens were deserted. The dark shapes of fallen warriors littered the ground.

Taking a breath, he bounded up the last step and sprinted to the nearest palace doors. Inside, more bodies covered the halls. Blood coated the flagstones, sticking to his boots as he ran. At one fallen palace guard, Erzion stooped and swiped up a dagger and a sword. His feet pounded down the corridor, he took the left fork, then burst outside through the door that would take him to the front of the king's tower.

He needed to make sure Lexon got out of the city.

In his haste, Erzion did not see the squad of warriors protecting the base of the tower. He skidded to a halt, blood trickling down his temple from the bang he had taken to his head.

Griana turned to face him, her now gold wings armoured and catching the light. A slow grin spread over her face. "Well, well, Erzion," she stated, studying him with narrowed eyes. "Where is Lexon? Lovers tiff?" she asked, indicating the blood on his head with a nod.

Erzion scowled and remained silent. He was trying to figure out a way to hide his disgust of this female and convince her—and himself—that he wanted to serve her. "Lexon is no longer my prince," Erzion growled, grateful his loathing of those words lent such an angry quality to his voice.

"Really?" Griana murmured, raising her brows. "What happened in those cells to change your love for the boy you have served all your life? And how *exactly* did you get out?" she asked, dangerously.

Erzion snarled to cover the seconds he needed to think. "It's *her* fault. The goddess came. She was weak from birthing her brat. She knew she would die soon, so she gave Lexon a way out—his promise to raise the child—in return for his freedom. The selfish bastard took it. He said he couldn't stand to be trapped here and used by you. He freely took a blood pledge." He swallowed as if in distaste. "She gifted him some of her magic to help him escape the city, before breaking the lock. That's how he got out. Then the coward left me there, saying he could get farther alone. After everything I have done for him. I gave him my life and he left me!" he yelled and thrust his sword into the ground where it swayed side to side.

Truth and lies, lies and truth.

Griana watched him. Weighing. Deciding. "Maybe. But that does not explain how *you* got out of a locked iron cell."

Erzion stood tall and snarled. He forced himself to seethe with anger, even though inside he was quaking with fear.

"Well, Erzion? What did that manipulative whore offer you to release you from your cage? Must you stay here and spy on me?" Griana asked.

Erzion resisted the urge to gulp or look guilty. "She offered me immortality, and I took it. But it wasn't to stay here, like I thought, and fight for my city and home; she told me that I would have to leave here. That I would become a guardian for her child, as I always have been for Lexon. I am a warrior! A good one! And I deserve better!" Erzion spat.

Griana had always resented her position as a guard for Noan. She had wanted to be recognised as far more.

She blinked, the only sign he might be getting through to her.

"Besides, my mother is my life. I will *not* leave her. Promise me my mother's soul will be safe from Erebos, and I will serve you however you wish."

Griana smiled a snake's smile. "And why would I do that?"

"Because my immortality means I can serve you for as long as you want me. I can lead your armies and give you someone you can rely on for hundreds of years. I will give you victory against the fae who will surely rise up against you—and I will serve your every order. I am a far better warrior than any you have under your control. Who else can you trust, Griana?"

Griana's smile was hideous, the greed in her eyes as she looked him over unmistakable.

Erzion pretended not to notice, instead he swiped blood from his right eye and looked around at the circle of warriors.

"These are my *Queen's* Guard. If I wish it, they will strike you down where you stand," Griana told him, observing every minute movement he made, but the challenge to prove himself was there, in her voice.

"Really?" he replied. His wide, arrogant grin hadn't fully stretched his mouth when he threw his dagger. Before it had chance to spear the male's throat, Erzion pulled his sword from the ground and killed the two guards nearest Griana.

Smiling with delight at the bloodshed, she slammed up a shield around herself.

All levity gone from his face, Erzion swallowed his self-disgust and guilt. He flipped into the air and fought the guards who followed him up. Spearing one on his sword, he used his armoured wings to slash off another's sword arm. Screaming, the warrior fell to the ground.

Erzion landed elegantly, still gripping his stolen sword.

Thick blood dripped from his wings. He eyed the screaming warrior coldly as blood pumped onto the ground near Erzion's boots.

Erzion stepped back. *Have I done enough?*

Outwardly he appeared unconcerned by killing his Avalonian brothers; inside he screamed and cursed the goddess for placing him in this position. *What other atrocities will I be forced to perpetrate in order to fulfil my blood oath?*

Griana fixed him with her icy green eyes.

Erzion's lower belly tightened, pulling his balls up painfully. *Don't bite me*, he prayed silently. He thrust his blade back into the ground and dropped to one knee before the new queen. "It seems you need a new guard, my queen. An elite force who can protect you. And perhaps someone to train them," he advised quietly. "I pledge myself to you for the rest of my eternal life, if you will save my mother's soul," he said gravely.

Before Griana could answer, a figure staggered out of the tower entrance.

Erzion's blood froze. "Mother?" he whispered in horror.

Mariel's face was swollen, her eyes just slits among the bruised flesh of her face. Blood trickled from her mouth and she held her ribs, stumbling forward.

"Mother!" he exclaimed again, catching her before she could fall.

Griana watched coldly, her lips a tight line.

"Who did this to you?" he hissed, his voice trembling with suppressed rage.

Mariel buried her face in his chest and sobbed. "L-Lexon" she cried, her words broken by pained sobs. "H-he took...the... princess. He took her from me. I-I couldn't do...anything. He-he killed all the...guards."

Erzion roared his rage, but the painful pinch of his mother's fingers on the skin of his forearm kept him grounded, reminding him of his glamour. With an enormous amount of effort, he controlled his magic. Instead, he stretched out his glorious golden wings and shook them violently. Anger stole his reason.

How could Lexon do this?

"P-please. Stop them. He is trying...to...leave the...city," she sniffed and gulped. Her eyes opened wider as she spoke and Erzion saw the message in her gaze. He chose to ignore it. Not even Lexon could be forgiven for harming his mother this way, no matter the reason.

Erzion laid Mariel gently on the ground. She stared up at him, sorrow in her eyes. Erzion ground his teeth and turned to Griana. He stalked up to her, gold magic swirling around his hands. Commanding it back into his body, he pulled his blade from the ground and bowed his head to his new queen.

"Let me hunt him down. I will kill the child if you desire. Let me go, and once he is dead, I will serve you forever," he pronounced, his voice unwavering but full of anger and the promise of violence.

Griana's responding smile was triumphant. "Forever?" she rejoined.

"Yes," growled Erzion. "My immortal service is yours, if you let me kill Lexon—and you keep her safe." He nodded to Mariel.

Griana snorted. "Make no mistake, Erzion, this throne is mine. Even when my Lord Erebos arrives here, I will be queen. That child must never get chance to take it back. I demand your service and absolute loyalty for the remainder of your immortal life. In return I agree to let you—and your mother—live." Griana dropped her magical shield and spread her wings. "Come. We shall find them together, then you will kill them both. After it is done, I dare say we can come to some arrangement about the terms of your service, *Master Commander*, and how you will best serve me," she remarked, raking her gaze over him from head to toe before she glanced meaningfully at Mariel.

Erzion avoided looking at his mother; instead, he smiled as though nothing were more pleasing to him than serving this hideous female for the rest of his life. Forcing a look of desire on his face, he returned the favour for Griana, deliberately appraising her curves. "I dare say we can," he growled.

Armour clattered across their wings and together the Queen of Avalonia and her new Master Commander launched into the sky.

CHAPTER 10

ERZION

Erzion kept his face hard and scanned the city. Deep inside, though, he was having real problems reconciling his sudden change in circumstances and allegiance.

Scanning the warren of tiny streets below, he swallowed the fear that coated his mouth and throat. *Has Erebos triumphed?* There was no sign of the Lord of Souls within the city, only pockets of fae loyal to their king, fighting fae now under false loyalty to Griana.

How could she control so many minds simultaneously?

Trying to ignore the carnage of bodies in the streets. He released a slow steadying breath, taking control of his emotions and mind.

"This way," stated Griana.

Erzion glanced at her in question.

She wrinkled her nose. "I can smell Lexon's stink. My Lord's gifts aren't all as grand as immortality," she bit out, her voice muffled by the rush of the wind.

Erzion merely nodded and followed her, not sure now his anger was settling, what he was going to do if they caught up with Lexon.

The tang of brine was heavy in the air, but only moments later Lexon's scent assaulted his nose too.

Griana glanced at him from under her lashes.

He snarled, pretending not to notice her scrutiny.

They passed over a tiny quay. Fishermen and city folk alike watched them wide-eyed. Then he saw a lone figure scrambling over the slippery rocks. The loner's objective was clear. A small fishing boat bobbed nearby, waiting to take Lexon and the baby out to one of the waiting ships.

Erzion narrowed his eyes, anger heating his magic. He remembered his mother's beaten face, quelling the voice of reason that told him Lexon would never willingly hurt Mariel.

Lashed by the ocean wind, Lexon seemed unsteady on his feet, clearly unbalanced by his lack of wings. He glanced up, and his face tightened in panic as he saw Erzion and Griana approaching.

The tattoos on his skin glowed as he put the bundle he carried into a crevice in the rocks.

Erzion did not give his friend the chance to call upon the full force of his magic; he promptly hurtled a wave of gold magic down upon Lexon.

Lexon bellowed and cast a shield over himself and the child. Erzion's magic bounced harmlessly back into the air. Tanelle began to cry, a high pitched squeal that grated on Erzion's frayed nerves.

Griana chuckled then yelled out, "Give yourself to me now, prince, and I will let the baby live. Defy me, and you will both die."

Lexon's answer was a shimmering, hot blast of magic. Clearly not expecting such a powerful onslaught, Griana was slow to raise her shields. The magical bolt knocked Griana from the sky, and she slammed into the ground. She grunted but her shield remained raised.

Erzion swore under his breath; he hoped to get a chance to end her.

Lexon immediately turned to Erzion. "So, you truly have chosen to follow your immortal path?" he asked.

A carefully phrased question.

"Did you find your mother?" Lexon added, his voice low and dark.

"Yes, I did, you bastard! How could you? After everything she has done for you. Your betrayal has broken our friendship. I will never serve you again," Erzion said, but something in his friend's eyes caused him to hesitate. Realisation punched through his gut.

Lexon nodded, then smiled sadly. "I know you won't."

Griana screeched and pushed her chest off the ground. Dirt and blood covered her face and clothes. Snarling, she lifted one hand. Magic hurtled towards Lexon. It slammed into him, sending him staggering; but instead of killing the prince, the blast of energy seemed to make his magic grow stronger.

Erzion watched Lexon shake the surprise from his shoulders and right himself. With one hand, the prince sent burning, red magic crashing down on the queen.

Griana met his magic with a green and gold surge.

Power exploded as their magic collided, a shadow swirling through the warring forces.

Erzion's heart thumped. Erebos was helping Griana. Somehow, the Lord of Souls was boosting her magic with that darkness.

Sparks flew and the energy burned the air, sucking away the oxygen.

"Talk to your mother," grated Lexon. "Please learn to forgive me for what I did to her. It was necessary. Now we can both honour our pledges."

Erzion nodded once and meaningfully looked to the infant, but he knew the queen was still watching. He had to act. He had to look like he was defending the new monarch. "I will always honour my pledge to my queen!" he bellowed, sending a surge of power at Lexon. His aim was sloppy. As if Lexon had deflected it, his gold magic slammed into the ground at the prince's feet.

Lexon's throat bobbed and his eyelids flickered. "Then I will leave you with this parting gift!" he roared.

Magic slammed into Erzion, knocking him to the ground next to Griana. His chest wouldn't expand properly and his lungs burned.

Griana snarled and redoubled her efforts, sending wave after wave of power crashing into Lexon's magic.

Sweat rolled down Lexon's forehead. He grunted and swore.

Erzion knew Lexon had far surpassed the limits of his own immature power. He was using the goddess's gift now, but Erzion had no idea how long it would last.

Sweat streamed down Lexon's face and chest. For a moment, he closed his eyes, looking pained before he snapped them open again. When he spoke, his voice was almost unrecognisable. "I will not weaken myself fighting you. You *shall* rule, Griana, but you will forever be trapped here in this city."

Almost as if someone else grasped his magic and his thoughts, Lexon's eyes dimmed. Archaic, harsh sounding words poured from his mouth.

Erzion inhaled sharply. The language of the guardians! Master Yagus had taught Erzion enough to recognise it, but as far as he knew, Lexon had never learned to speak that sacred language.

Wisely, Erzion did not to show he understood every single word Lexon uttered.

"False queen." Those words said. "For your part in trying to kill a child of the goddess, of the very blood we protect, you *will* suffer." Lexon lowered his sword. Raising his other hand, heat and a strange kind of energy shimmered through the air.

Erzion's eyes watered, his chest heaving, once again, barely able to breath. His magic dwindled, smothered by whatever power this was.

"You will never know the love of a child," Lexon continued, his voice hard. "Your body will remain as barren as your heart until destiny decrees otherwise. On the single longest night of the year—the Winter Solstice—you will be granted a single chance of conceiving new life. But that child's love will never be yours."

A hot flare of magic burned even Erzion's skin. He shied away, protecting his eyes. When the air cleared, Lexon swayed on his feet and panted hard. His naked body was slick with sweat, and his tattoos were dimming.

Whatever curse Lexon was weaving was rapidly draining the strength Lunaria had given him.

Erzion wished he could help but knew he could not, not without exposing his wizard side.

Griana grunted and increased her efforts, pummelling Lexon's weakening shields. "Get the child," she ground out, pointing toward Tanelle.

Erzion stood, only to be knocked down by Lexon, right on top of his new queen.

Lexon's eyes blazed as he deflected the magic Griana and Erzion hurled at him.

Griana screamed in frustration, hitting Erzion in the ribs to move him off her. Erzion rolled off, deliberately staggering, hoping Lexon had a way of finishing this.

Before he could even form his next thought, a mighty roar shook the air.

Out of the gloom of dusk, a green and gold dragon slammed down onto the rocks behind Lexon. Maw stretched wide, Vaalor roared. Sulphuric breath filled the air, and acidic saliva sprayed against the rocks.

Erzion slammed his magic forward to augment Griana's shield. He had to play his part. Now and always.

A woman sat upon the beast's back. She had long dark hair and the palest skin Erzion had ever seen. In her hand she carried a golden staff. His heart missed a beat—several in fact. It was Lunaria's spear! How had she gotten it?

Vomit surged up his throat. The answer was staring him in the face. Vaalor was here. Lunaria...and Noan, were gone. He swallowed his nausea and grief, hoping that Erebos, at least, had been beaten.

Urgently, the woman beckoned to Lexon.

Vaalor's constant barrage of gaseous belches and acid ensured the queen and Erzion were unable to attack Lexon as he dropped his magic and swooped down to grab Tanelle. He staggered toward the fireless dragon and, once within touching distance, reached out a hand, slapping it onto Vaalor's body. That connection ignited the air around the city of Valentia.

With the help of the woman, Lexon hoisted himself onto the dragon's neck.

As a shimmering curtain of energy and magic descended from high over the fae city, the last thing Erzion saw was the spear clutched in the woman's hands, its runes glowing brightly.

The guardian roared and launched itself to the skies.

Erzion could do nothing when that shimmering curtain hit the ground, stretching as far out as the Rift Valley and out over the ocean waves.

The air imploded, throwing him and every other citizen in Valentia off their feet. Erzion's head cracked against the rocks, pain exploding inside his skull. Through the descending darkness in his mind, he heard Griana choking and coughing. Allowing himself a small smug smile, he let her, hoping she would drown in her own blood. The sound of a dragon's roar was the last thing the red wizard heard as he gladly fell into unconsciousness.

CHAPTER 11

LEXON

Lexon blinked, his eyes raw. The wind had dried them out completely. Under his aching thighs, scale and muscle rippled.

Vaalor was injured.

Lexon could see huge gouges of ripped scales and torn flesh. It looked like claws and teeth had penetrated his armour coating. Lexon swallowed. He would not allow himself to think about what evil creatures had the strength to do that, of how his brother may have died.

Fighting his tears, he sent a prayer to Eternity, begging the guardians to care for his brother's soul.

Another shiver racked his frozen, half-clothed body. He was so cold. They had been flying for hours. Dawn had come and gone. Now the sun rose high in the sky, though it provided very little relief from the freezing wind.

He hated the thought that the dark-haired girl sitting behind him had full view of his mutilated back. Lexon's nostrils flared. He had wondered at first whether he could trust her. But it was clear Vaalor did—and she hadn't stabbed Lexon—yet.

Her spear had confirmed his worst expectations; his brother

and his queen were dead. Sadness tore his heart, his shoulders caving inward with the weight of his grief.

Below them the forest thinned until it disappeared altogether, and they soared over rolling grassland. Even the air became marginally warmer.

Lexon hardly noticed; he was fighting a bone-deep weariness and concentrating on gripping Tanelle with one arm and the dragon with the other. He hoped he would not fall asleep and drop her. With that thought, he shook himself for the umpteenth time.

A small tap on his right shoulder made him jump. A welcome heat warmed his cold skin as the girl leaned in so she could yell in his ear. "I can take her for a while, prince!"

Lexon didn't answer. He couldn't. He just shook his head.

Tanelle was his to protect. His only surviving family.

"Fine," he heard the girl mutter before she leaned away.

Lexon almost groaned. He wished she would stay there, pressed up against him. He was so cold, his teeth chattered.

Vaalor released a short shriek of warning and angled down towards the ground.

Lexon narrowed his eyes, blinking furiously in order to peer at the distant outline. A huge, grey stone castle. A fortress by the ocean.

He had been here once before.

Stormguaard. The mortal king's seat.

The girl leaned in again. "Vaalor says I should hold onto you and the little princess," she told him. "He thinks you might fall off when he lands."

Lexon would have liked to disagree, but he knew she was right. His arms—his whole body—were shaking so much he could barely hold himself upright anymore, let alone be certain he wouldn't drop Tanelle. Reluctantly, he nodded, hating that he had to rely on this stranger for help. He had never relied on anyone but Erzion—and his old friend was gone now.

Exhausted and overwhelmed by his circumstances, Lexon couldn't stop the tears that blurred his vision. He barely registered the warmth of the female's arms as she leaned forward to wrap around him, her front pressed up against his back. Her fingers whitened as she grabbed on hard to Vaalor's protruding scales.

"You just concentrate on keeping the baby in your arms. I won't let you fall," the girl said firmly.

Lexon looked at her slim arms and wrists and wondered if she had enough strength to keep herself on the dragon's back, let alone him too. But he merely nodded.

Vaalor screeched again as if in warning. They dipped sharply from the sky. The ground soon levelled out; the golden, grass-covered fields rushed by below. Soon Vaalor glided over the wide and bustling city streets. The aroma of spiced meat hit Lexon in the face. Saliva rushed his mouth, and he groaned. He couldn't remember the last time he had eaten. His heart squeezed anxiously; he didn't know when Tanelle had last eaten.

Faces gaped upward, and people pointed with an equal mix of awe and fear. Lexon gulped when suddenly the buildings disappeared and the ground dropped away. They soared out over the rough ocean that sparkled in the sunlight.

Vaalor roared loudly, almost as if greeting the soldiers and warriors now crowding the castle walls. He dipped a wing and circled above the castle keep, lowering them gently until he hovered over a large stone terrace, his massive wings thudding against the air.

Vaalor swung his great head backward, his elongated pupils flickering.

"He asks if you are ready to land. He says the princess needs sustenance—and so do you. He wants you to know you can trust King Oden."

Lexon nodded. He didn't really want to land at all, he wanted to head out over the ocean and far away from Griana. She would send Erzion after them. It would be her way of testing Erzion's loyalty. The thought that Erzion now served that female was painful and, though he knew his friend would not willingly harm either of them, Lexon could not face fighting Erzion again.

Vaalor flapped his wings and turned his head, his eyes rolling. He snarled, clearly impatient.

"Yes, guardian. I'm ready to land," Lexon lied, watching the armour-clad men who stalked out of the castle and stared up grim-faced.

Vaalor landed with surprising smoothness on the castle terrace.

Lexon's face burned as the girl straightened, leaving his naked torso completely open to the scrutiny of these hardened warriors. Dirt and blood cracked on his skin as he moved. Tanelle began to whimper. For a moment she distracted him from his own embarrassment. With a shaking finger, he pushed the blanket from her face. The poor little mite looked shockingly pale, dark shadows under her eyes. Lexon's stomach lurched with anxiety.

He did not want to be subjected to the questions and judgment of these men, especially the young king—who was handsome and powerful, who ruled his home and kingdom, who was *whole*—everything Lexon was not. But Lexon pushed those jealous, useless thoughts away. Tanelle needed milk, and this king could provide it.

Trying to control his stiff and shaking limbs, Lexon straightened his spine.

The girl jumped nimbly to the ground. "Pass me the princess, then you can get down."

Lexon eyed her suspiciously. He trusted no one. Tanelle was his responsibility.

The girl sighed. "Prince, I am not going to hurt her. I know you are exhausted and have lost much, but if I wanted to harm either of you, I would have done so by now."

Lexon knew she was right. Without another word, he passed Tanelle down into her waiting arms.

Knowing his back would be totally exposed to the scrutiny of the watching males, Lexon hesitated further. His eyes flicked to the man standing at the centre of the group. Pity flickered over the king's handsome face.

Determination flared in Lexon's chest. He would *not* be pitied.

Flinging his leg over the protruding spine of the dragon, he dropped, glad to be free of the beast. His feet crashed into the ground, the impact making his knees buckle. Cursing his body, he forced himself to stand straight—to appear strong, no matter how he was crumbling inside.

The group of men watched him warily, their eyes straying to the dragon. Vaalor huffed huge, stinking breaths into the air but was otherwise silent. The creature lowered his huge bulk until he was lying on the ground and his head drooped onto the stone-covered terrace, which had cracked under his weight.

Lexon recognised the despair and guilt in the dragon's eyes and felt a sudden surge of empathy for the creature. Yes, Vaalor had failed to protect Noan and his beloved goddess, but still...

His eyes.

It was like looking in a mirror. Vaalor had already lost his family and now his goddess; his purpose in life was gone. Erebos and Griana had timed their attack well. Vaalor had been too weak to fight an army of monsters and the dark god.

Lexon had always been terrified of this fire-breathing dragon. Ever since being a small child, he had been convinced this creature would burn his bones to dust. He still didn't trust it completely, but his heart went out to the beast. Briefly he rested his hand against the creature's chest wall. Vaalor rolled his eyes towards him then huffed, his focus shifting back to the king.

Right, Lexon thought. *I need to talk to them.*

Not knowing what sort of reception to expect, he took a steadying breath. They had all seen the extent of his humiliation at Griana's hands, and he knew there would be an inevitable barrage of questions about what had happened.

Vaalor huffed again, this time nudging Lexon.

"Fine! I'm going," he muttered at the beast.

He knew the girl by his side was watching him too. For a moment, Lexon's eyes snagged on the bundle of cloth that swaddled Tanelle. She was deathly quiet once again. Lexon's stomach turned with apprehension. He knew nothing about caring for a baby, about raising a child.

He looked at the girl, but her deep brown eyes weren't looking at his face, they were grazing across his naked chest. She must have sensed his attention, because her eyes flew guiltily to his.

Lexon flushed about the same time she did. Inwardly, he groaned, acutely embarrassed by his red cheeks, which in turn, only made them redder.

He knew he wasn't as heavily muscled as many red wings but his confidence in his appearance had grown these last weeks. Now, all that new found confidence had been destroyed—by Griana. The stumps on his back were hideous, and all he wanted to do was cover himself up.

Lexon wiped his damp palms down his filthy leggings and controlled his urge to run from everyone's gaze. "Is she alright?" he asked the girl instead.

The girl nodded, her cheeks still pink.

That was then he noticed her braided hair was not black as he first thought, but a deep shade of auburn, which shimmered with red as the sunlight caught it.

He turned away from her; he would find out who she was later. Right now he had to beg a king for help. He hoped Vaalor knew what he was doing, and that this king was trustworthy. Though Lexon really had no choice. He needed help with Tanelle; a wet nurse or someway of feeding her before he continued their journey.

"King Oden?" he said, facing the welcoming party.

The king looked to be in his late twenties. Like the Arjuno family, he had clearly chosen to forego wearing a crown in favour of wearing a sword. His body was that of a warrior; broad shoulders led to a narrow waist. He had a hard, chiselled jaw and deep brown eyes that narrowed as he assessed Lexon and the girl by his side. The king's gaze lingered on the girl, who had stepped up beside Lexon.

Lexon didn't blame the man; even in Lexon's distressed, exhausted state, he knew she was beautiful. He bristled, though the goddess only knew why; he didn't even know her name.

Unbidden, a slight snarl curled his lip. Shocked at his reaction, Lexon immediately curbed his desire to stand between the girl and the other men, especially the handsome king. From the corner of his eye, he saw her turn her head and stare at him.

For the first time ever, Lexon cursed his fae heritage as his magic surged, heating his eyes. He had never reacted this way because of another person, never.

Without asking, and to give himself time to cool his response, he took Tanelle from the girl's arms, making sure to avoid her gaze.

Focusing back on the king, Lexon settled Tanelle in the crook of his arm. His exhausted body was almost ready to collapse, and he stumbled forward.

King Oden's guards immediately drew their swords.

"No. Let him approach," instructed King Oden.

Lexon did, until he towered over the king, who was not small by human standards. Lexon, however, was tall even for a fae, and with his black hair and sapphire eyes, he was immediately recognisable to most people.

"Prince Lexon Arjuno," the king said, fixing Lexon with a narrowed-eyed, assessing stare. "So I take it Erebos has finally attacked your city?" he asked.

"Yes," Lexon answered, still unsure what sort of reception this was to be.

"So why are you here?" King Oden asked, his eyes once again travelling to the girl at Lexon's side.

Lexon looked down at her too. She was looking at the king as if weighing him up. Lexon didn't know why he moved, but he angled a shoulder slightly in front of her, effectively closing off the gap between her and the king.

What the hell is wrong with me? I don't even know who she is, he berated himself.

The girl glanced up and raised her brows in question.

Uncomfortable once again, Lexon ignored her, not sure how to explain his actions.

"The guardian and this girl brought me here...erm," Lexon paused, suddenly wondering how he should address this man. It was true he was a king, but Lexon was still a prince—wasn't he? Feeling completely inadequate all of a sudden, Lexon stumbled over his words. "I-I—er—majesty. I'm afraid I find myself in need of your help…" Lexon's voice faded. He cursed himself for sounding so unsure in front of these men. His brother wouldn't have; neither would Erzion.

"Of course," interrupted King Oden, his voice kind, understanding even. "Whatever you need. You will be given somewhere safe to rest and food too—as much as you require. But first, tell me what happened to your family. Who now sits on the throne of Avalonia? If you are here with the guardian, it is no longer your family or the goddess."

It was a statement, a hateful fact that Lexon had to swallow bitterly. Whilst he was still trying to form words, someone else spoke.

"Majesty. The prince is exhausted and I have information he does not," the girl piped up from behind Lexon. Taking a breath she looked the king right in the eye. "My true name is Alethia…"

They all gasped.

"What!" Lexon burst out incredulously. "You are Lunaria's

sister? The Goddess of Truth?" He was no longer stuttering. Shock had dissipated his nerves.

Tanelle's tiny body jerked at his raised voice. Her soft face turned into his chest, desperately rooting, trying to suckle. Lexon readjusted her, guilt washing through him that she was so hungry. Denied, she was soon squealing pitifully.

Alethia frowned, defiance sparking across her face at his questions. "Yes, prince, I am." Dismissing him, she turned back to the king.

Lexon snapped his gaping mouth shut and, with effort, swallowed his irrational resentment. The silky softness of Tanelle's blanket rubbed his skin as he rocked her and forced himself to listen.

"I am here on the instruction of my father, the High Ruler of the Guardians of Eternity. My father has seen the path both your world and mine may take. Only shadow and death await us all. He has ordered me to write his vision in a scroll. It must be kept safe and secret until fate declares it ready to be found once again."

"A scroll? You mean you brought me here to serve your own agenda? Not out of concern for Tanelle?" Lexon bit out.

Alethia turned to him. "Yes. King Oden must be the bearer of this scroll to its true custodian. But both you and Tanelle need care and rest. You are exhausted and Tanelle is dangerously dehydrated," she said, worry colouring her voice, but that tone changed when she spoke to the king again. "King Oden? Prince Lexon's family have perished at the hands of the new queen—and the goddess is no more. There was a terrible battle against the Lord of Souls, one which would have left this world at the mercy of Erebos had he won." She swallowed hard, tears shining in her eyes. "So many died. I have never seen such carnage."

Lexon fisted his hands. He wanted to comfort her, but didn't know if she would allow him to, or even if he was capable of such an act right now. So he just stood there, useless in the face of her grief.

"Erebos had winged demons on his side," Alethia continued. "Terrible creatures that have never been seen before. They were built for death and destruction. The guardians could not let Erebos release them on this world with no resistance."

"You mean *all* the guardians came?" Lexon asked, incredulously.

"Yes. All of us." Her attention drifted to Vaalor, whose eyes were closed and his breathing laboured.

The slash wounds were not healing. Lexon could smell the festering lesions from where he stood. *And yet, even with all their power, Noan still died, and Vaalor is gravely injured,* Lexon thought bitterly.

"The Ashmea. That is what Erebos called his winged demons. Lunaria ordered Vaalor to destroy them. He fought so hard alongside us. But he is the only one of our kind who has fed from the rivers of fire. He alone turned many to ash with his flame before it flickered out."

"What happened to the goddess?" asked the king, his voice quiet, but Lexon did not miss its slight tremble. A frown creased the skin between the king's brows. Clearly he was anxious and already planning how to protect his borders and people from such a threat.

Alethia swallowed hard. "When we arrived at the battle, my sister was fighting to protect Noan's soul. I have never seen her so weak. Erebos and his wraiths, his soul collectors, worked together to diminish her," she spat those words with hatred. "Still, they could not best her. By the time we had fought our way through the Ashmea, she was spent, no magic left. Her spear was the only chance she had left. I saw her throw it."

A tear ran down Alethia's cheek.

Lexon stiffened. He could almost feel her pain—her loss. His own was roiling inside him just as fiercely.

"It missed his heart. And in that moment, we all knew she was lost."

"You mean, all of the guardians together could not stop one god?" Horror filled King Oden's eyes.

Lexon felt his anger burn at the accusation in the king's tone. "You were not there. You cannot judge," he growled in Alethia's defence before his common sense could stop the words.

The king's men immediately stiffened.

Alethia didn't look at him, but her warm fingers grazed his cold arm. A warning. And, he thought, gratitude.

"I didn't say that," she replied, her voice thick with emotion. "My father channelled our combined power. He encased Erebos in a cage of ice and crystal. He could not run and he could not fight. Our magic sucked him dry. Then I saw it...a huge portal in the ground. It opened under King Noan," she looked at him her eyes dark and swimming with regret. "His body was taken."

Lexon's heart stopped beating. He was falling, just as his brother had.

Alethia swallowed hard and continued. "That void was full of nothing but darkness and screaming and despair. It was a portal to Chaos." She looked to the grieving dragon. "Vaalor unleashed all he had left of his flame upon the dark god. He sent Erebos back to his vile kingdom. But it was too late for my sister. The wraiths grabbed her. When Vaalor's fire faltered, she was gone."

Stunned quiet descended.

"What happened to my brother's soul?"

Alethia turned to him. Her fingers curled gently over his arm, though he barely felt it.

"Lunaria sacrificed herself to save his soul. My father has taken him to Eternity."

Lexon felt his already hot eyes burning with unshed tears now. He needed to get away from them all. He needed to scream and shout and cry, without an audience.

"Perhaps you would like to take the little one to my mother,

Prince Lexon? She will help you find a suitable wet nurse. Please stay. Recover your strength. Tanelle will be well cared for, and you will have chance to make proper plans for your future," the king advised. "I will help any way I can. You will be safe; my men will inform me if they see the new queen's troops approaching."

Lexon inhaled then blew out a long breath, simultaneously relieved to be able to rest and impatient to get as far away from this continent as possible.

The dragon stirred and looked to Alethia.

They locked eyes, a silent conversation taking place.

"He says you should stay and recover, that you are the guardian of Lunaria's line now." Her brows furrowed as they continued their silent communication. A clear sign she was unhappy. "Vaalor will not be accompanying us any farther," she said, her nostrils flaring, much as Vaalor's were doing. "He refuses to say why."

"Really?" interrupted Lexon, suddenly angry, and perhaps disappointed. He turned and fixed the dragon with a red-eyed, glowing glare. "Well, you *should* go farther. You are bound to protect this little princess with every part of your soul, guardian. You cannot fail her, not like you did her mother. She needs you," he growled, magic swirling in a storm around his body.

Vaalor turned sad eyes toward him, but it was Alethia who spoke again. "He says he was not chosen as Tanelle's guardian. You and your heirs were," she added in a softer tone.

Warm fingers once again curled around his skin. His upper arm, this time. Her touch, her very presence, seemed to calm his magic, though he did not know what to do with his anger. He wanted to strike out at something. Instead, he gulped as he looked down at her slim fingers resting on the muscular contours of his arm.

Vaalor huffed softly, looking between them before he curled into an even tighter ball and closed his eyes once again.

Tanelle began to wail pitifully. Lexon pulled his arm away

from Alethia's touch before he began to gently rock Tanelle—trying to calm her and his own tumbling emotions.

The king watched their interactions with shrewd eyes. His gaze flicked to Alethia. But the Goddess of Truth didn't notice the king's scrutiny; her attention was solely on Lexon.

"I would greatly appreciate your mother's help with this little one, Majesty. I-I haven't a clue about what to feed her or how to care for her other needs. Perhaps your mother could show me?" Lexon asked, hating his inadequacy.

The king merely nodded, his face a pleasant mask. Lexon had no way of knowing if he was being judged. He found he didn't care right now. Exhaustion almost had his knees collapsing.

"Of course," answered King Oden, before ordering one of his guards to escort Lexon to his mother's chambers.

Lexon gladly followed the soldier, leaving Alethia with the handsome king. He did not look back, no matter how much he wanted to.

CHAPTER 12

GRIANA

Griana sank her sword into the belly of yet another defiant fae. Fatigue dogged her. Her muscles burned and trembled, but still her dark-laced magic raged strong, lending her strength.

With unrelenting focus, she thrust out a wave of magic. It barrelled into six burly warriors, sending them crashing from the air into the ground. She snarled, satisfaction warming her. She ensured their bones broke painfully. Their screams joined the cacophony of terror and agony that filled the city streets.

Beside her, Erzion mercilessly cut down those opposing her. His skill far outmatched anything she had seen before; even the old fae king had not been this fast or talented. He was a natural with a blade, but it was the way his body moved—fluid and smooth—that made her want to stand and watch. She wondered at his magic being only gold. He fought so powerfully and instilled such fear in the attacking soldiers, she could have sworn he would be a red.

Her troops cut down any who challenged the new queen. Blood ran in thick streams down the sloping streets of the ramshackle city. It pooled against the soles of her boots, bringing the stink of death with it.

Griana inhaled. It was a welcome stink. She would purge this kingdom of any she could not control, though she avoided looking up at that hateful shimmering shield, her cage. Its power over her life sickened her.

After Lexon had escaped on the back of that hideous beast, Griana had launched herself towards the shield, Erzion by her side. Screaming and yelling, she had beat her fists against the impenetrable wall of magic until they were burned and raw. It had made no difference. Even her ever-growing power could not punch a hole in it. It was only when she saw the guardians coming for her that she had stopped. The High Ruler of the Guardians of Eternity had sent these beasts from Eternity, to destroy her Lord—and now her.

Erzion had also looked petrified by the sight. Stunned, he had just watched them approach. Screaming her defiance, she had hovered, snarling at them, magic gathered at her fingertips, ready to fight. There had been no point in trying to escape; she knew it, and so did Erzion. But then a miracle had happened.

She laughed out loud at the memory.

The biggest one had hovered, staring at her as if he could see right through to the remains of her soul. With his horned head, he had bade two others forward. Without pause, they had rammed their barbed metallic tails into the shield—over and over.

She had landed and fallen to her knees, her uncontained mirth making it impossible to stand. Tears of laughter streamed down her face at their efforts.

Lexon may have used the goddess's gift to imprison her, but the fool had also inadvertently saved her. *Even these celestial creatures could not break through!*

Erzion had landed close beside her, sword in hand. His large frame rooted to the spot when a great beast had screeched and stared right at him. Its glowing, multi-faceted eyes rested far longer on him than they had on Griana. Erzion had snarled at the beast and shook his head, as if to rid himself of something.

Lifting his sword, the warrior had stared down at her. She had waited then, to see if he would make a move against her. When he didn't, she pushed her hands into the dirt and stood tall. Resting her hand on his muscled chest, she had stood in front of him and grinned.

"They cannot enter the city. It is mine! Help me take it, Erzion." And with that, they had begun to fight in earnest to subdue the territorial fae. Erzion had not left her side since that moment.

Keeping her face cold, she stalked up to the kneeling warrior Erzion now held in a headlock. Magic could have easily held the big male, but it was far more satisfying to see him thrash against Erzion's strength. Horror swamped the man's features at her approach.

Griana smiled, showing her second set of needle-sharp green teeth.

"Pull his head sideways," she instructed Erzion.

Blank-faced, he complied.

Griana inhaled, enjoying the scent of fear from the big red fae. "That's right, be afraid. You are mine now," she whispered into his delicately pointed ear. Savouring the moment, she slowly sank her teeth into the pulsing vein in his neck. Hot, thick blood rolled over her tongue. She swallowed, lost in ecstasy as both he and his magic thrashed. When she heard Erzion grunting with the effort of holding the male still, she released her venom.

The male went limp. She pulled her teeth from his neck and retracted them.

Erzion dropped the male unceremoniously to the ground. Disgust rippled across his stone cold features. It was so fleeting, Griana wondered if she had imagined it. She focused on him. But he remained unconcerned as his eyes flickered around the remaining warriors. They had stilled their resistance when their commander had fallen. Pale-faced, they looked at each other, their eyes darting about, looking for an escape. A smile stretched her ruby stained mouth. There was no escape.

The male on the ground began to stir.

Griana waited impatiently for him to regain full consciousness. It was a powerful feeling to take hold of his mind, to control him completely.

He scrambled onto his knees, looking utterly confused that his body moved without his consent.

"That's right, commander," she said, tugging on the link to his mind. "Your body belongs to me. *You* belong to me. You shall retain your own will—most of the time, but you will serve me and follow my every order, or I will make you do things that will sicken your soul. Do you understand?"

Pale and sweating, the warrior gulped. Full of hatred, his gaze rested upon Erzion.

Dominant and utterly cold, Erzion held his gaze, his fingers tightening on his sword.

After only a moment's hesitation, the warrior nodded.

"Good. Now, a little demonstration is in order, just so you fully understand my power over you."

She turned, the soles of her boots sticky in the clotting blood. Her eyes alighted upon a likely victim. A young, injured gold-winged fae lay quivering in a pool of his own blood, his gut sliced open.

Griana smiled. This fae would be of no further use. His injuries were too severe. It was a kindness to end him. "Kill him," she instructed, pointing at the dying warrior.

"No!" her new slave spat.

Griana huffed a dark chuckle. "I thought you might say that."

Instantly the warrior's eyes became dark, his brown irises swallowed whole by darkness. Griana did not watch his following movements, she knew what he would do; it was Erzion she surreptitiously watched.

His face remained blank, even as the warrior's blade plunged into the gold-wing's heart.

"Does it not disturb you to see your own kind kill each other?" she asked, genuinely curious.

"No. Why would it? They are nothing to me now. I am immortal, they are just a temporary stain on our city," he answered coldly.

"*My* city, Erzion," she corrected him sharply.

He bowed his head, chastised. "Of course. You shall forever be the queen of this kingdom, this city and me," he said.

His use of those words sent bliss through her body. "Yes, I am your queen; I am *the* Queen. Please don't forget that or, immortal or not, I will end you," she warned him. Magic shot from her hand and grabbed him by the throat. Even then his face remained unchanged.

Well, alright. I guess you aren't acting, she thought to herself. *You really must have lost your heart, maybe even your soul, when you lost those you loved.*

Satisfied, she released him.

Erzion immediately bowed before the Queen on one knee, lowering his head. "I will always remain loyal to the Queen and this city," he said gravely, his voice hoarse from her rough touch.

"Good. Now stand," she ordered.

He complied.

The Queen released the other warrior's mind. It was no effort to instruct him to stand before her. She rested her hands on either side of his hips and smiled up at him.

The warrior was shaking, his eyes clear, but it was obvious he dare not move away from her. Her eyes rested on Erzion.

"Master Commander Riddeon, you will train this warrior to become one of my personal guard. I want only the elite of my soldiers protecting me and doing my bidding. You will personally choose thirty men from those we fight in the coming days. I will ensure their loyalty, and you will ensure their skill."

"Yes, my queen," he replied, bowing his head.

Dismissing Erzion, Griana ran her hands up the warrior's waist, across his chest and cupped his face. His eyes darted to his warriors, who watched in horror. Fear and disgust glazed his eyes, his whole body tensing, his fingers clenching into fists at her continued touch. His hair was silky to her fingers as she pulled his face down.

"That's right" she whispered in his ear. "They will be the first to die—by your hand, if you dare defy me."

He swallowed hard. "Yes, my queen," he answered hoarsely.

Griana pulled back and grazed her lips over his. He tasted of blood and gold magic. Her heart bloomed at the power she now wielded over him.

"You will stay by my side and protect me with your life," she told him.

Turning away, the Queen of Avalonia missed the fire of hatred in Erzion's eyes before his gaze settled to golden brown once again.

∼

A week of bloodshed and near constant fighting passed. Hunting down the powerful commanders of the fae army had become a priority. Many had chosen to camp out beyond the shield, in the depths of the forest, mistakenly thinking this would protect them.

Some Erzion had succeeded in talking into her service. Her Master Commander may not be a red wing, but he had an air of authority and danger about him that easily dominated other males. Plus, his skills with a blade could not be outmatched. He had killed any who would not bend the knee to their new queen, using a coldness that impressed even her.

Now Erebos was gone, she had no real interest in killing her countrymen indiscriminately. No, she would only kill those who defied her rule, or the ones whose magic she needed for youth and immortality.

A half-smile curled her lips. *And there would be many of those*, she reflected.

Hovering above the battlements of the marble wall, Griana rubbed her tired eyes and stretched her aching body. A vicious wind froze her toes and stole her breath. Ignoring it, she slowly reached out. When her fingertips made contact with the shield, sparks flew.

She snatched her hand back and rubbed her burned fingers.

Inwardly she screamed and swore; outwardly she would not show such weakness.

Griana flew down and landed elegantly on the battlements. Her elite guards landed around her. She turned to Erzion. Filthy tunic and leggings still covered his large frame. It was covered in yet more blood.

She curled her lip. Her Master Commander should have clothes and riches befitting his station, she decided.

She still did not fully trust this warrior who had once belonged to her enemy. But he had shown no emotion since his friend had left. Even his mother had deserted him. Griana stopped the smirk from reaching her mouth. After all that pleading on his mother's behalf, the traitorous bitch had left him; just disappeared into thin air. Perhaps being betrayed had taught him a valuable lesson in the weakness of love and feelings.

Griana didn't much care where his mother had run to. After Erzion's blood pledge, he could never betray his queen. That very first night she had challenged him to swallow her blood…and show his devotion. He had accepted.

"What is it you wish me to do, my queen?" he asked now, dipping his head.

Griana met his golden stare. It would be easy to bite him and ensure his loyalty, but it was so much more fun to control someone without the aid of magic. "Find Commander Edison. I believe he has taken his squad of red wings north. Take a legion and bring him back to me before he gets too far. Kill as many as you need to ensure their submission to my rule, but do not kill the commander. I have use of such a skilled leader. Once you have him, return to me. I have other orders for you to fulfil."

"As you wish," Erzion said, his face remaining in its customary blank mask as she turned to three of her newly turned commanders.

Unable to resist, she ran her tongue over her teeth. The blood of so many new vassals thickly coated her tongue. It had become so easy to control them. Once she commanded that venom bond, their minds blossomed open like the petals of a flower.

Their eyes became dark and unfocused as she planted her orders in their minds.

With no further words, Erzion rose into the air. In formation, the others followed him. Griana watched him go, the cold wind whipping at her tired body.

Nodding to her remaining guards, Griana lifted into the air. She was buffeted about cruelly, but armouring her wings stabilized her. She manoeuvred to face the island city.

Over the ocean, the huge globe of Tu Lana hovered. Every day it sank lower to the horizon, heralding the winter storms. Soon horseback would be the only safe way to travel.

Her eyes flicked to the distance where Erzion was now just a speck. She had almost not sent him after Commander Edison, but she needed the powerful commander under her wing. He would cause far too many problems if left to grow his following. So she had pushed aside her impatience for revenge, though she hoped Erzion would return quickly. King Oden had sent word; Lexon was sheltering at Stormguaard. And it seemed even Vaalor had deserted him.

Griana folded her hatred for the dragon inside her heart;

instead, she silently thanked him for leaving her prey totally alone. It was fortuitous, too, that the human king seemed to want to protect his borders far more than he wanted to protect a deposed prince and princess. A wise move.

Way off in the distance, the pink tower loomed over the island city. The ramshackle buildings had remained largely intact, but Griana would raze much of Valentia to the ground. If she was to be stuck here for the foreseeable future, the city would need to improve. More grand buildings. More culture and theatres. More trade with the other kingdoms.

Once the bloodshed was done, rebuilding could begin.

As her wings ploughed powerfully through the turbulent air, Griana turned her attention to her own circumstances. She would tear out that throne room and build a new one, something more fitting for a conquering queen. Once she had a throne, maybe she would find a suitable male to serve her and it. Perhaps she would make Erzion her consort. He was strong, powerful and immortal. He would not age or become weak, and he dominated other fae males without hesitation.

She immediately dismissed the idea. With a stubborn set to her jaw, the Queen of Valentia determined she did not need a male by her side to rule. She would use as many as she pleased, as often as she pleased, and have only the strongest and most powerful serve her.

Erzion will remain my immortal commander. But the power to rule will be mine alone.

Behind her, she felt the presence of her guards and a smile stretched her lips. *Oh, Lexon, I wonder if you realise you have not thwarted my ability to have a child, merely delayed it. I have an eternity to conceive an heir. And I now have a never-ending supply of the strongest warriors in this kingdom. Winter Solstice shall be the most enjoyable night of the year for me, for eternity.*

You, on the other hand, will die, as will that little half-goddess. We all know immortality is never inherited.

CHAPTER 13

LEXON

Lexon watched the sunrise over the distant ocean. The dark blue waters sparkled, as if scattered with jewels. A warm breeze fanned his body through the small open window. He leaned his head out, studying the part of the castle wall he could see.

The fortress of Stormguaard was an austere and huge place, built of immense grey stone walls, towers and keeps. It perched upon the high cliff edge as if daring the winter storms and the powerful ocean to knock it down.

The large central keep was protected by an outer keep, which backed onto the sheer cliff edge. Granite towers protected the sides and front of the castle, all joined by wide ramparts.

For almost two months now he had explored the castle freely, taking in the garrisons of soldiers patrolling the wall and camping on the grasslands outside the city. Lexon had no idea if that was normal. The thought that he may have put this whole city at risk by staying here made him feel sick.

He gazed back at the beauty of the bright fireball rising from the dark horizon of the ocean. Such beauty was a testament to the power of the goddesses who had created this world.

He sighed with contentment, his magic all but purring through his veins. Dawn always fed his magic and strength. Closing his eyes, he absorbed the heat and light of the new day, imagining the beauty and perfect features of one particular goddess. One who was said to have the power to read the truth in any words.

He open his eyes, cracked his neck side to side, then raised his hands over his head and stretched. No matter how strong he felt, it was still hard to ignore the sensation of the sea breeze grazing his back.

He often had a naked torso whilst in his room. He had not told anyone that his stumps were sensitive to the point of agony —not even Alethia, who spent much time with him. He couldn't stand the feel of any armour against them; even fabric was agony after a while.

He dressed in a loose cotton shirt every morning, but as soon as he could escape the king's court and the combat training sessions, he ran back to his room and stripped.

The toned and growing muscle across his naked chest and abdomen rippled as he loosened his stiff body. His training sessions were brutal, and none of his human or warrior opponents gave him quarter because he was a prince or younger and less battle-experienced than them. Nor did they mention his wingless state or show any pity when he stumbled or overbalanced and fell on his arse. For that he was grateful; even learning to rebalance his body and stance to fight without wings had been like learning to walk all over again. It would take him months, if not years, to get back the high level of skill he'd used before. He clenched his jaw. It didn't matter how long it took, he would do it.

He lifted his hand, letting sparks of fire play between his fingers. To know he could still use his magic, even if he couldn't fly, had boosted his damaged self-confidence.

Wistfully, he watched the gulls soaring on the wind. Their

plaintive cries never stopped. The cliff face under the window was plagued with the birds. Tears suddenly stung his eyes as he watched them glide and dip and roll. He swiped the wetness away with the back of his hand. There was no longer a place for self-pity in his world. What had happened couldn't be changed, no matter how much he might wish for it. He had a baby to raise and a kingdom to find.

Leaving as soon as possible, today even, was the best choice. Staying here much longer would be dangerous. Spies worked in every court, in every kingdom, and this one would be no different. Griana would surely know where he was by now. For the last few days it was almost as if King Oden had been simultaneously trying to keep him here and encouraging him to leave.

Lexon's brows drew together, trying to decipher the intent of the king. In front of his court, the king loudly told Lexon to treat the palace as his home; when alone, he had told Lexon about the secret escape tunnel, which led from the guard tower to the ocean.

Lexon tried not to overthink the king's behaviour, but he was determined that today he would visit the docks. He needed to get Tanelle across the ocean where she would be safer and harder to find.

Griana could not leave Valentia, and for that Lexon thanked Lunaria. Even now, he had no idea how he had caste the curse that had surrounded the Rift Valley and Valentia; he only knew that the words had fallen from his lips as if someone or something had put them there.

His sapphire eyes narrowed, reflecting the sun's rays in their hidden red depths.

Erzion would be ordered to hunt them down, Lexon was sure of it—and that would be disastrous for them both. His heart squeezed. He missed his friend so much. He wondered, not for the first time, how Erzion was enduring serving that murderous viper. Lexon did not curse Lunaria often, but the whisper that slid from his lips was vicious. Erzion did not deserve to suffer for an eternity with the new fae queen—no one did.

A knock at the door had him tensing and grabbing the Silverbore sword that King Oden had gifted him. The metal was iron-free and extremely rare. The only known mines were in Ice Witch territory in the north. When Lexon had asked the king how he had acquired it, the king had merely smiled and replied that some things were best kept secret.

Sword in hand, Lexon approached the door, though it should only be the wet nurse returning Tanelle after feeding.

His big hand grabbed the handle and pulled the heavy door open. The creak of old hinges echoed down the hallway. Colder air rushed in, brushing his skin and raising goose bumps across his torso.

His breath caught in his throat. It was not Lara, the wet nurse, who stood before him, but Alethia. Her dark hair had been tied in an intricate and pretty braid that hung over her shoulder. She wore a simple blue tunic and dark breeches, which hugged her curves in all the right places. Lexon thought her the most beautiful female he had ever laid eyes on.

His heart began to race. He hoped she couldn't hear it, though there was no hope of him

hiding the way he instinctively inhaled her scent. His chest expanded, his large shoulders lifting before he exhaled in a rush.

He cringed, even as his face heated in mortification. He had never reacted to anyone like he did her. Every time he was near her, it was as if he could not control his body. He tripped over his words like an idiot and had to breathe deeply just to calm his racing heart. The more he was with her, the harder it became to hide his need to touch her, to wrap his scent around her.

Damn it! She's a goddess. She will never be interested in someone like me. Mutilated and only half a male, with stumps instead of wings, he scolded himself for the umpteenth time.

He needn't have worried. Alethia seemed transfixed by his

naked chest. Her throat bobbed as her eyes travelled over him, lighting a fire on his skin wherever that beautiful gaze rested.

Lexon's mouth instantly dried out. It was impossible to hide the heat in his own gaze when she met his eyes. Her face flushed so red he thought she might catch fire. A half-smile curled his lips as he saw this ancient, immortal goddess become more flustered than him.

Deliberately, he stepped closer. It was an effort to appear calm and in control. His palms were slick with sweat and taking a breath became difficult; he felt as if he had run miles.

They stared at each other. Tension crackled in the air between them.

Lexon wanted to kiss her. Badly. But he didn't know how to act with her. She was so small, so perfect compared to him.

She has probably had hundreds of lovers, he told himself. *Why the hell would she want me?*

No, he would not pursue her and risk making an utter fool of himself.

He took a step away from her, deliberately breaking eye contact.

She sighed and shook her head as if frustrated, then walked over to the window.

He push the door shut and turned to watch her. Slowly, he walked over to where she stared out of the tower window, the wooden floorboards smooth and warm under the soles of his bare feet. He stopped beside her, watching the light play on her shining auburn hair.

She didn't look at him.

Lexon turned and leaned his shoulder against the wall so he could gaze down at her. Her face was troubled. She bit her bottom lip, worrying the flesh with her teeth. His gut tightened instantly. Gods, he wanted to do the same thing.

"What's wrong?" he practically growled. Then almost rolled

his eyes at himself. *Why does my heritage have to make it so obvious that I want this woman?*

Her teeth pushed a bit harder onto her lip before she looked sideways at him. Her fingers gripped the stone window ledge so hard that Lexon thought she might break her nails. Appearing calm and in control, he pried her fingers away from the stone and held her hands. They were so small in his. His thumbs grazed her soft skin, a frown furrowing his brow when he felt them shaking.

"Alethia? What's wrong?" he asked, suddenly anxious. Grief had put him in a dark place these past weeks, but he had tried to keep it confined to his own heart and mind, not subjecting this gentle goddess, or anyone else, to his morose mood.

"Nothing," she denied, shaking her head.

"Then why are you shaking so badly? Has something happened? Did someone hurt you?" he demanded to know, his magic beginning to flare despite his best efforts to contain it.

Alethia's brows furrowed immediately. Quickly she pulled her hands from his and cupped his face with both hands. "No, Lexon, I'm fine," she whispered.

Her touch was like a brand on his skin. His eyes widened, a huff of disbelief rushing from his lungs, both at her words and the effect such a connection was having on him.

"Really," she added, the warmth of her breath fanning his lips.

"Then why are you shaking?" he half-whispered, half-growled back.

She swallowed, then took a deep breath. "Because you are standing so close to me—and you are half dressed," she answered, a flush creeping up her cheeks.

Lexon tensed as her hands dropped to his shoulders. He could barely believe what she'd just said.

She met his eyes—and held them. "And I have never seen such a beautiful body," she said softly, making him shiver as she tentatively ran her fingertips over the contours of his collarbone, following the deep russet coloured tattoos that swirled down his chest. Mesmerised, she watched his muscles tense wherever she touched him.

Lexon's mind almost ceased to function. Her scent was changing, becoming sharper, more intoxicating. "Alethia?" he whispered hoarsely, not quite sure what to do. His hands curled into fists. Her closeness, her scent— it was driving him to distraction.

She jumped at the sound of his voice, snatching her hands back as if she had been burned.

At that moment, a knock resounded on the door.

Tension simmered between them. Lexon found he couldn't tear his eyes from her face. He didn't care who was outside.

Another knock.

Alethia blinked.

"Prince Lexon? Are you there?" asked a musical voice from the other side of the door.

He swore. It was Lara.

Breaking Alethia's beautiful gaze, he stormed over to the door and yanked it open. "What!" he almost bellowed in his frustration.

Tanelle's little arms and legs jumped as he startled both her and the wet nurse.

"I-I'm sorry, prince," the nurse stammered. Her feet shuffled backward. Warily she held Tanelle tighter, staring at him like she might bolt.

Lexon instantly calmed himself, realising his pounding heart, flushed face and surging feelings were not this poor woman's fault. "I'm sorry, Lara. I did not mean to startle you," he apologised. "Here, let me take my niece. Thank you for caring for her so well."

"Y-you're welcome, prince." Lara passed Tanelle into his waiting arms, hesitated then took a deep breath. "Erm, when you leave, prince, I was wondering how you are going to care for this little one?" she asked.

Lexon frowned. It was a question that had been plaguing him

since they had arrived here. And the main reason he hadn't left yet.

"I am not sure," he admitted.

"Well, if I won't be in your way, I should like to come with you. My husband died before my own baby was born. My son, he's about the same age as the little princess, so I have plenty of milk for them both. Besides, the poor little mite will starve if you try and cross that ocean without a regular food source for her."

Lexon turned back into the room, the blanket Tanelle was wrapped in smooth against his skin.

Alethia walked over. Although she was still flushed and avoided his attention, a loving smile curled her lips when she looked at Tanelle. His heart squeezed at her soft expression. A surge of yearning rendered him speechless for a moment.

"That's kind of you, Lara," he managed to force out. "I know the king has offered us passage on a ship to Houria, but he has been vague about when that might be. I am hoping to find a ship's captain who can take us to Gar Anon, maybe even as early as tomorrow," he told Lara. "Though I doubt it will be easy."

"Really?" asked Alethia, her eyes lighting up. "That might actually be easier than you think. King Oden was telling me of the Silk Road. It's a trade route that runs across the Southern Hotlands. The High Wizard has built it to transport silk and other goods from the Sky Desert to his main port of Ion Tua. There is a trade delegation here right now."

Lexon cocked his head. *Why hadn't the good king seen fit to mention that yesterday when I saw him?* He was suddenly grateful he had retraced his steps to the escape tunnel after going there only once with the king. He now knew the way to the guard tower and the old tunnel with his eyes closed.

"It seems the High Wizard is protective of his new palace at Ion Kugat. He has sent his people here rather than ask King Oden to go to the Hotlands," continued Alethia, oblivious of the suspicion growing in Lexon's mind. "And, much as you did with

Valentia, he has done with his capital city. He has surrounded it in a cloak of spells and trickery that hides it from view and persuades the mind to travel a different way. Only those escorted by a wizard can enter. All other traders have to go to Ion Mah."

"Ion Mah?" questioned Lexon, trying to curb his jealousy that Alethia had spent so much time conversing with the handsome king.

"Yes, it's his second seat, and his main trading city. It sits on the borders of the jungle and the Sky Desert."

Lexon filed the information in his mind. Gently he rocked Tanelle, who was making contented gurgling noises. His heart squeezed painfully, not for himself, but for Noan—who would never hold his beautiful daughter in his arms.

It should be him here, not me, Lexon thought, his eyes burning. He leaned in and brushed is lips against Tanelle's soft, downy forehead.

"Lexon?"

He had lost all concentration for a moment. "I'm sorry," he said guiltily. "What did you say?" he asked, swallowing his grief.

"Where are you intending to take Tanelle?"

"The Fire Mountains," he answered gravely, holding Alethia's lovely eyes with his serious gaze.

"Oh," breathed both women at once.

Lexon looked at them both in turn. "It's where the goddess wanted me to go. That's why I needed the guardian with me; he is the only living being with a claim on that land. Now I will have to hope that I can somehow claim it and build an army with enough magic wielders to beat back any challenges that arise from the neighbouring kingdoms."

"Oh, sir. I think that's a wonderful idea. From what I have heard, the guardian's lair stands empty. It should make a good fortress for the young goddess to grow up in. I will be honoured to make the journey with you—and serve you both."

"Thank you, Lara. I gratefully accept your offer—as long as your king is willing to let you go. I will talk with him today."

Lara nodded, her loosely tied back hair falling over her shoulders.

Lexon realised she was probably no older than him, nineteen, perhaps twenty. He was glad of it. At least she would be strong enough to survive the long, arduous journey to their new home. Lara smiled as she left, promising to immediately sort out her affairs and belongings.

"Vaalor will never return to the lair," Alethia told him.

He had wondered, but he just said, "I guessed as much."

He did not ask where the guardian had gone. It made no difference; if the creature had truly given up on them all, he was better off crawling into the shadows to fade away.

Lexon knew he was being uncharitable, but he didn't care. Guardians were supposed to protect, not slink away and hide like cowards.

"Have you spoken with King Oden about your plans to go to the Fire Mountains?" Alethia asked.

"No," Lexon responded, his voice tight. He had no reason to mistrust the king but still... "I'm glad that is where Lunaria wanted me to take Tanelle. My magic will be strongest there, near the heat and rivers of fire."

He wondered, not for the first time, about Alethia's magic and if it would help him to protect Tanelle.

His heart sped up again. He wanted to ask her to come with him. But he daren't. Instead, he cursed silently as his gut started to twist in a most uncomfortable way. What if she said no—what if she wanted to stay here with the king? Lexon angled himself away from her.

Then it will be her choice, he told himself. He had no right to ask her to take such a dangerous journey with him.

"Here, let me put Tanelle down, then we can talk," Alethia said.

Lexon loosened his grip on Tanelle and allowed Alethia to take her. He watched her settle the tiny princess gently in her wooden crib. Tanelle gurgled happily as Alethia stroked her soft cheek with feather-light fingers.

Lexon's heart squeezed. His traitorous mind wondered what it would be like to see her settle their own child to sleep. To cover his longing, he went to the small window and stared out across the ocean again.

He had tried not to fall for Alethia these last weeks, but the more he denied himself her company, the stronger his feelings had grown. Embarrassment at his injuries had made him evade her those first few days, but she had still seemed to be able to find him, no matter where in the huge castle he tried to hide. Soon he did not even attempt to avoid her, let alone want to. He wanted to dominate her time and attention—and he had. He smiled—when she had let him.

Lexon placed a hand on the stone wall next to the window. It was cool against his palm. He knew he was near experiencing the full force of his *urge* but he *wanted* to be with Alethia. Yes, her scent, her smile, her body, drove him crazy, but he adored *her* too. The Goddess of Truth's inability to lie had led to some interesting conversations, which had him laughing out loud. He loved the soft curve of her lips; her gentle, loving nature; the way she looked at him, like he was the only person in the world she wanted to be with.

He squeezed his eyes tightly shut. She was the most beautiful and enchanting female he had ever met, and the thought of losing her—or of her choosing to leave him—had his heart squeezing painfully in his chest.

Warm hands touched either side of his waist, making him jump. He inhaled sharply, curbing his surprise as desire punched him in the gut. Though he tensed under her touch, and he desperately wanted to spin around and kiss her, he didn't move a muscle lest she startle and pull away. Those warm fingers slid forward, then her palms were touching him. He couldn't think, couldn't breathe, as those hands continued their journey across the flat planes of his stomach, stopping just below his navel. The softness of her cheek on the skin of his disfigured back almost undid his wavering self-control.

"Do you have something you wish to ask me, Lexon?" she whispered, the warmth of her voice brushing over the sensitive skin beneath his stumps. He shuddered, his groin tightening.

"No," he mumbled, still not ready for her rejection.

He felt her smile.

"Yes, you do," she said.

"You're right," he admitted. He was fast losing control of his body, and he needed to ask this before he did something he might regret. His voice shook with suppressed desire and apprehension. "I do. Will you come with me and Tanelle? Stay with us? Unless you have to go…back?" his voice faded, sick at the thought she may have to leave. *Would she return to Eternity?*

Lexon placed his big hands over hers, intending to remove her touch before the feel, the very closeness of her body undid him. His thumb caught the new scar on her wrist. He bristled, his muscles tensing instantly.

When she had said she had been sent to write a scroll, Lexon hadn't realised it would be in her own blood. He had almost ripped the door to her chambers off its hinges when he had smelt her blood in the air. Rage—and disappointment—had ripped at his heart, that metallic smell immediately making him think she had shared her blood with another. He had hidden in his room for a whole day, sulking and snarling, until he realised how utterly ridiculous he was being. Alethia wasn't the sort to give her soul to another so rashly, and even if she did want to take another's blood and mate with them, it was none of his business —no matter how much he wanted her himself.

He looked down at the soft hands that pressed against the ridged muscles of his stomach.

She has come to me, he realised, blood roaring through his ears. In a swift move, he pulled her hands off him and spun himself around so they faced each other. Then he wrapped his arms loosely around her lower back. By the look of her wide eyes, he had startled her. He prepared to let her go.

Then she smiled. "Yes. Of course I will return to Eternity. My father is there, as is my family—all except Lunaria," she said sadly.

Lexon swallowed the ache in his throat, his face falling.

Alethia raised her hands to cup his face, forcing him to look at her. "But I do not wish to return to my family yet. I love being in this world. I love the heat of the sun on my face and the coolness of the wind against my skin." She looked at the sleeping baby, her eyes turning wistful. "I love the laughter of children. I want so much to feel the joy of bringing new life into this world, to one day nurture babies of my own and see them grow." She turned her beautiful eyes upon him, pushing her body against his. Her voice became husky. "But most of all, I want the freedom to fall in love with whomever I choose. I want to feel the pleasure of their touch, of their body, warm against mine."

Lexon could not respond. His throat and chest had constricted so tight he couldn't breathe.

"I want that person to be you," she finished, her cheeks turning the most beautiful rose Lexon had ever seen.

"But you've only known me a short time." He managed to force out the words, despite wanting to follow his more base instincts.

"No. *You* have only know *me* for a short time. I have known you since the day you were born." She smiled and tipped her head back to look up at him. "My father is the High Ruler of the Guardians of Eternity. I am half-guardian, half-goddess. I can take either form. And just as my father can, so too can I see through the confines of space from Eternity. I have watched you every day of your life, Lexon. I loved you long before my father ordered me to stay behind in this mortal world. I *wanted* to stay. I promised myself I would find you. I have fulfilled my pledge to write the Veritas scroll for the one destined to find it, and now—" she stepped closer. "I can do what I really came here for."

"What's that?" Lexon whispered, still trying to process her words.

"This," she replied, sliding her hands up to cup the back of his head.

Lexon did not resist as she pulled his head down and her soft, warm lips alighted upon his.

Many feelings exploded through Lexon at that moment. Of their own accord, his hands moved—one to her lower back, holding her to him, and one speared through her silken hair to cup the back of her head. She filled every part of him—her scent, her touch, the very feel of her.

He groaned.

Soft and warm, she pressed her tongue through his lips, stroking and teasing his mouth.

His magic burned through him. He was on fire. She was in total control of him. For long minutes they devoured each other, touching and tasting, their moans filling the air.

But no matter how much his body wanted to take over, Lexon forced himself to slow. Breathing raggedly, he grabbed her hair and gently separated them. Satisfaction rushed through him when she moaned her disappointment.

"Are you sure?" he managed to growl, not recognising his own voice.

Alethia nodded, her eyes hooded, her chest rising and falling in a rapid rhythm.

Sparks flew across his hot skin where she trailed her fingers, following the dips and hollows of the hard-won muscle on his body.

Lexon couldn't stand it any longer. Sliding his hands lower over her curves, he lifted her. Heat engulfed his waist as she wrapped her legs around him. She weighed next to nothing. Easily, he carried her to his bed, trailing kisses up her neck and face.

"Don't move," he ground out as she dropped her legs from him, and he placed her down on her knees on the soft mattress. He left her only to untie the bed curtains around the four poster bed. They dropped in a whisper, affording them a little more privacy and warmth. On his knees, Lexon faced Alethia. His sapphire eyes glowed red with the magic and desire that heated his blood.

He wanted her to be his completely. It didn't matter that he hadn't known her long. This goddess was his soulmate. He had never felt such overwhelming need or love for another person. He wanted to spend the rest of his life showing her how much she really meant to him, not just this moment.

Swallowing the lump in his throat, his eyes burning as he looked at her beautiful face, he knew he couldn't ask that of her yet.

"Lexon, what's wrong?" she asked, shuffling close enough to touch him.

It was so soon. Too much, too quickly. But he had to tell her. "I want you so much, Alethia," he whispered, running the back of his calloused fingers down her soft cheek.

"Then take me," she said simply.

"No," he breathed. His hands dropped and clenched into fists. "You don't understand..."

She quickly placed a finger over his lips. "Yes, I do. I understand."

Lexon stared at her wide-eyed, his mouth dry.

She smiled. "Lexon, remember how old I am. Just because I have chosen to save myself for the one I love does not make me innocent or naive. I want a mating bond with you, as much as I think you want it with me. I want to take your blood and bind my soul to yours for eternity."

He couldn't speak as she shuffled closer.

His mind reeled with shock that she hadn't given herself to another.

Her fingers shook as she pulled a small knife from his waistband. He let her take it, his breath coming in short, quick gasps.

"Lexon, I love you. But I know you believe it is too soon to for us to share our blood. I understand, really I do. But I won't change my mind," she told him, understanding softening her face.

"It is not me I worry about. You might only think you love me," he replied, trying to convey his feelings.

"No, I know how I feel about you. But I want you to trust in both your feelings and mine. When you are sure, we will seal our souls together. Until then…" she pushed her body against his, and dropped the knife over the edge of the bed. "I want to give my body to you."

Lexon swallowed.

"I want a mating bond with you too, but I need to be sure you truly want such a permanent connection, too. Do you understand?" he asked, worried she might feel hurt or rejected.

Alethia merely nodded and began lightly running her hands over his arms and shoulders. Exploring. "Of course. But I will soon convince you I am certain of what my soul wants, just as I am certain of what my body wants."

Lexon's gut tightened. With his senses full of her scent, he leaned in and kissed her, slowly tasting her lips and brushing her tongue with his own. He was painfully aware that she had saved herself, that she had chosen him, so even though it killed him, he made himself move slowly.

Gently, he pulled away, smiling when she moaned and gripped his shoulders, trying to stop him. He pushed her down against the softness of the mattress, lowering his body until he hovered over her. His hungry gaze dropped to her swollen lips. Unable to stop himself, he kissed her, still trying to rein in his need. But

Alethia was having none of it. She grabbed the back of his head, pulling him closer.

"Please..." she murmured against his lips, crashing her soft mouth into his, and undulating her body against his.

Her fiery response took his breath away. He felt like he was drowning in her touch, her taste—the very *feel* of her. Pulling away, he stared at her, his chest heaving.

The swell of her breasts rose and fell rapidly under her tunic. A kaleidoscope of colours flickered in her eyes as she studied him from beneath hooded lids.

Fingers shaking, he peeled off each item of her clothing, worshipping her body with his hands, his mouth and his magic. As his soulmate cried out his name, as she lost control and trembled under his touch, his magic flared, wrapping them in a cocoon of red, shimmering heat.

Without taking his eyes from her, he discarded his leggings and underclothes.

She licked her lips, her hair a tumbling mess of silk. Her eyes grew dark with need as he stood there and let her drink in his warrior's body.

Slowly, he lowered himself over her nakedness. The heat, the softness of her...he was losing himself. Her eyes fluttered closed, and she groaned at that contact.

"Alethia. Look at me," he demanded, his voice raw as he fought to stay in control.

Her eyes opened. He felt like he was drowning in their starry, violet depths. Her lips curled into a seductive, inviting smile. Her hands slipped over his waist. When she wrapped her legs around him and urged him forward, he was lost. Heat surrounded him, a long low sound of pleasure ripping from his throat. Their eyes did not stray from each other's, their bodies moving in unison until they lost control and tipped into an oblivion of pleasure. One Lexon never wanted to leave.

CHAPTER 14

ERZION

Erzion gripped the stone balustrade and watched the Hourian ship fade into the distance. He was certain no one else could see the large vessel heading out to sea at great speed, its sails rippling in the ocean winds.

Not one of the fae warriors with him pointed it out or raised the alarm.

Face smoothed into a blank mask, he smothered his sigh of relief. Lexon had been on that ship. He was sure of it.

Cool, salt-laced wind blew Erzion's loose hair from his face. The aroma of old blood, his own sweat and days of flying wafted up his nose. Despite bathing occasionally in the forest rivers, his clothes were still those he had fought in for weeks.

Gods, I must look a gruesome sight. And I stink! he thought, wrinkling his nose in disgust.

Erzion could still feel the blood of his kinsmen on his hands and face. He would for the rest of his immortal life.

He tried to take comfort in the knowledge that the bloodshed had stopped, for the time being. The fae had accepted the Queen as their ruler—for now. No one referred to her as Griana any longer. No one even called her Queen Griana. She was simply the Queen, and her rule was absolute.

Warmth from the sun caressed his hidden magic. He had missed the sun's strength once Tu Lana began to drop in the sky. The more northern forests of Avalonia had already begun showing signs of winter when he had hunted down Commander Edison. The leaves had begun falling from the trees, leaving them mostly bare, which meant less camouflage for the fleeing red wings.

The screams of the warriors he had killed still rang in his ears; even now, in the stark light of day, they did not fade. He had done his duty and found Commander Edison within a few days. But the commander and his men were true warrior fae—loyal and territorial. They did not listen to his reasoning or his pleas for peace.

It had taken hours to bring them to heel. A slaughter, on both sides.

Erzion shuddered, the agonised screams of those he cut down momentarily stealing his ability to think clearly.

As soon as he had delivered the injured Commander Edison to the Queen, she had ordered Erzion to make haste to Stormguaard. It seemed the king was providing succour to Lexon, a young woman and a baby.

Erzion was to kill them all.

What would I have done if Lexon had still been here when I arrived? It didn't bare thinking about.

Trying to shake off his guilt and self-loathing at what he had become, Erzion cast his eyes back across the sparkling ocean.

Once again he thanked his unknown father for his wizard blood. It seemed the ship had been cleverly glamoured.

Erzion did not allow his eyes to dwell on it for too long. It would not do for anyone to suspect he had seen something untoward.

Turning on his heel, he pulled his wings into his back and faced the mortal king.

Astute eyes narrowed, taking in Erzion's dishevelled appearance. Erzion ignored such scrutiny, keeping his broad shoulders squared and his head high. He towered over the king, though the man did not appear small or weak.

Erzion held in a smile. This king would have seemed small in comparison to Lexon.

Erzion was exhausted and simmering with a constant, dull anger at his current situation. If he could, he would thank the king for giving Lexon protection. But he was not that fae anymore; he was the unfeeling Master Commander of the Avalonian armies. Besides, it seemed this king was astute enough to know the Rhodainians needed the Avalonians as allies. He had betrayed Lexon to ensure amicable relations with the Queen continued.

The treaty to provide warriors and arms to the Combined Army needed to remain intact. Not even the Queen would want to risk the potential escape of the Wraith Lord from the Barren Lands because of war with Rhodainia.

Other kingdoms would fight each other for land and power—and Erzion had no doubt he would see more than one war during this damned immortal life—but none would go to war with Rhodainia itself.

It was really the safest kingdom to be in. It was certainly safer than Erzion's own precarious existence.

He would not think about what he had done to ensure the Queen believed him loyal to her. It sickened him to his core. A shudder of disgust tightened his muscles as he felt the ghost of her hands on him.

No. He would not think of that now. Besides, he had a lifetime to condemn himself for his heinous actions and to suffer his nightmares.

The night the shield descended, Erzion had almost killed

Griana, but that damned guardian had told him to endure, to forgive himself and follow Griana. Erzion wondered, when he eventually died, if that same guardian would grant him entry to Eternity or if he would be condemned to suffer the realm of Chaos for everything he had done.

For a moment, Erzion glanced back over his shoulder at the disappearing ship, unconsciously wiping his hands down his leggings. He envied his friend his freedom, his servitude to their true queen. He wondered where Lexon go with the child and how many new and wonderful things would he see in his short life.

It was hard to hold in his tears. His heart ached for the loss of his friend and his freedom.

Erzion nodded, pulling himself together. His exhaustion made his raw emotions difficult to hide. "I believe the Queen has a right to know why you were harbouring her enemy." His voice remained just the right side of respectful—just.

He already knew Lexon would have stopped for Tanelle's comfort. But he also knew his friend would have left far sooner if there were not another reason for delaying. That made Erzion curious—and worried. Delays could be due to infections setting into Lexon's wounds or something to do with the stunning woman who had ridden the guardian.

He glanced around the terraced gardens, then down. Under his boots, cracked flagstones bore long claw marks. There was no other sign of the great beast. With Lexon aboard that ship, Erzion wondered where Vaalor had gone.

King Oden strode forward, turned and leaned his back against the balustrade. The man did his best to appear relaxed, but Erzion saw the slight stiffness in his shoulders, the way he loosened his fingers before resting his elbows on the stone. Yes, this man was indeed a fighter, and he was ready to move.

Erzion waited, hoping it wouldn't come to that.

"You were friends with the red prince, were you not, Master Commander?" asked the king, somewhat disparagingly.

Erzion slowly turned his head and stared at the man. "Indeed I was—until he betrayed me," replied Erzion coldly. "I do not forgive betrayal."

Now it was the king's turn to stare at Erzion. "Even your own?" he asked softly, his brown eyes piercing Erzion's. "It did not take you long to bend the knee to a new ruler and murder your own kind, did it?"

Erzion used a little of his magic to push against the king's body, but the king merely gave a half-smile.

"You will not gain my subservience like that, Master Commander. I am too used to living among magic wielders. Besides, I expect you have your reasons for obeying such a beautiful woman as Griana—and we all have our priorities. Mine are my people and my lands, in that order. Betrayal is all part of the games we rulers play."

Erzion forced himself to dip his head in acquiescence. *Hmm, perhaps I don't want to thank you for helping my friend. Perhaps I want to punch your goddess damned face in for betraying him to the Queen, no matter your game—or reasons.*

Their guards loitered nearby, ready to strike at a moment's notice. Erzion had already noted the king surrounded himself with a mixture of men and fae, maybe even some with shifter blood.

"At first I gave them shelter so the little princess could be fed, but then I persuaded the prince to stay and regain his own strength. As more news reached me of the Avalonian queen, I felt it would be prudent to allow her the opportunity to apprehend them."

"Indeed," responded Erzion neutrally.

The king gave a small smile and continued. "As it happens, the woman who came with him also had a purpose. She wrote this scroll." His calloused fingers reached inside his finely made tunic and pulled out a rolled up piece of parchment. "She asked me to be keeper of it until the little princess comes of age—and returns here for it." The king paused.

Erzion waited patiently, though he tensed, his eyes alighting on that parchment. It smelled of blood—and magic. Invisible fingers walked down his spine.

Take me, a voice whispered in his ear. *Protect me.*

He hid his shudder. Just his imagination, surely?

"I will give this scroll to you, if you will be so kind as to pass it to your queen. I would like to ensure peace between our kingdoms."

Erzion's face remained blank. This man was clever enough to know his kingdom was safe from invasion. There was another reason behind handing him the scroll. Erzion was sure of it.

"Why? Who was this woman?" he asked, not bothering to hide his curiosity.

The king swallowed hard, looking mildly uncomfortable now. "The Goddess of Truth," he informed Erzion quietly.

Erzion raised his brows but bit down on his surprised exclamation. He merely held out his hand. "Let me see it then," he said.

King Oden almost seemed relieved to hand it over.

Erzion untied it and broke the wax seal. The metallic smell of old blood burned his nostrils. With steady fingers he unravelled the stiff parchment. His eyes scanned the contents, then he rolled it back up. There was no way he was handing this to the Queen. The mortal king, however, did not need to know that.

Erzion stared steadily at the man. "You have done the right thing giving this to me. I will ensure it reaches the Queen. She can decided what she wishes to do with it. Who has seen this scroll?" he asked, his voice now infused with ice.

The king immediately met his gaze—and held it. "No one," he responded, his voice almost a growl, his nostrils flaring.

"And you?" Erzion asked, allowing his golden eyes to glow.

The king paled, though he held Erzion's magic-filled glare. "Alethia called this the Veritas scroll."

The whole of Erzion's body tensed. Veritas. Truth—in the language of the wizard's. Maybe it had been left for him, not the Queen.

"Alethia wrote this alone and gave strict instruction that the Veritas scroll should remain sealed until the person she left it for was here to lay eyes upon it," King Oden replied, his voice as hard as stone, his gaze holding Erzion's.

The half-wizard couldn't help but wonder if the king knew Erzion understood that word, that the scroll might very well have been left for him. "Good," replied Erzion coldly, not allowing his relief to show. "It would be—unwise—for anyone else to have seen it and unwittingly share its contents. Don't you agree?"

If the king had admitted to having seen its contents, they both knew it would bring his death. The king would believe Erzion threatened his life out of loyalty to the Queen. That couldn't be farther from the truth. If the king had seen the contents of the scroll, there was a small chance he would mention it to the Queen in his lifetime.

Erzion could not allow that.

The details written in the blooded scroll were meant for Tanelle—or her descendants—not the Queen. Erzion would make sure the details were passed on—even if it took a thousand years.

The Queen would get a scroll—but not this one.

"Indeed I do, Master Commander," the king answered gravely. "As I said, my life is my kingdom and my people. I hope our alliance will help me keep *both* of our kingdoms safe. Please be sure to tell Queen Griana my loyalties now stand with her."

"Of course," Erzion agreed with a respectful nod of his head.

"Thank you. Now, if you'll excuse me, I have a council meeting in a few moments. I trust you have all the information you require and will be returning to your queen," the king said meaningfully.

It was not a question.

Erzion had to admire the man's bravery. They both knew the legions of Avalonian red wings should be able to annihilate the mortal army. Although, when observing some of the king's soldiers, Erzion's suspected some of the king's army originated from across the rough seas. Magic of different kinds prevailed there. Erzion was hiding his true power. It stood to reason others might be too.

The King of Rhodainia marched away, surrounded by his guards. The sound of their footsteps beat against the stone until they disappeared into the gloom of the castle.

For a moment Erzion remained where he was, studying the castle. Moss grew over the shaded sections of the ramparts. Even here, where the sun shone and it was warm most of the year, darkness lurked.

Cool air eddied around Erzion. It had changed direction and was no longer salt-laced and fresh from the ocean. The stink of old fish and sewage from the large city hit him straight in the face.

Erzion grimaced. It was definitely time to leave.

Stretching out his wings was normally a relief, but right now, his muscles were so stiff it made him hiss. Keeping his face averted, he stretched them a little. He needed to hide his exhaustion from his warriors. They may show him respect, but he had killed many of his own kind—sons, fathers, friends. He was not stupid enough to think his life was safe.

The Queen's elite guards flanked him. The hairs on the back of his neck raised instantly. He ground his teeth, but did not let them see the snarl curling his lips. His new monarch had sent a squad of her new warrior dogs for his *protection*.

Spies.

Despite all his recent actions, it was going to take some time to gain her trust.

Ploughing through the air, Erzion slipped the scroll within the confines of armour. The weight of it felt far heavier than it really was.

The guards had witnessed him with it, so the Queen would expect to receive a scroll. Fear coated his mouth; he had to keep it out of her clutches. It seemed the war with the Lord of Souls was not yet done and would not be for many years to come.

Clenching his fingers to stop their shaking, he wondered who the poor soul would be who was destined to save the Eight Kingdoms.

His own loyal red warriors, now glamoured with gold wings and brown eyes, fell in formation behind him.

Replacing the scroll would require preparation—and the skills of a master forger.

Erzion halted high over the city, his golden wings resplendent in the sun. Hovering in front of his men, he barked out his orders. "Gather our troops. We will make our way up the coast until dusk falls. I do not wish to camp on this army's doorstep. Captain Orrec, organise a hunting party and ensure we are fed and watered tonight. Captain Lerstin, your squad is on guard duty once we land. The rest of you inform your troops to remain vigilant. At first light we will head for Valentia," he instructed his warriors.

Saluting briskly, they complied.

Erzion tensed his stomach, lifted his legs and pushed his head and shoulders down. He began to pick up speed. Soon he was soaring over the sprawling, crowded streets of the city. Below him, farmers and traders bantered across stalls and wagons. Horses whinnied in fright as they caught site of the warriors overhead. Old crones and young mothers alike weaved among the crowds—buying, selling, stealing. Stormguaard was a thriving city, and with the port of Garrison only three miles distant from the city gates, it was bound to grow.

Erzion sped out over the outer city walls and headed inland.

They would gather the rest of his men and then head back out towards the coast.

Behind him the Queen's guards shadowed his every move. Erzion gritted his teeth. He would talk to his own men tonight and plan how to ditch these annoying bastards. He wanted to see his warriors, and he needed to see Master Yagus. The Veritas scroll needed to be preserved for its rightful owner.

And Erzion would do anything to protect the information he now held.

That night he looked up at the stars and prayed to the goddess and the guardians that he could endure the Queen, that he could honour his blood pledge until destiny decided the time to rise and fight was upon them.

CHAPTER 15

LEXON

Another huge wave crashed against the ship, sending it listing and making Lexon stumble. He swore, soaked to the skin.

Why did that damned stupid captain have to get sick while we're on his ship? The idiot shouldn't have got so goddess damned drunk...

Lexon cursed loudly. Cold seawater drenched him again, nearly knocking him off his feet. He shivered violently as the wind chilled his sodden clothes.

It seemed the captain had a liking for the corn liquor sold on the black market at most port towns. The evil stuff could render a man useless for days if he over indulged.

Lexon spat his disgust, along with a mouthful of seawater, over the edge of the ship. And the captain had definitely over indulged. He was currently a sickly shade of yellow with a belly twice the size it should be.

Oh, Lexon was grateful to the Hourian captain for spiriting them away from Stormguaard. Controlling the waves and the appearance of his ship had been an amazing show of power.

That same power had kept them safe until they were days

away from shore. This morning though, the captain had not emerged from his bunk.

It had been Lara who had gone to seek him out.

The first mate had just shrugged off the captain's absence. "Let the prick pickle his brain and balls alike. This ship will be mine then," he had laughed.

Throwing the sailor a harsh look, Lara had stormed off, swinging agilely down the wooden steps and disappearing below to the captain's cabin. Lexon had soon followed, after a sharp look by Alethia made it clear he should.

The cabin had been awash with vomit and the stink of liquor. Lexon grimaced at the memory. Surprisingly, Lara had not balked or stormed out in disgust; she had clicked her tongue in disapproval but had stayed with him.

A week later and Captain Guerra was still alive, but only through the experienced ministrations of Lara.

Lexon snorted, hawked and spat as another wall of water hit him. The ship listed, then slammed upright as the first mate's magic commanded it. It was all Lexon could do to hold on, gripping the balustrade until his numb fingers went white.

Lexon's feet slid on the wet deck, his heart in his mouth as he made his way to the main deck. He had wanted some air. Now he was saturated and shivering, he wondered why he had even bothered. It was lethal out here for someone who had never been on a boat of any kind, let alone a ship in the middle of the Rough Sea. Cursing, he slipped down the steps of the quarterdeck and landed in a heap on the main deck.

He was petrified of falling in the water. Like most other fae, he couldn't swim.

Maybe that is something else I can learn to do now I have no wings, he thought bitterly.

The ship groaned in protest as the bow raised skyward. Lexon flung his arms around the stair rails and gripped on.

A pair of sodden black boots came into focus in front of his face. Lexon looked up.

The first mate grinned down at him. Water dripped from his forked, beaded beard but his deep grey eyes looked alive.

Lexon scowled, feeling foolish and inept. A stinging pain on his head told him he'd hit it when he fell.

"Here, *prince,*" the swarthy Hourian sneered. "Let me escort you to the hatch. Your kind of magic will not protect you from the ocean and, as you cannot fly above the storm and would drown below it, you need to stay in your cabin. Don't want you washed overboard before we get the rest of our money. Now do we?" He chuckled, darkly.

Lexon let the man help him up; there was no other choice.

All the crew members were walking about the deck as if their feet were glued to it. Clearly the first mate's magic was doing a fine job of keeping them safe, but the ship still wasn't his.

Lexon had learned an Hourian ship would only fully respond to the magic and control of its captain.

Still, this man had managed to keep the ship off the Dragon's Spine, a group of small islands between Stormguaard and Ion Tua.

Lexon tried to be grateful to the arrogant arse, though it was getting harder by the day. The first mate had been provoking him since the captain had first brought him, Alethia, Lara and the two babies aboard.

Lexon hadn't asked Captain Guerra how King Oden had secured their passage, he was just grateful to be off the mainland.

King Oden had led them out through the ancient tunnels under Stormguaard the moment news reached him Erzion was drawing close.

His gut as cold as his skin, he knew Griana would never give up; he would forever be looking over his shoulder—and he would have to teach Tanelle the same vigilance.

The first mate hauled Lexon by his arm across the deck and

practically shoved him down below. Lexon's boots slid. Up went his legs and his back hit the soaked wooden steps. Fiery pain shot through his body as skin was scraped off his stumps. Swearing, he slithered down and landed feet-first on the lower deck. Lexon straightened to snarl up at the man.

The first mate just laughed again, gave a mock salute and slammed the wooden hatch shut.

Lexon took a breath and calmed his temper. He wanted to slam his fist in that man's smug face, but Lexon needed the man. If the captain did die, the first mate was the one who would get them to Ion Tua. That reality left a bitter taste in his mouth.

From Ion Tua, the biggest trade port in the Southern Hotlands, they could take the Silk Road to Ion Mah. Lexon knew he would find a guide and some sellswords in a busy trade port like Ion Tua. It would be rife with them. If he could pay them enough, they may even stay on after Ion Mah.

Sodden and dripping water in his wake, Lexon muttered a vicious curse as he banged his head on a low beam. He hunched his shoulders and ducked his head down. Grumbling about the lack of space, he made his way back to his cabin. Alethia was there with the two children. Another shiver spasmed through his body, nausea rolling in his belly as the ship undulated beneath his boots. He wondered briefly why he had even bothered leaving the warmth of the lower decks. Then an angry cry rang out, loud even above the din of the angry sea.

That is why, he thought ruefully. Babies caused so much racket with such little lungs.

Taking a calming breath and steeling his patience, he pushed open the door and smiled at Alethia.

~

For two more days the captain stayed below, recovering under the watchful eye of Lara. After emerging on deck and delegating command of the vessel to his first mate, the captain had just concentrated on using his recovering power to push the ship through the ocean at a brisk speed, catching up on the days they had lost. For days he sat up on deck, not speaking to anyone other than Lara or his first mate. He left only to see to his personal needs—that was it.

When he was not propelling the ship onward, he was watching Lara with an intentness that bespoke of something far deeper than just curiosity. For her part, Lara was the one who ordered him when to eat, drink and rest. To the clear surprise of the first mate and their crew, the captain complied.

They had left the storms behind and now sailed in calm seas. Blue sky, peppered with soft, high clouds stretched as far as Lexon could see. The sun beat down upon him, feeding his magic until its ember smouldered with contentment deep inside his soul. Much as Lexon welcomed the fiery heat, he still sighed with relief when a gentle breeze seeped through the cotton of his shirt and cooled his hot skin.

Now that the deck was steady, Lexon loved to stare over the rails into the crystal clear waters to watch the sea creatures that followed in their wake. The rail was smooth under his fingers. Trusting its solid strength, he leaned forward and stretched the stiff, underused muscles across his wide back. He groaned, deciding he would find something physical to do today.

The captain sat under a canopy the crew had rigged for him. There was an air of determination about the man this morning that surprised Lexon. His eyes were bright and his jaw set.

Later on that day as Lexon practiced some sword work with one of the crew, the captain stood and made his way over to his first mate. They were in deep conversation, and not a happy one by the looks of it. Ignoring the rivulets of sweat that ran down the grooves of his chest and spine, Lexon watched them. His eyes narrowed as the first mate nodded stiffly and started barking orders. There was a snap of sails and the zing of magic increased a little.

Lara appeared from below and carried the captain a tray of food. The captain's tight features softened at her approached. Meekly, he followed her back to the canopy.

Lexon glanced at Alethia and raised his brows. She just shrugged and smiled back from where she was watching over the two young ones. Tanelle and Jacob, Lara's baby, now lay upon the blankets Lara had taken from the cabin to make a little nest under the canopy. As had become their routine these past weeks, once Lara had fed both children, Alethia took charge of the babies. The joy on her face warmed his heart as she rocked and played with both children.

Lexon picked up a large bucket of seawater and doused his head, sluicing away at least some of the sweat from his skin. He shook some of the water off his head, sending water droplets shooting into the air. Feeling refreshed, he grinned and handed the bucket back to his training partner. Still smiling, Lexon prowled over the deck toward the canopy. He didn't look at Alethia, but he was painfully aware of her gaze burning into his bare skin.

"We should reach Ion Tua tomorrow," the captain informed Lexon as he flung his practice sword down nearby. Lexon could not hide his relief. This journey had been long and arduous. He just wanted to reach land, feel firm earth under his boots and get away from the sticky film of salt that stuck to his skin. What he wouldn't give to bathe in fresh water...

He lowered himself next to Alethia, deliberately shaking his head. She squealed as cold water splashed onto her hot skin.

Lexon grinned at her.

She was staring openly at the ridges of his chest and abdomen. He inhaled deeply, then wished he hadn't. She swallowed hard when she noticed his fingernails digging into the deck.

It was damned torture not to touch her.

Sharing a cabin these last weeks had been ecstasy and hell. He had held her every night, inhaling her sweetness; however, there was so little room and even less privacy that they had both agreed to do no more than that. Lexon wouldn't be bothered if anyone walked in on them, but Alethia was mortified by the prospect. It was true that Lara came in and out whenever Tanelle cried, and even when she took the babies into her cabin and they were alone, there was no escaping the way sound travelled through the ship.

"Where will you go from there?" asked the captain. There was something in his voice, something far deeper than curiosity.

"I'll need to find us a means of travel. Some horses and sell-swords for protection. There should be plenty looking for work near the docks."

The captain nodded his agreement. "Yes, there always are. I can take you to the right inns. I know a few places where they go to wait for traders. I speak Ionian, so can help you negotiate a decent deal."

"Do most people speak Ionian then? Not the common language?" questioned Lexon, raising his brows.

"Depends. People in the trade towns like Ion Tua and Ion Mah generally speak both, though many indigenous folk go to those cities to find work, so it pays to speak Ionian. The wizards who took their lands use it too, for obvious reasons."

Lexon was suddenly glad of the language tutoring his father had insisted upon for his two sons. The king had always believed it was essential to understand what visiting dignitaries conversed about when they believed you ignorant.

Lexon silently thanked his father. At least now he would be able to glean information for himself. The captain didn't need to know that though.

"So, are you fully recovered?" Lexon asked, downing a full

pitcher of sour wine, then grimaced. Fresh water was in short supply after so long at sea.

The captain nodded towards Lara. "More or less—thanks to Lara," he said, resting his eyes upon her like they wanted to be nowhere else. "I always knew that stuff would kill me. But it's a hard habit to break—unless you have a reason," he added, almost to himself.

Lara's cheeks flushed, but she carried on playing with Tanelle as if she hadn't heard. Lexon bit down on his smile but couldn't help wondering what would happen if Lara had feelings for this weathered captain. She might leave Tanelle to stay on board with him.

"I've been thinking," continued Captain Guerra, fingering the beads in his forked beard. "I have been at sea most of my life. It's been a good life and has allowed me to use my magic unfettered, but it has also been a lonely life at times." His voice became thick, but he coughed it away. "It seems I have become a liability to my ship and crew, which is the last thing I want." He hesitated, his voice becoming heavy with emotion. "It seems my ship wishes for a new master, and I will oblige her. This life is unforgiving and harsh and no longer for me. I have learnt how precious having someone to care about, and to care about me, can be."

Lexon smiled as Lara blushed bright red and stared at the captain.

"Perhaps an adventure of a different kind is on the cards," the captain said, grinning widely and winking at Lara. Then he turned to Lexon, his face serious. "I should like to come with you, prince."

Lexon hid his surprise. "Our journey will be a long one. It will also be far from any water for months at a time. You need to be sure leaving this—" Lexon swept his hand out indicating the deck and the ocean, "—is what you truly want."

"It is," the captain replied without hesitation. "My first mate is a strong seaman. Once I pass my ship to him, his magic will be enough to keep her happy. When we disembark at Ion Tua and I leave the ship, he will become captain and set sail up the coast up to Houria," he said, then looked directly at Lexon. "So, if I am to come with you, I cannot keep addressing you as *prince*. Neither can you address me as captain, as I will not be one. My name is Varil."

Lexon nodded. "Varil it is. As for myself, you may call me Hisel. I don't know what to expect from these new lands, but having another who is able to wield a sword to help protect the princess will be welcome indeed. Know that I cannot guarantee your safety, though. It is my intention to travel through the jungle and skirt the blue dunes of the Sky Desert. We may very well have to fight our way across, if anyone discovers who we are. I expect Griana has issued a handsome reward for our heads."

Lara gulped, though she still had not taken her eyes from Varil.

As if feeling her regard, Varil turned and grinned widely at her. "Sounds like an adventure—Hisel," he said. "Count me in."

CHAPTER 16

LEXON

Lexon swatted a mosquito on his wrist and fastened his head scarf tighter around his head and neck. The damned insects were feasting on them all. He was eternally grateful to Varil, who had suggested buying the headscarves to both protect them and cover their identity. They had also purchased some fine netting to protect the babies.

They had been suffering the tiny irritations for weeks while trekking along the Silk Road, but it would have been more hideous without that protection. "Road" was a loose term for the dirt track they followed, which had been cut from the thick jungle that lined it.

Lexon huffed a laugh, his hot breath trapped behind the confines of his scarf. A bead of sweat ran down his spine. He absentmindedly rubbed his lower back where his damp waistband irritated his skin.

From horseback, he had a clear view of this straight section of roadway. He checked in front, then he twisted, his saddle creaking as he looked behind. A train of carts, horses and men that they had passed a while ago were disappearing into the distance.

They had passed other groups of traders along the road, most headed toward the coast, their carts loaded down with swathes of silk and other goods. They too were protected by sellswords, who watched Lexon's group pass with narrowed-eyed suspicion.

Robbery was clearly a problem out here.

His focus landed on the others who were ahead of him. The hooves of their sturdy beasts kicked up fine red dust with every step.

One of Lexon's hired swords guided his chestnut mare far too close to Alethia. Her horse whinnied unhappily, startling Tanelle. Alethia dipped her head to hush Tanelle, who rested in a sling across her aunt's chest.

The man closed in. Alethia reined in her horse and spat a sharp comment his way. The man grinned widely in response.

Lexon bristled. He had seen the sellsword trying to talk to her several times over the past weeks, but these past few days he had become more insistent. Every time Lexon left Alethia's side, the sellsword moved in.

Lexon hadn't interfered, not wanting to anger Alethia by being possessive. But his inherent need to protect his mate was hard to control. It was clear to him the man didn't only want pleasant conversation. Even the other sellswords were eyeing him darkly, before glancing warily back at Lexon.

Red hot magic boiled through Lexon's blood as the man reached out and touched Alethia's cheek. She slapped away his hand and glared at him.

Lexon didn't hide the aggressive snarl that twisted his features. He had not been able to bed Alethia since their first—and only—time together, and his frustrations were beginning to get the better of him. His fingers curled into fists, one around his reins, one where it rested on his thigh. He cricked his neck, itching for a fight.

None of these men were particularly honourable; some were clearly predators hidden beneath robes and scarves, probably no better than thieves who preyed upon this road. They respected physical strength only when they had to, and money only when it was enough.

He waited, wondering if she would at last show her power, whatever it may be. She could stop this man dead in his tracks.

Her beautiful gaze met his. Anger, and perhaps shame, filled her eyes before they dropped to the ground.

Apparently she didn't want to reveal herself yet.

He ground his teeth. That didn't mean this man should get away with his lecherous behaviour.

Lexon noted how close Varil rode to Lara. Clearly the ex-sea captain was just as worried for her.

The sellsword followed Alethia as she trotted away, chuckling delightedly to himself.

Lexon bared his teeth. *Enough!* A little lesson in respect was due. Red and glowing, his eyes met Varil's narrowed gaze. Varil grinned and nodded.

He reached out and pulled Lara's horse to a stop. They both watched as Lexon urged his horse forward.

Lexon charged past Alethia and the sellsword, yanked his reins, and whirled to face them. Smoothly, Lexon bolted down from his saddle, his feet slamming into the dirt in front of the man's horse. Before the man could react, Lexon took two swift strides, grabbed the man's robes and yanked him out of his saddle. The man stumbled as his feet hit the ground. Lexon released him, straightened his spine, squared his shoulders and glared down at the swarthy sellsword.

The man snarled, though his face paled, and there was no hint of that self-satisfied grin any longer. Lexon noted the man's fingers moving to grip his sword hilt.

Time for a show of dominance. He hadn't ever needed to do this before. As a prince, his warriors always respected his position.

Lexon gave a wide, evil grin—one that spoke of the pain he

was about to inflict and the satisfaction he would get from it. He could use magic, of course, but he decided it would be far more fun to use his fists. His body was clamouring for release, not this kind of course, but it would do—for now. Besides, he would prefer to keep his magic secret.

The man stepped back, drawing his sword as he snarled.

Lexon tilted his head, surveying his prey. This would not take long. This man might be a sellsword but he was heavy footed, his movements slow.

"You should not have touched her," Lexon growled.

"Why? The whore isn't yours. You haven't bedded her all these weeks. That means she's fair game," the man spat back.

Lexon became utterly still at the insult in those words. Realising his mistake, the man raised his sword. Lexon allowed him time enough to swing his blade. Light footed and swift, Lexon spun away. As the man overbalanced, Lexon slammed a fist into his face.

With reluctance, he pulled his powerful strike so as to leave the man alive and conscious. Still, bone splintered and blood sprayed as the man's nose broke.

A pained scream rent the air and the man sagged to his knees, dropping his sword.

The other guards laughed raucously.

"You stupid bastard. Told you not to mess with the women," jeered one of them.

"Idiot!" yelled another, storming over and smacking the man on the side of his head. It was the sellsword who seemed to have been elected spokesman for the others. "If you mess this job up for the rest of us, I'll kill you myself!" Barom spat.

The man scowled as he forced himself to his feet. Blood streaming down his mouth and chin, he glared hatefully at Lexon.

"We will reach the next town tonight. You will leave us there," Lexon told him coldly. "You will be paid for your time. If you come near us again after that, I will kill you." Leading his horse, he strode up to where Alethia had dismounted. "Walk with me?" He did his best to make it a question, not a command.

"Of course," she murmured and took hold of her reins.

Leaving the injured man to stagger along behind, the others closed ranks around Lexon, Alethia and Lara.

~

It was almost dusk when they walked into the outskirts of the town. Its lime-washed buildings glowed softly in the remaining light.

After so long away from civilisation, Lexon revelled in the sound of children laughing, men shouting and the general noise of the busy streets. The aromatic smell of spiced food laced the air. The whole group groaned. It had been weeks since they had eaten anything but unseasoned dried meat and stale flatbread.

They wandered through a small but bustling bazaar. Stalls and brightly lit shops displayed their wares, their goods glittering and unusual enough to catch his eye. Lexon tried to watch the people around him, but it was easy to become distracted by this new and colourful place. The lilt of a stringed instrument eddied through the melee of Ionian. It was bright music that lifted Lexon's mood. He inhaled deeply, smiling at the aroma of spice and tobacco that surrounded them.

Groups of men gathered outside small refreshment rooms, smoking from large floor-standing pipes. Some watched the group curiously but not aggressively, others completely ignored them, totally focused on their own pleasure and conversation.

Farther into town, the streets were busy but not too crowded. No one paid much attention to one group of travellers among many others.

Lexon's belly rumbled loudly as they led their horses past a stall selling spiced meats. Alethia giggled and glanced sideways.

"I can hear yours too," he smirked, tapping his ears, which were hidden under his scarf.

She rolled her eyes, hitching Tanelle up in the sling before sliding her warm hand into his. Lexon held it tightly, enjoying the feel of her touch, anticipation tightening his gut. That one night had not been nearly enough.

It didn't take long to find a large inn on the outskirts of the town. Only a few inquiries led them to where they stood now.

The building stood three stories high and seemed secure within its own white-washed walls. It even appeared to have a separate bath house.

Lexon glanced at the rest of his party. They were all as dusty and stank as badly as he did.

Varil grinned. "That place is going to be mighty busy tonight."

Lexon grinned back. "Yes, it is. But I'll pay for us to get in there first," he promised, glad he had sold the Silverbore sword King Oden had given him. It had paid for their supplies and sell-swords, with plenty still remaining.

They clattered into the sizeable courtyard, dragging the weary horses along. Varil went with one of the guards to negotiate a price for stabling the animals.

Lexon, Lara and Alethia trudged up the steps into the inn.

A dark-haired woman greeted them in a flurry of Ionian.

Lexon looked suitably confused. He didn't yet want to reveal his understanding of the language. He had picked up much from the guards as he exploited their belief he was ignorant. Though, they were more careful around Varil.

It had come as a shock to learn of the war between the wizards and the Ionians. Most of the fighting was centred around the trade town of Ion Mah, which was precisely where they were heading. The guards hadn't mentioned it so far, and Lexon had yet to figure out how he was going to find more supplies without heading there. He would give Barom a little longer to confess he was taking them to a war zone. What Lexon wouldn't do was risk these very same guards robbing them blind. He would cut every single one of them down to get away safely.

Using hesitant, single words, Lexon managed to secure two rooms and a visit to the bath house each. He desperately wanted to be with Alethia tonight, but he could not just assume Lara would be happy to share with Varil. It was clear there was something between them but Lexon had no idea how far it had gone.

He dropped two coins into the fat landlady's upturned palm. She grunted in thanks, not even looking at him. She shoved two keys across a wooden table at him. Scooping them up, Lexon turned to the others.

"We have two rooms, a visit to the bath house and a meal," he informed them.

Both women squealed with delight, then Lara's soft brown gaze alighted on the keys Lexon now dangled from his finger. She looked right at Varil and then Alethia and smiled mischievously. "Thank you. I'm sure Alethia and I will be very comfortable in our room."

Alethia pressed her lips together, unsuccessfully hiding her amusement as Lara took a key from a disappointed Lexon.

"Come," Lara said, her face now completely straight as she took Alethia's arm. "We will care for the little ones tonight. I'm sure you would appreciate some time to rest," she said to Lexon.

The landlady busied herself tidying some papers nearby, trying to appear like she wasn't listening to their every word.

Lexon ignored her. It was safe to assume she was as ignorant of the common language as he was of Ionian.

"Err, y-yes," he stuttered. "I would." Though it was hard to hide his frustration. Part of him had hoped Lara would take pity on him and offer to share with Varil.

Lexon tried not to sulk as the women ascended the stairs, each holding a baby. Varil followed them, turning on the top step and winking.

Alethia caught him and snorted a soft laugh.

Scowling, Lexon followed behind.

The men's own room was opposite the women's. Varil said a cheery goodbye to the ladies and followed Lexon.

"Well, it's better than the dusty ground," Varil commented, peering around the sparsely furnished room.

Lexon could only grunt, which sent the other man into a deep chested chuckle.

"Just remember it was you who negotiated the rooms, not me," he commented.

Lexon growled in response.

Varil laughed again, his eyes sparkling. "Lara is certainly a force to be reckoned with, isn't she?" he grinned, throwing himself down on the bed and tucking his hands behind his head. "Gods, that feels good. Right, I'm taking a nap, prince," he informed Lexon.

"No, you're not," rumbled Lexon, rubbing the beard that now covered his chin. "You stink. As do I. I've booked the bath house for us all. The ladies can go in first, but we go and watch over them."

Varil sat bolt upright and waggled his eyebrows. "Watch over them, you say?"

Lexon groaned. "Pigs balls, Varil. Not like that! We'll wait outside—just to make sure they're safe."

"Of course, prince. Of course," Varil agreed, grinning like a fool.

Lexon sighed and shook his head. "Come on, *captain*. Let's go and escort our ladies and keep them safe from men like you."

≈

Full to bursting after gorging on a meal of spiced roast boar and perfumed rice, Lexon groaned and sat back in his chair. He stared intently at Alethia; he couldn't help himself.

Her hair shone brightly in the light of the lamps. Newly

washed, it looked like liquid silk falling around her shoulders. He itched to touch it, to run his fingers through it. Every time she moved, her scent wafted around him, driving him to distraction.

He swallowed and fisted his hands in his lap. He couldn't sit this close to her and keep hold of himself any longer. "Well, I'm ready for a soft bed," he informed them all gruffly and downed his ale in one long swallow. "I'll bid you goodnight."

Without a backward glance, he strode across the wooden floor and up the creaking stairs.

Once in his room, he threw off his shirt. Sweat prickled his newly washed skin and his face was tight from shaving off many weeks' worth of beard.

The heat was stifling, even for someone with red magic. He flung open the slatted shutters and let the warm breeze blow over his naked torso.

The smell of horses and dung and cooking wafted up from below. *Better that smell than baking in this heat,* he thought with a scowl, listening to the raucous noise of the inn below.

Leaving the shutters wide, he paced the floor. There was no point in laying down; he was so tense he didn't stand a chance of sleep. He stopped his pacing and gazed outside. Stars peppered the endless night sky. He always thought the dark night so beautiful and peaceful. His magic still flickered with life when the sun went down but it was more settled. He closed his eyes, wishing with all his soul for the release of flying, of feeling the wind rushing beneath his wings, of pushing his body through the air until he ached from exhaustion.

A soft knock made him jump. He spun towards the door, tense and suspicious, until a soft citrus scent wafted over him. He halted, swallowed hard, then took a deep steadying breath. Slowly he released it from between pursed lips.

Alethia.

She smiled as he opened the door, her hair glinting in the flickering light of the sconces, her eyes burning and wholly focused on him. The way she was looking at him—like she wanted to *devour* him.

The ability to speak deserted him.

She breezed in, running her fingers lightly over his chest as she passed.

He closed the door—and locked it. Before he had fully turned, she said, "Lara and I thought you and Varil had suffered enough," she chuckled softly, the sound raising goose bumps on his skin.

"Suffered?" he queried hoarsely.

"Yes. Some cruel amusement at Varil's expense, I'm afraid."

Lexon just cocked his head. Slowly, his gaze smouldering, he ran his eyes over her curves, which were barely hidden by her silk shirt and long flowing skirt. "Really?" he growled.

She stepped right up to him. "Yes," she whispered. "She wanted to teach Varil a lesson, though I think he knew what was going to happen tonight. He did not seem the least bit bothered by the room situation. You, however, did."

She brushed her lips against his chest. Small shocks of pleasure made him groan.

"I have loved every night you have held me close, but that isn't nearly enough," she said, her eyes hooded. "I want your hands on my skin, your body on mine." She ran a finger gently around the contours of his lips. "And I want this mouth on me—everywhere," she whispered.

Lexon's self-control snapped at those words. Wrapping a hand in her silky auburn tresses, he crashed his lips into hers.

The bed was indeed far softer than the jungle floor, but the light of a new day was staining the sky by the time Lexon allowed either of them to fall asleep on it.

CHAPTER 17

LEXON

Undulating and vast, the blue desert disappeared into the distance, its dunes sparkling like they were strewn with jewels. It was impossible to see where the sky ended and the sands began.

The Sky Desert, indeed.

Beautiful though it was, Lexon was beginning to wish they had taken the coastal path instead of the Silk Road. Risking attack by the slavers on Gar Anon's borders seemed almost easy compared to the route they now had to take across this barren and unforgiving landscape.

There had been no more good-sized towns, only villages. None sold the amount of supplies Lexon needed to get his group across the desert and to the Fire Mountains.

Squirming on his belly and sending an avalanche of sand skittering to those below, Lexon looked over the ridge of one of the big sand dunes. The Silk Road continued on its way, meandering between the towering hills of sand and in through the city gates of Ion Mah.

Ion Mah had been a beautiful city, built upon a neat grid and protected from the encroaching desert by a tall city wall. Wide streets, lined with palm trees and small regular shaped buildings, led to a large oasis that glinted in the unrelenting sun.

Thick columns of black smoke billowed into the skies, flames devouring the homesteads that sat in and outside the protection of the city walls. Screams and the clash of swords reached Lexon's keen ears. He grimaced. It didn't take much to imagine what was happening down there.

A stream of curses fell from his lips.

There was nowhere to go. It wouldn't be long before Barom double-crossed him and tried to take what was left of the money Lexon had attached to his waist. Shifting his position allowed Lexon to better keep an eye on the sellsword, who lay only a few feet from Lexon's shoulder.

Dust filtered into his eyes and mouth as he breathed. He ignored it, watching the scene playing out below.

Soldiers dressed in loose-fitting robes and pants—but armoured with plates on their shoulders, back and chest—ran from house to house. Upon their heads they wore slightly pointed helmets, which marked them as military. Each warrior carried two curved swords. Without mercy, they cut down any who tried to run. Lexon felt his gorge rise. These were unarmed people, and no threat to the soldiers.

Among the soldiers, men dressed in red flowing tunics, which were secured by leather straps and belts, seemed to be commanding the sand and the air, even nearby objects were becoming airborne and used as weapons.

Wizards.

Lexon tensed as a group of soldiers cornered two figures dressed in dark fighting garb. The soldiers slowed, approaching cautiously. The wizard at their centre chanted loudly. Lexon couldn't hear his words, but he could see the wall behind the two men begin to crumble and sway.

Before the wall could tumble, the two dark-clad figures attacked. They did not go for the soldiers, but leaped directly for the wizard. The wizard reached for a short-bladed dagger strapped to his thigh. Before he could even draw it, he fell to his knees, clutching his neck. When he fell to the ground, Lexon could see why. A shiny piece of metal, shaped like a star, protruded from his neck.

The two black-clad figures did not miss a step. They did not flee. A swift and savage dance of death began. The two twisted and moved, so fast he lost sight of them. Then they both came together and turned to face down the remaining three soldiers who were left alive.

Barom hissed, either in approval or horror.

In the fighting, the headscarf one of the men wore became dislodged.

Lexon blinked.

Blue metal.

It wasn't a helmet or any other kind of protection. The metal was actually inlaid in the man's skin.

With a roar, the soldiers attacked the robed men, and within seconds they were dead, their body parts and blood staining the sand.

Lexon inhaled at the brutality of it, inadvertently sending fine grains of sand up his nose. He cursed, then sneezed, sending sand streaming down the dune.

Below, the man nearest snapped his head up.

"Shit!" cursed Lexon, ducking down the same time Barom did.

Varil slithered back from farther along the dunes, followed by one of the other men. "The whole damned place is overrun with soldiers and wizards!" he panted, a sheen of sweat glistening on the bit of forehead visible under the swathes of cloth he had wrapped around his face and head.

Lexon nodded and gestured down to where the others waited under the glaring sun.

They half-slipped, half-ran down the steep dune.

"We need to leave," panted Lexon to Alethia when they reached the bottom. "And quickly. There are soldiers swarming everywhere."

Barom swore. "We *all* need to get far away from here," he said, meeting Lexon's suspicious glare. "It will be safer if we remain together. The High Wizard will not allow this attack to continue. He will retaliate with force and cut down whoever is responsible. We should work our way over to the mountains and follow them until we reach the Fire Mountains."

"Have you ever taken that route?" enquired Varil, his voice deceptively soft.

Lexon appreciated the mistrust in Varil's eyes, though he had no intention of staying with these sellswords. His magic would keep them safe.

Barom held Varil's gaze, a smirk playing on his lips. "No. But it seems the shortest and most direct route. And it is less likely to get us killed."

"Is it? You have no idea where you are going or what you might meet," replied Varil in a harsh tone. "Why not go the route you profess to have travelled before, across the desert? We can bypass Ion Kugat if it's dangerous."

Barom laughed coldly. "My friend, you cannot bypass Ion Kugat because you won't even know it's there. The High Wizard has it glamoured with spells and enchantments. Only those accompanied by a wizard can enter. And believe me, we are more likely to die going that way, now there is a war. The desert road will be watched by both sides."

"I'm not your friend, and how is it you forgot to mention this war *before* we got here, sellsword? Hmm? Why is that?" Varil's voice became harder, sharper. It was the voice of someone used to a lifetime of giving orders—of doling out punishment. "Do you think you'll get more money out of us if we're desperate?" he sneered.

Lexon did not react, but he watched Barom closely. Varil knew

Lexon had intended to ditch the sellswords in Ion Mah, and clearly the captain had reached the limits of his tolerance for these lying snakes.

The skin around Barom's mouth tightened as he fought back a snarl. "I will never turn more money down if it's offered," Barom replied. "But I have delivered you safely to the agreed destination. Which—" he grinned without amusement, "—is right here." His eyes drifted up to the sun. "Right now."

"What do you mean? That you're going to leave? Go ahead, we don't need you—"

Lexon release a growl. Tension simmered in the air. It wasn't a gentle warning sound, but a full-on dominant fae snarl that rattled his chest. Whilst the two men argued, the other sellswords had slowly spread themselves out into a line.

This is it then.

His gut churning with anxiety for the others, Lexon looked meaningfully at Alethia. He couldn't lose his new family. He couldn't fail them.

She nodded calmly and passed Tanelle to Lara. With a baby in both arms, Lara was left vulnerable, but there was nothing to be done about that. Lara stepped behind Lexon, Alethia and now Varil, who had realised what was happening and moved closer to them all.

Barom's grin widened.

"So, do you think to kill us?" enquired Lexon. Anger, and a small amount of magic, gave his voice a harsh rough quality. "Why not just take your money and leave with your lives?" he asked. Reaching into his tunic he plucked two bags of coins from his money belt. They landed with a thud at Barom's feet.

Barom looked at them, then guffawed. "What!? You really think that amount of coin would persuade me to travel all this way during civil unrest? No, *prince*," he sneered. "I'm not interested in that piss poor amount," he said, kicking the bag sideways. "I have a far better offer. One I made as soon as you hired me."

It came as no surprise Barom had worked out who they were.

"What offer?" grated Lexon, even as he pooled his magic around him like a shield. It swirled against his arms and hands, begging to be released.

When Barom didn't react to Lexon's show of magic, Lexon's stomach turned to ice.

Barom was still grinning like a smug bastard, as if he had already won this fight. "Oh, from them," Barom answered, triumph glinting in his eyes. With a grand gesture, he swept his arm to the summit of the dunes that surrounded them.

Lexon swore.

Barom's men hadn't tried to circle them. It became clear their role was merely to block the way to the road.

There would be no running from whatever was coming.

The clamour of metal echoed eerily through the dunes as hundreds of soldiers mounted the summits. They peered silently down at the small group of travellers.

Alethia gasped, Lara released a strangled, terrified squeak and even Varil paled.

"Shit!" the captain mumbled.

"Shit indeed," replied Lexon, slamming a shield of red magic down over them as around twenty red robed wizards stepped in front of their soldiers.

Lexon swallowed his fear; he could hold his magic for minutes, maybe even hours, but Erzion had always found a way through Lexon's shield with his spells. These wizards would too. He turned to Alethia. "We will have to fight," he said solemnly. "It doesn't look like they're in the mood for negotiations. They either know Griana will pay handsomely for my head and Tanelle's death, or the High Wizard wants us for political negotiation."

"I know," she gulped. Her shoulders rose and fell in a shaky breath but she held his eyes. "I will change into my guardian. Maybe I can get us all out."

Relief made his legs weak. He had wondered if he would ever see this part of her. But the time for concealing their identity was past.

She eyed him warily. "I know you mistrust Vaalor, but please don't fear me, I will never harm you," she told him.

Lexon nodded, gaping at the dragon that peered from her eyes. "I do not fear you," he said.

One long slow blink told him she understood.

He panted, his breath burning in his lungs as the wizards began to chant, pounding his magic with spells. Inside the shield was blazing hot and the babies, now grown enough to be heavy, began crying and kicking. Lara struggled to hold them, her face a mask of terror.

Lexon twisted to Varil, his voice commanding but calm. "Alethia is a shapeshifter—she is not from this world."

"What are you?" Varil asked, turning to her.

But Alethia's focus was outside their shield, eyeing the men nearest to them with a predatory intent.

Lexon tried not to cringe at that look. "A guardian," he answered.

To their credit, Varil and Lara did not fall apart at that revelation.

"And she is about to give these men the shock of their lives. When she changes; run to her. She will not harm you. I need you to get yourself and Lara on her neck. Hold on and stay low, it will not be a smooth ride," he warned, thinking of his time on Vaalor's neck.

Varil quickly took Tanelle from Lara then nodded to Lexon. Varil's body tensed and he pulled Lara down to a crouch on the ground. A smaller target.

Barom watched them from nearby, his shrewd eyes narrowed.

The wizards began to shout and push harder when they realised the group were planning something.

Lexon took a deep breath. *"Now!"* he bellowed, dropping his shield in front of them. A split second later his magic exploded into the ground, sending clouds of sand skyward. Simultaneously he blasted a hole in the chests of the nearest wizards. Blood shot into the air and men began screaming.

Arrows whined as they were released.

Alethia leaped into the air.

Light burned Lexon's eyes but he did not stop attacking. When it faded, a stunning silver dragon stood before him. There were no horns around her head, but ridges of silver gleamed and her silver scales ripple as muscle moved beneath them. Solid. Powerful. Her silver claws sank into the blue sand.

Lexon blinked, stunned, but he had no time to study her beauty.

She roared, sweeping her powerful tail and taking out half of Barom's men. Limbs and bodies broken, they went sailing through the air, their screams cut off when they thudded into the ground.

Alethia snapped out a wing and swept her head to roar at the pale-faced soldiers. Many staggered back, some fell to their knees, clearly begging forgiveness from this deity. But some panicked and began firing arrows at her.

Alethia swung her head their way, her molten eyes flickering. She roared, her displeasure.

Her wing stayed extended, arrows harmlessly bouncing off the silver, armour-coated membrane. It provided much needed protection for Varil and Lara, who were already on their feet and running forward.

With a vicious swipe of her other wing, Alethia sent Barom and the remainder of his men flying through the air. They screamed. Their bodies thudded as they slammed into the sand.

Lexon grunted with satisfaction, but he couldn't risk looking. The wizards were working together now, attacking from all sides.

A thin young man, more a boy, led the wizards down the dune. He barked orders loudly. His cruel features were set in a mask of rage and determination as he honed in on Alethia.

Lexon concentrated his attacks on the young leader. His power was repelled again and again until the wizard couldn't cast spells quick enough. Then Lexon's magic found its mark. The boy staggered back, spittle flying from his mouth when magic hit him square in the chest. Only his magic-infused chest plate saved him. Two other wizards ran and jumped in front of him, blocking him from view. They worked together, slamming up a wall of sand.

Alethia lowered herself to the ground and dropped her wing.

Varil and Lara climbed up as quickly as they could, their ascent made awkward by holding the babies.

Lexon growled as he thrust his magic outward to provide them with a shield; at the same time, he ran toward Alethia.

"No! Stop him! Aim at the beast's eyes! No armour on the eyes!" screamed the boy who had escaped his protectors.

Lexon's heart raced with terror as hundreds of arrows were loosed. Hissing through the air, they rained down upon Alethia's silver head.

Lexon tried desperately to shield her. He thrust more red magic forward.

Concentrating on protecting his friends on so many sides had its cost. Sweat ran down his shaking body, his palms slick with sweat. Without realising it, he weakened the shield to his back. The wizards behind him noticed and immediately sent a spell crashing into it.

Strange power began to eat at his. Lexon grunted. It was painful, like ants swarming and biting. It sent him sprawling to his knees in the sand. Roaring, he fought it. But it cost him. The shield over his friends suffered.

Varil yelled as an arrow slammed into his shoulder. His body was forced back into Lara, then he slumped forward.

"Go!" yelled Lexon at Alethia.

Molten silver eyes flicked at him. She roared her anger, swiping her tail in a huge arc. Bodies flew in all directions.

"Go! Please," he whispered desperately.

That spell flayed his magic as he pushed himself up. He couldn't stop it. The well of his own power was waning under the onslaught. Panic gripped him when he couldn't find Lunaria's gift.

Arrows whined, thudding into the sand beside him. He shored up the shield over his head, but it left his body vulnerable.

An iron arrow thudded into his thigh, its force sending him staggering. Instantly, its poison began seeping into his blood. It began to smother his power.

His magic flickered.

No. No. No.

He couldn't, he wouldn't fail Tanelle or Alethia.

He took a breath, commanding his magic. He did not think again about failing, only saving those he loved. Ice cold calm washed over him. If he was to die here, he would do everything in his power to save his family.

And that is how he thought of them. His family.

In desperation, Lexon dragged up his remaining power. He looked one more time at Alethia, and mouthed, "Leave."

She screeched, her response calling to his aching heart.

I love you. He willed her soul to hear him.

Lexon tore his eyes from his soulmate and sent his remaining magic in a fiery surge that crackled through the air, scorching the sand.

Alethia had no choice but to launch herself upward or risk her passengers being caught in his onslaught.

Pale-faced, Lara sat behind Varil, clutching onto him desperately, whilst trying to keep the babies secured between them.

The downdraft from Alethia's wings stirred the sand into a storm of blue dust. Lexon ducked his head, trying to hold his breath. When he looked up, she was gone.

Good. Good that she won't see me die. His heart shook at the realisation he would not see his friends again.

With that thought, the well of magic Lunaria had gifted him broke open, flooding his body with light and power. He did not allow it to heal his own body, but gathered it about himself like a lightning storm.

Ignoring his bleeding leg and the iron burning his flesh, Lexon forced himself up.

Shapes began to materialise from the blue storm of sand.

Lexon squinted and blinked. Sand blew in his mouth; grit scratched his eyes. He scanned the desert. The last thing he had expected to see as the dust cleared was this wizard army fighting another foe.

Grunts and screams accompanied the clamouring of swords and the dull thud of bodies falling.

Though he kept his magic simmering around his body, he did not throw it outward as he had planned.

Black-clad figures twisted, kicked, struck and slashed with efficiency. Their lithe bodies moved like the wind, disappearing and reappearing where they willed. More appeared from thin air and over the precipice of the dunes.

None seemed intent on attacking him, and the wizards were now too occupied with saving their own lives to bother with his.

A bloodied figure caught his eye. Barom had dragged himself up. His left arm hung loosely by his side, and he limped badly. No matter his injuries, he was slashing and fighting his way through the melee of blood and death.

Lexon did not hesitate. Uncompromising will tuned his face to stone. Magic barrelled from his hand.

Barom toppled forward and landed face-first, a huge hole in his back.

With a satisfied grunt, Lexon quickly tore a strip of cloth from his tunic. Gritting his teeth, he wrapped it around his hand, then curled his fingers firmly around the shaft of iron protruding from his leg—and pulled.

Blood pulsed, soaking his leggings. Sparks flew across his vision. His knees sagged, unable to support his own bulk.

It was a dangerous place to be injured and vulnerable—in the middle of a battle, not knowing who his enemy was.

Lexon forced himself to stay conscious, sinking sideways and landing hard on his rear. He forced his magic to obey him. Fingers of red flames reached out, cauterising the wound. A guttural roar rattled his throat, sweat soaking his tunic and head scarf.

Two figures began stalking toward Lexon while dragging a semi-conscious wizard. The captive's boots left lines in the blood-soaked sand.

Lexon tried to hide his trembling hands as he unbound his head. His breath was too hot, his skin feverish.

Air. He needed air.

Without considering it, he pushed.

Magic flared from his tattoos, those streams of flame burning clean through his robes and tunic. Their remains fell from him, leaving only a fine covering of dust on his sweat-slicked skin.

Around him, the black-clad warriors continued to fight.

Across the body of the dune and stretching across the summit, warriors forced their captives to kneel. It seemed the soldiers were far outmatched in their fighting skill. Only the wizards continued to cause any real damage to their enemy but they were realising they were outnumbered. And casting took time, too much time for mortal soldiers to protect you.

"Do not fret, red prince. We mean you no harm," said one of the approaching warriors, his astute eyes resting on Lexon's red eyes and glowing body.

Lexon glowered at the black-clad figure. It did not matter who they killed; trust did not come to him lightly.

Heat beat down upon his skin and he did not attempt to suppress a shudder of pleasure as his magic sought to replenish itself from the sun's fierce touch. He grinned humourlessly, his eyes blazing. "Oh, I am not fretting. And you are right, you will not harm me." He found he did not care that his tone was arrogant; the words were true.

Blue metal gleamed on the man's wide forehead and bald scalp.

A sun!

It hit him then, who this man was.

A Fire Priest.

The priest's exposed ebony skin shone with sweat as he returned Lexon's grin and scrutiny. Perfect white teeth gleamed, and his deep brown eyes sparkled with approval as he chuckled. "It seems not. You are not the weak second son I was expecting."

Lexon kept his expression hard. "I had to grow up quickly." He sent a small blast of magic into the sand in front of the man, halting his progression. "And I am learning not to trust anyone—including Fire Priests," he rejoined.

"It is both a good and bad way to be," the priest agreed.

In one vicious thrust, the priest shoved the dangling wizard forward.

The captive growled and cursed as if his voice had been unleashed. "You cannot harm me! My father will hunt you down if you do. He will destroy you for this. For murdering his men."

Lexon peered closely at the raging figure. The cruel-faced boy.

Lexon opened his mouth to ask who the young man was, but no words emerged. He clutched his throat, his eyes wide. The air was being sucked from his lungs! Shards of pain racked his body, his muscles rigid as an uncontrollable spasm crashed through them.

His magic was being shredded from all sides.

The cruel face of the boy twisted into a parody of laughter. "Now it is your turn to die!" he screeched, spittle dribbling down his blood-streaked chin.

Lexon could do nothing but watch as a figure materialised from thin air in front of him. His eyes blurred, losing focus, at the same time overwhelming weakness commanded his limbs.

As he fell unconscious to the soft blue sand, Lexon's last thought was for the beautiful silver dragon and the woman who was his mate.

CHAPTER 18

ERZION

Erzion held his mother tightly, her body tiny in his embrace. He pulled her closer, absorbing her warmth deep into him, unwilling to let her go.

Garnald stood close by, watching them. The green wing had hardly left Mariel's side these last months whilst they had been in hiding in these caves.

Erzion met Garnald's gaze, overwhelmed with gratitude for the fae who had fought so hard for his mother, who had proven how much he loved and adored her.

They all knew Garnald would have died of his injuries but for Lexon's ministrations. Erzion squeezed his eyes shut, eternally grateful to his friend for using his magic in this manner. He still felt such guilt at believing, even for a short time, that Lexon could have beaten his mother out of pure wickedness.

He pulled back a little, cupping his mother's shoulders in his big hands. "When you find Lexon, remind him we are, and always will be, more than friends," Erzion said, his voice thick with emotion. "We are soul brothers." He swallowed against the lump in his throat. This hole inside him would never close. It was utter agony. The more people he allowed himself to love, the more his desolation would feed that void when they finally left his life.

Eternal existence was going to be hell.

I will never love deeply again. My heart will only ever belong to me, he promised himself.

As if reading his mind, Mariel smiled gently and cupped her son's cheeks between her hands. "We will see you again, my beautiful son." Then her expression saddened. "I know you will live far longer than any of us, and that you will harden your heart against grief. But please, do not turn your back on love completely. No matter how many losses, how much pain you go through, please leave room in your soul for it. I should hate to think of you becoming cold and soulless, like the one you are forced to serve." She looked into his eyes, holding his face with such strength Erzion could not look away. "Promise me," she insisted as he stared at her, his jaw muscles tensing.

How can I promise that? The grief and loneliness he would suffer if he did not protect himself overwhelmed him. Still, he had no desire to become like Griana, intent only on her own power and goals; with no heart, save one filled with cruelty.

He swallowed and made the hardest promise of his life. "I promise to love, Mother, but I will not promise how often or even when." He looked away from her to where a small brown-haired boy clutched his father's hand. The trust, the adoration in the little boy's face…

Pain lanced his chest. It surprised him how much it hurt, to know he would never allow himself to hold his own child. "And I cannot promise I will allow myself to have a family. I do not know if I could bear to outlive them…to watch them die."

Tears dripped down Mariel's face at his words. "I understand," she told him softly. Pleading crossed her eyes. "But don't decide that yet. Loving someone, especially your children, even if it's for a short time, is such a gift. One worth any amount of pain."

"That's enough, Mariel," Garnald said gently. "Leave Erzion to make his own decisions in that regard. Goddess willing, neither of us will know how it feels to outlive our children."

Erzion smiled at the male who was now his mother's lifemate. The support almost made him crumble, but he merely nodded his thanks. "It's time for you to go, Mother. The ship needs to leave with the tide."

They all turned to watch as another large group of fae headed across the ocean towards the waiting ship. Mariel had worked hard with Garnald and other strong figureheads to arrange this exodus. Fae who were still loyal to the Arjuno line had flocked to the coastal caves. They had been hoarding food, weapons and other supplies for months.

Erzion had done his part, feeding misinformation to the Queen and her spies. He had known she spied on him. He had *felt* her presence in the darkest shadows of the city as he feigned searching for his mother.

Master Yagus had glamoured the caves from view, and Erzion, who had known the Queen would watch his every move, had led her on a merry dance of deception.

Only fae were allowed anywhere near the caves, shifters or humans were kept away—by any means necessary. And fae who joined the caves were not allowed to leave for any reason.

At first Erzion had fought his mother's desire to help Lexon build his kingdom in the mountains of fire, but when it became clear to him how many fae were in danger from the Queen, Erzion knew he had no choice. Already she had incarcerated many reds and greens for supposed crimes against the crown.

It sickened him that he could not save everyone, that he had to be part of their demise in any way. Erebos would surely rejoice in taking his soul for all the heinous acts of omission he had and still would perpetrate against his own kind.

Thousands had waited for the arrival of these ships. Even with the security of spells and enchantments, as more fae arrived, the more dangerous it became and less likely it was that their secret would remain intact.

Erzion had visited his friend, Lord Firan of the Wetlands, when he had been sent on a mission to hunt down green-winged fae. Pleading with his friend had been the only way he could secure enough vessels to take this many fae away from here. No fae could fly as far as Gar Anon's shores without stopping. Besides, the winter storms were upon them now. The skies, as well as the Rough Sea, would be more dangerous than ever until Tu Lana began to rise into the sky again after Winter Solstice.

Firan's father had recently died in an attack by a sea serpent. Even an immortal could be killed by decapitation. His death had left Firan as ruler of the island nation. These ships were his, as were the blue-and green-skinned crew who manned them. Firan had sworn he would be Erzion's ally for however long it took to restore the throne to the rightful heir. They had sealed their promise with blood, and Erzion would be forever in his debt.

Erzion watched as more and more fae flew out to the ships. The ships floated calmly in the sheltered bay, and the fae seemed to be landing without problems.

Erzion frowned. He hoped Garnald and the others would have the means to sort their survival on the other side of the ocean. He studied the green-winged fae as the male kissed Mariel chastely on the cheek.

Then he turned to Erzion. "Goodbye, Master Commander. I wish you well. So—until we meet again," he muttered. Looking mildly uncomfortable, he held out his hand.

Erzion grinned and embraced the other male. "Until another day," Erzion agreed. "Thank you." His voice was heavy with meaning as he pulled back and looked to his mother.

"No thanks necessary. It is my honour," Garnald answered, quietly enough only the two of them heard his words.

Erzion felt his eyes burn. Knowing his mother was loved so much overwhelmed him.

Without further words, Garnald firmly slapped Erzion's shoulder in a gesture of friendship and farewell before launching himself into the watery dawn light and towards the ships.

Erzion could not stop his tears now as he said farewell to his mother. He embraced her, holding her to him as sobs racked his body. "I love you," he choked out.

She gently kissed his cheek. "And I you," she whispered back. "Don't let her turn your heart to ice," were her final words.

His heart breaking, Erzion watched as Mariel spread her gauzy wings and lifted elegantly from the ground. Wiping her own eyes, she blew him a kiss, then turned and left.

~

Erzion stood on the lip of the cave watching the horizon long after the ships had disappeared from view. He did not heed his body's need for food or relief. He just stood, watching the storm clouds build and the misty haze of rain where the sky blurred and the ocean began.

A reflection of his life.

A bitter smile twisted his lips. The line between good and evil was never clear; he hoped that would excuse him for all he had done, all he would do. He considered his pledge and—trying not to hate himself—smothered his desire to fly after those ships in order to be with his mother and best friend, to be the warrior he always wanted to be, not the monster he had become.

As the sun began to drop from the sky, the first splats of rain hit his face. He blinked, awaken by the cold droplets. Driven by the fierce stormy wind, they stung his face.

Erzion shuddered. He hadn't realised how cold he had become. Stiff and aching, he turned and wandered into the darkness of the cave. The remains of the camp lay strewn about —abandoned.

After the noise of his kin leaving, the cave seemed eerily quiet. Even the boom of the waves and the howling wind could not dispel the hollowness.

Erzion swallowed hard. He was totally alone now. Every person he had loved was gone from his life. His lips tightened into a solid, thin line. Such emptiness in his heart was surely a feeling he would get used to.

He squeezed his eyes shut and remembered his promise to his mother, vowing he would strive every day of his life, no matter how long it turned out to be, to remember that promise—to eventually love.

His boot connected with an old cooking pot. It clattered across the floor, the metallic sound echoing into the darkness. Erzion cocked his head and listened to the continued echo.

Behind him the sea and storm raged. He could not fly back to the city yet. With nothing else to do Erzion, prowled forward into the darkness of the cave system.

His fingers brushed the parchment hidden beneath the folds of his cloak. It had been on his person since returning to Valentia.

Erzion peered into the beckoning darkness. Perhaps he might find a place to hide the Scroll of Truth inside these caves.

Master Yagus had helped him forge a duplicate of the scroll. Erzion had wanted to remove the information about how to bring back Erebos from the Chaos realm, but the stubborn old goat had argued and worn him down. He knew the wizard was right; it had to contain some information that was important enough to leave for the heir of Valentia's throne, otherwise the Queen would never believe in its authenticity.

He fingered the smooth paper, thankful that they had seen eye to eye on removing the most important piece of information.

The Queen had since hidden her copy in the palace vaults. Even Erzion was not allowed to enter—only her Elite Guard.

Erzion smiled grimly, hoping the goddesses would forgive him for forging and changing Alethia's words.

Using his magic to light his way, he wandered on. He lost track of time, his boots crunching and slipping on the ancient rock. Soon the signs of any camp disappeared. None of the fae had come so far into the caves.

Eventually the cave narrowed down to little more than a fissure in the rock. He almost turned back, but the darkness seemed to whisper to him,

Go farther. Go farther.

Unable to explain why, Erzion tucked his wings in tight and squeezed through the gap. The unforgiving rock scraped him as, grunting and swearing, he forced his bulk to pass through. The sounds of the ocean had faded and the air was quiet and still, his rasping breaths the only sound. It was disconcerting.

Not wanting to scrape his wings further by going back, he continued, squeezing through gaps and trudging along pitch-black tunnels.

Erzion paused.

Go on. Go on, urged that voice in his head.

Something tingled against his skin and tugged at his chest. A sense of urgency and excitement gripped him.

Onward he went, the tingle growing stronger.

He stumbled into a large tunnel. He looked left, then right. Right would take him back towards the city—albeit, under the ocean; left would lead to—Erzion cocked his head. *Where does it lead?* he wondered.

The tunnel was large enough for three maybe four fae to fly side by side.

Gods, he thought with sudden excitement, *a guardian could fit down here!*

Erzion's heart thrummed in his chest.

Yes, agreed that voice.

With no more hesitation, Erzion expanded his wings and set

off. After about twenty minutes of steady flying, he found himself in a huge cave. It extended well past the illuminating capability of his magic.

Though he could not see it, he could *feel* its vastness dwarfing him.

He absentmindedly rubbed his arms. The tingle of magic increased. Erzion gulped, the overwhelming size of the dark space pressing in on him. Slowly he turned in the air.

To go up or down?

The question was answered for him. A bright bluish-green glow caught his eye. His heart lurched. Using his wings to hold himself steady, Erzion peered downward toward the source of the flame.

As if waiting for his gaze, deep in the cave a huge arc of light glowed, flanked either side by two burning pyres.

Feeling the power pull on him, Erzion beat his wings. The closer he got, the more he could feel its magical touch. Soon his keen eyes picked up a huge shadowy structure.

Under his scrutiny, it flared to life. The runes adorning it glowed brighter at his approached. In turn, Erzion felt a surge in his blood. It seemed the structure could amplify his own magic. Grinning at the feeling, Erzion forced his magic to use that extra boost. With ease, he pushed outward, igniting his life-force, his energy, with his magic. Such power bathed the cavern in a red glow from floor to roof. Protruding from the ceiling were huge, glistening stalactites.

Lexon would have hated the way they looked like a dragon's teeth. He huffed, a small laugh.

Slowly his head turned, taking in the sight of the colossal cave.

Beneath his feet, huge scratch marks scarred the smooth dark rock.

Erzion swallowed. They weren't just the marks of one or two beasts, but many.

He thought about the stories circulating from the warriors who had survived the battle with the Lord of Souls and his winged demons. Some had spoken of mighty guardians ripping those armoured creatures to shreds with talons and teeth. Others spoke of them trapping the Lord of Souls and banishing him to Chaos, right before Lunaria was dragged into the land of shadow herself.

Perhaps this structure is how they entered this realm? Is this why I have been drawn here? To protect and guard over this gateway?

Lunaria's distant words came back to him. *"I will have this city and the power beneath it kept hidden and safe until an heir of my bloodline returns. Promise me."* Maybe she had meant for him to find this all along.

Inside his heart he knew she had. A strange sensation warmed his chest. Pride. She had chosen *him* to protect this secret.

He turned to face the huge cave. It yawned before him as he flew closer to those huge shining stalactites.

Tunnels on many different levels disappeared off into the rock face. *Do they connect?* A frown creased his brow. It would take hundreds of years to map these undiscovered catacombs and caves to find out where they led.

Then he realised the implication of his thoughts, of what he could *do* with such a place. His grin was wide, unrestrained. He had time. Tanelle was but a baby. That meant he had tens, perhaps even hundreds of years, to map and make use of this city of stone, especially if she was not the one destined to retake the throne.

Even the Queen had no idea this place existed. And if Erzion used his wizarding skills carefully, she never would.

He banked and dived and soared through the darkness. When he was satisfied he had a good idea of the layout of the cave, he returned to the archway. Its runes flared brighter as he tentatively reached out a hand and touched the strange, smooth stone. Its warmth surprised him. And though he could not say why, Erzion lay his cheek against it, enjoying a moment of peace as purpose flooded him.

This will be my purpose, Mother. Here I will build a sanctuary for all our kind. I will protect it with all my magic and all my heart. I will build our army, and when the time is right, we will tear down Griana's world and crush it beneath our might.

CHAPTER 19

LEXON

Awareness pricked Lexon's mind. He had a vague memory of a foul liquid being forced into his mouth—of it burning through his body, seeking out his wounds. Its disgusting taste lingered on his tongue.

Blood crusted his eyelids. It took several attempts before he could crack them open. Harsh sunlight sent searing agony to his brain. He groaned. The ringing in his ears made it difficult to think.

Am I dead? he wondered. Then a kernel of sense bloomed in his mind. Sore, aching muscles. A throat so dry he couldn't swallow. *Nope. If I am dead, I wouldn't feel such agony.*

His heart flipped. *Alethia!*

"Be still, prince," ordered a deep voice. "You will not like your body for the next few hours," it advised wryly.

Lexon huffed a breath, his torso heaving. Sand scraped his bare skin. "I do not like it now," he croaked.

A deep throaty chuckle. "Indeed. Here. Let me help you sit up. You need to drink."

Lexon did not fight as capable hands helped him drag his bulk upright. The movement caused his head to pound and nausea to roll through his belly. He swallowed the bile that stung his throat and closed his eyes again. Digging his fingers in the hot sand seemed to centre him, to give him a sense of who and where he was.

Alethia! Varil!

He tried not to think of them, just trust that Alethia had got them all somewhere safe.

Breathe...in...out...

It took a while for the pounding in his head to settle enough for him to risk opening his eyes again.

Warily, Lexon scrutinised the ebony-skinned man, who in turn studied him right back. His dark brown, almost black eyes glinting with amusement and curiosity.

Up close, the metal sun inlaid in the man's forehead was like nothing Lexon had ever seen. Long tendrils of greenish blue metal reached across the man's bald scalp, winding down the back of his neck. Across his forehead fingers of fire stretched, reaching down his temples and cheeks to beneath his jaw bone.

Lexon couldn't help but stare.

"My name is D'thy. I am a priest of Ionia," the man rumbled, his voice deep and rich.

"Hello," croaked Lexon. "I'm..." He hesitated, considering lying.

D'thy smiled, understanding immediately. "I am glad to have found you, Prince Arjuno. The great guardian has honoured me by guiding me here." His dark eyes travelled over the killing ground, his mouth becoming a grim line. "I was searching for you when my brothers and I found Ion Mah in flames. We could not leave the people to suffer alone."

An angry, high pitched voice screeched, echoing off the mighty dunes and interrupting their conversation.

D'thy smiled almost cruelly.

"That is Prince Kalib. All these deaths, all that..." He swept his hand in the direction of the dark cloud of smoke that marred the perfect blue sky. "That is his doing," he growled.

Lexon turned to look, his hands grinding into the sand, and watched as Kalib yelled obscenities at the two stone-faced wizards who held him.

Something tickled his skin. Lexon looked down, then flicked a fat, glistening fly off his forearm. He grimaced. More of the hideous things swarmed around him, landing on the glassy-eyed dead or the bits of bodies that lay nearby. The stench of blood was overpowering and sickening.

D'thy snarled as he followed Lexon's gaze. "Too many have died, on both sides of this war," he said.

"They always do," Lexon breathed, thinking of another time, another place. He swallowed against his sore throat, then stiffened.

How stupid was he being? Had he not learned from his recent past?

Barom had betrayed him; he should not be sitting here waiting for it to happen again.

"No," D'thy said, shaking his head at Lexon's dark expression—the way his fists curled, the way he angled his body. "I have no interest in betraying you."

"Then what do you want?" questioned Lexon, eyes narrowed upon D'thy's. "I don't believe you are with me out of the goodness of your heart," he said, suspicion pouring off him.

D'thy sat back on his haunches and held out a water skin. "Drink," he advised.

Lexon stared at the skin dangling between the priest's fingers. *Poison?* he wondered.

"It isn't poisoned, prince. If I wanted you dead, I would have left you to suffer your fate at that cruel boy's hands," D'thy pointed out dryly.

Accepting that truth and being desperately thirsty, Lexon took the water skin and drank—deeply. He groaned as the warm but sweet water rolled across his tongue, washing away a little of the rotten taste and dust between his teeth.

Lexon handed it back, bent his knees then rested his forearms on them. "Why did you help me?" he asked, cringing as another high pitched squeal of rage rent the air.

The wizards were hauling Kalib away. They held him firmly. No matter how much he fought or cursed, they ignored him, staring forward like he wasn't there.

Curved swords rested upon their hips. Leather straps and buckles held their armour secure and cinched in their loose tunics at the waist. Nothing covered their heads, though scarves were bunched around their necks, and each had a long plait that reached down to the small of their backs. One with almost black hair, one with completely white hair.

"Since it has become known the last guardian of Lunaria no longer occupies the lair in the Fire Mountains, these past months have become chaos for this land," D'thy told him. "Over one hundred years ago, when the wizards came from the north of your lands and invaded ours, the guardians helped bring peace. That peace has been crumbling." His dark eyes narrowed, observing his fellow priests, who Lexon noted stood in a protective line behind them. "My brothers and I worship the guardians above all others, even the goddesses who created this world. I was told by the guardian to be here for you."

"Vaalor? Why?" Lexon asked.

"No," D'thy spoke softly. "The High Ruler. He—" The priest hesitated as if unsure how much to say.

Lexon held his gaze and waited, though his heart was pounding. *Alethia's father! Here!*

"He came to me. I am to be your guide to your new home—and perhaps beyond."

Whilst D'thy spoke, Lexon was gently testing his magic. A familiar warmth seeped through his belly, reassuring him with its touch. It was hard to hide his sigh of relief.

"Since news reached the High Wizard of the battle in your kingdom, he has taken it upon himself to send his army to demand more goods and taxes—and slaves from our people. As there is no longer a guardian to ensure he uphold his ancestor's promise for peace, it seems the wizard has become greedier." D'thy's face became hard and angry. "Building the Silk Road has expanded Ion Mah into a prosperous trade city, and with that has come all the scum you would expect—from many kingdoms. Like moths to a flame, they seek their own fortune. They terrorise the weakest in our communities and take what they want by force. Our villages have burned and our silk farms have been invaded. These barbarians enslave our people, then sell them to Gar Anon's slave trade. And the wizards just get fatter and richer. My people have begun to fight back." His jaw tightened. "But these last months the bloodshed is escalating; the wizard believes my people are the cause of the unrest and is condemning them—killing them. Many have come to our sacred caves asking for help from the Fire Priests—and we have answered. My brothers are scattered throughout the Sky Desert. If peace cannot be found, we will fight."

Lexon did not let his expression change. In those seconds it had truly registered what D'thy was, and how badly the Ionians must need the Fire Priests if they had come out of the seclusion in which they normally lived. He had learned about the Fire Priests as a boy. Very few people ever saw one, let alone met one. They were legendary in their devotion to the guardians and their worship of the sun, believing its fire to be the mother of the great beasts. It seemed stories of their unique fighting style and prowess had not been exaggerated.

And the Fire Priests were ready to go to war.

Lexon wrinkled his nose as he glanced at the bloodied sand and the dead bodies. More flies swarmed. They buzzed, landing on the gore of wizard and priest alike, their fat bodies pulsing as they feasted. The stench of blood and excrement had become stronger in the heat.

Lexon felt his gorge rise.

Pulling his gaze away from the gruesome sight, he anxiously searched the skies. He had lingered too long. This was not his war. He needed to find his family.

D'thy looked up too. "I also wish for your mate to return," he said quietly, but deadly serious.

"She's not my mate." Lexon stated, but even as the words left his lips, his gut twisted. *Liar!* His soul screamed. The thought of losing her before he had uttered the sacred mating words, before they had shared the blood that would entwine their souls, sickened him. His heart and mind already belonged to her.

The sun began to drop lower.

Lexon forced himself to stop gazing at the skies and to continue listening to D'thy. The more he understood about what was happening, the more likely he was to find a way out of this situation, for the attention of the wizards was sure to land back upon him sooner or later.

"The guardian and your friends, even the little princess, will be safe. You can trust me, prince. I have no interest in helping a foreign queen capture or kill you or the little princess. And I would never ignore the responsibility I was given—I will only ever help you."

"Really?" quipped Lexon.

He looked toward a group of wizards, who knelt in front of a regal-looking man. Only his back and intricately braided white hair was visible, but his bearing was unmistakable. It was that of a man used to being obeyed, of having and using power.

He appeared to be questioning the wizards, and none too gently. One of them began to beg and plead. The white-haired man simply flicked his wrist dismissively and the wizard's mouth healed over, effectively stopping any further speech.

Lexon stared in horrified fascination as the wizard worked, sealing each man's mouth after he had been questioned.

It was like nothing Lexon had ever seen.

Lexon considered running. He scanned the blue sands, weighing up the wizards and the Ionian priests that surrounded him.

"Do not worry, prince," D'thy nodded toward the white-haired wizard. "My promises are not empty. You will come to no harm. The High Wizard is powerful, but we can move through the desert far faster than he can cast his spells."

D'thy looked to his fellow priests, both men and women, all with their heads shaved, all tattooed with a sun. None other had an inlaid metal sun like his.

Lexon couldn't help but wonder at the significance of that.

"I must try and stop this bloodshed. I owe it to my people. We do not wish to fight, only to live in peace. But we will not be conquered or enslaved."

Lexon grunted his acknowledgment. "How will you do that?" he enquired, watching the High Wizard work.

D'thy smiled. "I have already made a start." He cocked a brow. "Whilst you were sleeping."

Lexon huffed but swallowed his retort.

"I reminded him of his pledge. You have brought a guardian back to these lands. Her existence persuaded the High Wizard to honour a truce. He is willing to negotiate, asking only that I give him time to talk with his men and his son."

Lexon swallowed his surprise, letting D'thy continued. "The High Wizard's pledge was to live in peace in these lands and protect the Ionians. It was made in the presence of the goddess and her guardians, and is the only chance we have to stop further bloodshed. I do not wish to fight a war where the cost to life will be devastating for both sides. But if we are forced to protect our lands and people, we will." His eyes shone with resolve when he met Lexon's gaze. "If the High Wizard will not reaffirm his pledge, we will destroy anyone in these lands not of Ionian blood, no matter their age, bloodline or purpose for being here."

Lexon admired the conviction in D'thy's words, though couldn't help but wonder how the Ionian's could fight such powerful spells. He nodded carefully even as his gut twisted at the thought of more lives lost. "I understand, but perhaps Alethia's presence will not be necessary for the High Wizard to honour his pledge. He could have continued the fighting if he desired. Instead, he has stopped. He looks far more like a man who is gathering facts than one planning further attacks."

"True," agreed D'thy, his focus now on the High Wizard. "I hope that is indeed the case."

"So do I," muttered Lexon. Not least because the people of this land would border what he hoped would become his kingdom and home. He needed the trust of both the wizards and the Ionians if he were to build an army so close to their borders.

∾

Lexon just had time to down the full skin of sweet water before the High Wizard finished questioning his men. During that time Lexon scanned the skies for Alethia. He wanted to leave, to search for her, but the legion of wizards who had materialised behind the High Wizard and his son made a peaceful escape impossible.

Something momentous was about to happen here, and Lexon did not want to destroy the possibility of peace by running. So he tried to quell his anxiety for his new family and concentrated on the wizard.

Behind D'thy and Lexon, the remaining Fire Priests stood silently. They were all once again swathed in headscarves. A hot wind had risen and was blowing fine particles of sand into the air. Beneath the swathes of material, their dark eyes unwaveringly observed their enemy. Being vastly outnumbered did not seem to faze them.

"Thanks," Lexon said, handing the empty skin back to D'thy. Sand covered his sticky skin. He snorted, blowing dust from his nostrils. In hindsight, burning his clothes had been a stupid thing to do.

Feeling much stronger, his magic buzzing inside him once again, Lexon stood, and attempted to brush himself down. He grimaced as sand scraped his skin.

The High Wizard turned towards the two guards holding his son.

He was slim and tall. Unlike all the other wizards who were armoured with tough leather plates and gleaming metal, this wizard wore nothing but gold and crimson robes. At the front of his head, his long white hair was plaited in an intricate pattern, his features so perfect as to be beautiful. There was, however, nothing beautiful about the look in his ice blue eyes as he honed in on Kalib as if he were prey.

Kalib paled, becoming almost as white as his hair. His throat bobbed. "Father?" he whispered.

"Get up," the High Wizard ordered his son coldly.

Kalib set his lips in a thin stubborn line and lifted his chin in defiance as the guards released him. He stood and squared his shoulders. No matter how he tried though, he was still a foot shorter than his father. Sweat glistened upon his upper lip. "But Father, this is the traitor prince the new queen searches for." His voice trembled as he almost whined his excuses. "He had the baby princess too. We can use her to negotiate a ransom large enough to rebuild our cities. Handing over that child will build an alliance with—"

"Quiet!" snapped the High Wizard.

Lexon could feel the power emanating from the wizard. His own power responded. Lexon allowed it to gather defensively just below his skin.

"You are not only spoilt and over indulged by your mother, but you have proven yourself completely inept at politics and benevolence. Negotiating a peace for our people with the Ionian council and saving our cities from ruin was a responsibility *you* asked for."

"But we need to prove our strength *before* approaching the Ionian council. They do not respect us, Father."

"No, they don't anymore, and that is down to you! I gave you a chance to stop this unrest, instead you have turned it into a war. I realise now the enormity of my mistake. You have proved to me, as well as the rest of my generals, that you are useless. You maybe my son, but you will never be my heir. And heed my words, Kalib, should you ever seek to threaten your brother, I will kill you myself," he stated icily.

Kalib's face turned an ugly shade of puce, and his eyes flashed with rage. Lexon might have laughed if he hadn't recognised the utter hatred in that expression. He pitied the brother who would be on the receiving end of that life of inadequacy and jealousy.

"You will return to the palace where you will give General Chix a complete report about your movements with my troops. He will know where you abandoned the wizard army I gave you; which villages, towns and cities you have ruined and where the cache of valuables and slaves are that you have amassed over these past months. And he will know *everything* by the end of the day. Do not try and hide any information. These men have imparted much and I want to know if you will be truthful. Make no mistake, Kalib, you will all be punished for bringing death to our lands in my name."

The High Wizard did not raise his voice at his son. His quiet, cold tone seemed far worse to Lexon.

Kalib only pressed his mouth into a tight thin line and stared defiantly at the stocky wizard who approached with a squad of heavily armed men.

General Chix, Lexon surmised.

Tattoos, similar to the whorls upon a fae warrior's wings, adorned the faces and hands of this group. These were neither just soldiers nor wizards. These were both.

Up close, General Chix appeared sun-weathered and tough looking. His hard eyes rested upon Kalib before they slid to his ruler.

The High Wizard nodded. "General, take him to the palace dungeons. Do what you must to learn the information you need. It seems we have much damage to repair."

"No! You cannot treat me like this, Father! I have claimed lands and people on your behalf. I have waged war to make sure these Ionian savages respect *us* now that the guardians are dead."

"Respect, you stupid boy, is earned, not beaten into people," pointed out the High Wizard coldly. "All you have done is destroy our peace and our lands. You have *enslaved* people, and you have murdered innocents in the process. *I* have to try and salvage our relationship with the Ionians. I was completely wrong to give you any freedom to act on my behalf. I had hoped...well, it matters not what I hoped. I will not make the same mistake again."

He looked to Lexon, a frown furrowing his brow, a clear question in his eyes and voice. "And unless all these men are lying—which I doubt, the guardians are not all dead."

Lexon swallowed. A nod of his head confirmed the truth.

The High Wizard gave a curt nod of thanks.

General Chix stepped purposefully toward Kalib.

Kalib stepped back.

The general halted. His eyes did not shift from the boy, who looked like he might bolt.

General Chix muttered some words. A spell. Slithers of blue sands squirmed toward Kalib. Kalib screeched with fury. Wild-eyed, he looked for a way out. Panicked, he turned and ran. It was futile; wizards waited on the steep dune. Realising it, he turned, raising his hands and chanting. The snakes disappeared only to be replaced by waves of super-heated sand. By the time it almost hit General Chix, it had become shards of glass.

The General shielded with ease and retaliated in kind.

Lexon got ready to drop a shield over himself and the Ionians, but he needn't have worried.

The High Wizard turned to him, not in the least concerned by his son's show of magic. "You and the Fire Priests will not be harmed, Prince Arjuno. My son will be dealt with."

"No. I will not *be dealt with*, Father! And I will never return to the palace. These foreigners are *my* prisoners. *Mine!* I found them. It should be me who ransoms them to the new queen!" Kalib yelled.

With a flick of his father's wrist, Kalib was airborne. He landed in the sand only feet away.

The High Wizard spat out some spells. A flare of blinding light.

Lexon blinked. A wall of blue glass encased Kalib.

At the same time the air cleared, an earth shattering roar rattled his ear drums. Alethia glided over the summit of the dune. Her wings flapped urgently, stirring up a storm of blue sand. Wizards and Ionian alike were forced to throw themselves face-first to the sand as she flew in low. A high pitched screech escaped her as she spotted Lexon.

He remained standing tall, a shield of red shimmering about him. He watched as she passed above, her silver belly almost close enough to touch. She raised herself back into the air and circled, banking shallowly to return. She backwinged, holding herself steady, her tail swishing dangerously close to the dune and the men cowering there.

Her big head dipped, her silver eyes like molten fire as they gazed down. It seemed she was weighing up the situation. She bared her teeth in a snarl as she noted the dead bodies and the young wizard now trapped in his glass cage.

The downdraft of her great wings stirred up a storm of blue sand, covering some of the dead nearby.

Kalib cowered against the sides of his prison, wide-eyed and shaking as Alethia landed, her head lowering until she was looking directly at him. Fire and wrath burned in that ancient glare. A hiss of rage escaped her scaly lips when Kalib spat at her. She lifted her head, snarled.

"No!" Lexon bellowed as she angled her head to swing at the glass cage.

Even his stomach tightened as that massive head and jaws whipped his way. Alethia growled as he shifted to stand between her and the cage.

Lexon held in his gasp as the High Wizard stepped up beside him and dropped to his knees. All the other wizards immediately followed.

"Great guardian, my son will pay for his treatment of your friends and all the people he has harmed over the past months. But I beg you not to kill him. There are too many things we must learn from him. Innocent people will die if we do not negotiate peace and find all those he took from their homes against their will. They must be found and returned to their families. Please. I wish for a land of peace, not war," he told her sincerely.

Alethia growled and fixed him with her stare. The Goddess of Truth weighing up his words.

Lexon wondered if the High Wizard knew she would kill him if he was lying.

She lowered her silver-scaled head. Watching. Listening. The fire in her eyes cooled just a little.

Lexon held his magic tightly under control. Ready to strike, to protect her if he needed.

Beside him, D'thy held two curved blades, and his priests had their hands tucked inside the arms of their robes.

Is that where they keep their weapons? he wondered.

The High Wizard stood, sand pouring from his loose clothing. No matter that it covered his hair and skin, he still looked regal.

Lexon suddenly felt self-conscious. His torso was naked, his wing stumps open for all to see, and he was covered in blood and sand. *Hardly prince-like, and certainly not kingly,* he thought in disgust.

"Guardian, will you let me release my son?" the High Wizard asked Alethia respectfully.

Alethia rolled her bright eyes to Lexon. A question.

Lexon nodded once.

Alethia huffed her consent at the wizard.

Lexon stepped forward to place a hand upon Alethia's nose. Relief washed through him as her warm breath fanned his skin. He was no longer afraid or repulsed by being near a dragon. In truth, he considered Alethia the most beautiful creature in this world.

Her silver eyes rolled down, as if seeing into his soul.

"Is Varil alive? Are they safe?" he asked fearfully.

Alethia blinked and lifted her head to look back over her shoulder. Worry gleamed in her eyes.

"We will find them—very soon," he told her solemnly, anxiety churning in his gut. It was the truth; no matter the cost, he would leave with Alethia.

Keeping his attention and magic open to the movements of those around him, he approached the High Wizard.

D'thy stayed close by his side. "I will come with you to find your friend. If I can, I will help him," he told Lexon, gravely.

"Thank you," Lexon replied, then dipped his head in greeting and respect to the beautiful man that was the High Wizard. "But I fear you may need to be here far longer than me."

D'thy nodded, his lips curling a little. "I am the High Priest and will liaise with the Ionian council," he agreed. He reached into a small pouch that hung on a leather strap around his neck and pulled out a small phial. "Here."

"What's this?" Lexon took the phial, studying it through narrow eyes.

"Petrified Fire Toad," grinned D'thy. "It's the foulest tincture in this world but also the most effective. It will heal your friend, just as it healed you. I just hope he has not lost too much blood."

"Thank you," Lexon said, sending a silent prayer to the High Ruler for sending this man to him.

"Prince," the wizard greeted, keeping a wary eye on Alethia.

And now the negotiations begin, thought Lexon. Silently, he thanked his father for his lessons in both history and diplomacy, though nerves roiled in his stomach as he wiped his sweaty palms on his breeches. "High Wizard," he replied.

Controlling not only his fear for Varil, but his apprehension at manipulating this situation to his advantage as a future ruler, Lexon took a breath and stepped forward.

CHAPTER 20

ERZION

Seventeen years later

Erzion stood with no expression upon his face, and his heart banged in his chest. He listened through the door, his glamour as a palace guard firmly in place.

It had been nearly ten years since he had last heard the Queen plot against Tanelle like this. He knew she had sent assassins to the Fire Mountains before, but thankfully he found out about most of them through his growing network of spies. He had even managed to send warning to Lexon. All the assassination attempts failed, and the assassins never returned to report to the Queen.

Lexon and Alethia had somehow warded the palace they were still building against those intending harm to its occupants.

With the High Wizard's help, maybe? wondered Erzion.

He had heard through letters sent by his mother that relations between the Fire Mountains and the High Wizard thrived.

Sorrow and loneliness speared his heart, which he quelled.

His true queen would soon be seventeen, he realised. A young woman. He wondered what she looked like now. Would she have long silver hair and bright blue eyes, like her mother? Or deep sapphire eyes and long black hair, like her father?

"The High Wizard is dead," the Queen continued, her voice breathy with excitement.

Erzion's heart lurched. *Dead?* That was not good news.

"His youngest son will challenge the High Wizard's heir to a duel on the thirtieth day of mourning. The girl is betrothed to the heir. It is a marriage that has to be stopped. *At all costs!*" she hissed. "That imposter king cannot be allowed to make a marriage alliance with such a powerful kingdom. Together they will become too great a threat to my own."

Erzion nearly choked, almost revealing himself.

Imposter king! She truly is mad! What in the name of Eternity does she think she is, if not an imposter?

"You must go, Lord Commander. Go to Ion Kugat. Prince Kalib has sent word; when the heir steps foot in the arena to be named the next High Wizard, Kalib will challenge for the throne. As their law dictates, there will be a fight to the death. Only one brother will walk away from the challenge. The girl will be there. She fancies herself in love with the heir. She will not stay away, not even to protect herself."

"Yes, Majesty," replied Commander Edison. "Am I permitted to take a small force with me?" he asked.

His rough voice grated on Erzion's nerves, even through the thickness of the closed door.

The commander had aged well, but he had still aged. His skin was more lined, his eyes dull and he had lost any semblance of kindness. Erzion wondered if Edison even remembered who he had been before the Queen had bitten him. That loyal warrior had certainly disappeared. Guilt sent bile up Erzion's throat. It had been his hand that had delivered this warrior to the Queen.

No. Erzion had done as his goddess and the High Ruler had bid him that night so long ago. He only hoped they were true to their word, and he would not end up in Chaos for all he had done.

Other than the Ice Witches in the north, Avalonia had almost settled to peace. Those rebellious of the Queen's rule hid out in the forests and were easy to hunt down.

Erzion allowed thoughts of his cave city to calm him.

Ultimately, there was always another choice than servitude or death, for those rebellious fae who wanted it.

"You will not need one," the Queen continued. "I have an assassin ready to deal with this. All you need to do is get the assassin to the arena. She will do the rest."

Erzion's blood ran cold at those words. His only hope was Lexon and Alethia would sense the assassin as they had all the others. But if Tanelle were outside the Fire Mountains…

"You will leave on the *Sea Wing* at dawn. It is an Hourian ship already in harbour. It will speed you and the assassin to Ducat city. From there you will fly her to the border of Gar Anon and into the Hotlands. Prince Kalib will have a force ready to meet you and escort you quietly into Ion Kugat. The Ice Witch is waiting aboard the ship for you."

"Can she be trusted, Majesty?" Edison asked carefully.

Erzion couldn't blame him for asking, the Ice Witches were Avalonia's enemy.

"Yes. We have a mutually beneficial arrangement. She takes care of the false princess, and I help her become one. Take what coin you need and do not return until the traitor is dead."

"Yes, Majesty," Commander Edison replied.

Disguised as a palace guard, Erzion stood silently on the other side of the newly carved and painted throne room doors. Large, gleaming serpents curled up the wooden doors, their gilded heads and green and blue painted bodies making him feel as though they were about to devour him.

He shuddered, suppressing his desire to run, to warn Lexon.

Footsteps approached.

Erzion kept his eyes straight ahead when the doors were yanked open.

Erzion turned and reached for the throne room door. He did not look in the Queen's direction, merely kept his eyes down on the floor until the heavy doors clanged shut.

∼

Erzion informed his red wing commander where he was going. No one else knew he was even in Valentia. As far as his army and the Queen were concerned, he was in the north fighting an uprising. If anyone required his advice or an audience, his network of faithful, glamoured redwings created a series of sightings and responsibilities he was attending to. Messages would be passed back and forth, and his second in command in the north would make decisions on Erzion's behalf.

It went without saying he could not get away with leaving like this more than once. The Queen would learn of his elusive behaviour. Questions would be asked.

Erzion silently thanked the Ice Witches who had declared war in the north. It was easy to get lost in the mess of a vicious war that spanned hundreds of miles, no matter whose spies were looking for you, though clearly the Queen had allies inside her enemy's ranks.

Exiting the caverns, Erzion stood in the same cave from where his mother had departed. This time, he was departing.

An accepting, if somewhat sad smile curled his lips. Despite travelling to Ion Kugat, he knew he would not have time to get as far as the Fire Mountains. He would not see his friend or his mother.

Down the coast a slight sea mist had formed, turning the sunlight hazy. Steeling himself for this long, arduous journey, Erzion glamoured his wings to a dull yellow, though he did not armour. His worn and simple clothes made him appear as nothing more than a forest traveller. None could see the throwing knives secreted under his clothes.

Stopping to sleep for only a couple of hours a night, Erzion made his way down the coast. He maintained his glamour the entire way, not dropping it even when he landed in the forest to drink at a stream or buy food from the small fishing villages on route.

The locals eyed him suspiciously but relaxed when he ate with gusto and answered their questions with a twang of accent similar to most fisher folk. He was heading down the coast to Stormguaard, to find work, he told them all.

After more than a week of near constant flying, Erzion reached his destination. A small outcropping of land that was the closest point to the Wetlands.

Sweat-soaked and exhausted, he plonked himself down on the sand. Leaning his forearms on his knees, Erzion watched the horizon and waited.

The sun was setting, its fire turning the sky a glorious pink by the time a small sail ship appeared on the horizon. The shore dropped away steeply into the ocean. Large waves crashed, the sea foam curling to just in front of Erzion's boots. He watched the water carefully, his excitement and nerves growing despite his shaking muscles and aching wings. He had never gone farther than the Wetlands, never travelled across the ocean to the shores of the other kingdoms.

A shadow. A flick of silver and blue in the clear water.

A grin spread over Erzion's face.

Bursting from the waves, Lord Firan flipped elegantly out of the water. Glorious blue and silver scales gleamed, reflecting the glow of the sun before he disappeared under the water, only to jump and spin again.

Erzion's breath caught at the feeling of freedom and beauty his friend's antics evoked in him. "Show off," he muttered, but he was still smiling as he pushed himself to his feet, brushing the sand from his clothes and hands.

Firan's blue-scaled body glistened as he emerged from the surf. Opening his hands, he commanded the water. It snaked around him like a living thing until he was covered in what looked like clothes of liquid blue silk. "Hello, wizard," Firan greeted, striding forward in his elegant way.

Erzion embraced his friend, swallowing hard. It had been so long, so long since he had seen *any* of his friends, held any of them. "Gods, it's good to see you, Firan," he mumbled, swallowing the ache in his throat, his fingers gripping the smooth silk of Firan's clothes.

"You too," Firan replied. Something unsaid zipped in the air between the two friends and understanding shone in Firan's deep blue eyes. Then he chuckled. "But if you don't let go of me, I'm going get worried you lied about going across the ocean and only want to bed me."

Erzion let go and laughed, waggling his brows. "Can't I want both?"

Firan snorted. "You do not have a hope with me—but some of my mers, well, they'd like to brag about bedding a fae warrior, I'm sure."

But all levity fell from Firan's face when he looked back in Erzion's eyes. Only understanding remained.

Hiding his heart normally helped Erzion keep the pain of losing his loved ones at bay, but it felt good to know Firan understood. Loneliness was a heavy burden to bear.

"So you want to go on your travels?" Firan asked, searching Erzion's tired and dirt smeared face.

"I wish it were just for my amusement, but it is not. My true queen is being lured into danger—away from the safety of her home. I need to stop the assassin."

Firan merely nodded. "It's time you crossed this ocean. No matter the reason. You should see Lexon again. He has become a fine king and father, Erzion. You would be proud of all he has achieved." Firan, who was as tall if not a little taller than Erzion, looked upon his friend and said gravely, "As he would be of all you have achieved in Avalonia."

Erzion dropped his eyes, wishing that were true but knowing it wasn't. His friend wouldn't understand all the things he had done in the name of bringing peace within Avalonia's borders and protecting Valentia for the Arjuno line.

Firan slapped his shoulder. Both a supportive gesture and a chastisement of sorts. "Do not be ashamed of anything you have done. Ever. Many people see the cruel Master Commander when they look at you, and that is who you are meant to be to them. For their sakes, as well as your own. It is who your goddess asked you to be. But never doubt that the people who love you will always recognise the goodness beneath the glamour."

"Maybe, but they will soon die. Then no one will know who I truly am," Erzion replied, unable to keep the sadness from his voice or the weight of that crushing knowledge from his shoulders.

"*I* won't. I am immortal too," Firan pointed out. "I will *always* know. And all those you save, that you offer a new life to, a better life, will know who you really are. Now," he said slapping Erzion's shoulder hard. "Let's get you to the Southern Hotlands."

∼

Erzion was still in awe of Firan and his men. Firan had chosen a non-descript trade vessel that was small and cramped. The crew was always respectful of Erzion, but never overly friendly. Wary, he supposed.

He didn't blame them. Wetlanders were a notoriously secretive society. Like his father before him, Firan had let no foreigners in his lands. Any outsider who went there was never seen again.

Erzion did not ask Firan what happened to them. It was none of his business how Firan ran his kingdom.

Sail or wind made no difference to the ship's progress. Firan's small army of Wetlanders powered the ship from below, their scaled bodies flashing and darting in the crystal clear ocean waters.

Despite their unending stamina and speed, it still took nearly twelve days to cross the vast ocean.

Erzion had not flown that whole time. A warm sea breeze stirred his hair and feathers. He gazed at the sky, aching to feel that breeze beneath his wings, lifting his body high above. *Soon,* he told himself, stretching his unarmoured wings wide and flapping them to relieve the stiff muscles in his back.

Knowing they would be reaching land soon, nerves churned in his belly. Under Firan's supervision he had briefly visited the shores of the Wetlands but other than that, he had never been out of Avalonia before; despite his education being delivered alongside Lexon's, he couldn't help but wonder what he would find in this new land.

He stretched his arms along with his wings and back. He was going to have to fly hard, and his muscles needed to be looser if he were not to cramp up.

Firan had handed him maps of the Sky Desert, and even Ion Kugat, at the beginning of their journey. And Erzion had studied them every day and night since. Memorising his route and the towns, even the watering holes he would visit.

A star-speckled night had fallen when Firan called his men aboard from the murky waters of the Liary estuary. Tu Lanah shone brightly, illuminating the shadowy banks that narrowed in around the ship as the wide mouth of the river became nothing more than an inlet.

The air over the water was damp and heavy. Sweat trickled down the grooves of Erzion's body, soaking the waistband of his leggings. His clothes seemed too thick, too hot, for this place.

Taking his tunic off had helped, but his wool leggings and linen shirt clung to his skin, moulding to his body.

The ship shuddered to halt as the anchor was dropped.

"Are you ready for this?" asked Firan, appearing beside Erzion.

Erzion jumped. "How do you do that?" he muttered tetchily. "No one other than Lexon has ever been able to sneak up on me."

Firan grinned broadly. "I know. That's why I do it. I like to piss you off," he said with a chuckle.

Erzion noticed the bundle his friend held. "What's that?" he asked.

Firan held them out. "Clothes. You should change. Yours will mark you as a foreigner immediately; besides, yours stink almost as badly as you do," he quipped.

"Thanks," Erzion said, rolling his eyes.

"You're welcome. There's some water." Firan pointed to some buckets. "You might want to strip and sluice down before leaving. That stench will draw all sorts of unwanted attention," he quipped with a grin.

Erzion cursed his friend under his breath, but he was grinning when he unabashedly threw his filthy clothes to the side and used the water to wash the days of sweat from his body and salt from his wings. Dried and dressed in the light, loose pants and tunic Firan had provided, Erzion cinched the material with a leather belt and turned to his friend.

"Here," said Firan, pushing something into Erzion's hand.

"What's this?" he asked, holding the small pebble-like object between his finger and thumb. It was completely smooth and shot through with veins of crystalline rock.

"It's a way to contact me when you're ready. I will return for you if you need me to. Just hold this in the ocean. I will hear its call, the same way I can hear the call of any of my people through the ocean."

"Thank you," Erzion said, awed that Firan could do such a thing.

There was an awkward pause. Erzion wanted to say more, to tell his friend how much his friendship and support meant, but he didn't know how.

Instead he pulled Firan into a hard, quick embrace before stepping back. Erzion threw out his wings, tucked the stone into the pocket of his tunic and grinned. "I owe you, my lord," he said sincerely and bowed low.

Firan shrugged, his scaled forehead gleaming against his moonlit blue skin. "Yes, you do, wizard. It's alright. I'll seek payment one day."

Erzion grinned. "I'm sure you will."

With that he stretched out his wings, bent his knees and launched himself towards the stars.

CHAPTER 21

ERZION

The arena was bigger than anything Erzion had ever seen. The sea of heads stretched around the terraced steps, seething with activity.

Wizards and Ionians mixed together; the stench of sweaty bodies was overpowering. Erzion glanced around. It seemed word of this death match had reached far and wide. The shield around Ion Kugat had been dropped for the day. People from all Eight Kingdoms mingled among the crowds.

Perhaps the fae here had been part of the exodus to escape the Queen.

Ensuring his non-threatening glamour was in place, Erzion cast his gaze around the expanse of thousands of people.

This is impossible, he thought, panic beginning to bloom. *How do I find one young woman among all these people?*

The voices surrounding him were a cacophony of different languages, amplified tenfold by the raised sides of the amphitheatre. He cursed his sensitive fae ears. People were yelling and chanting for the heirs to appear.

Their lust to see death disgusted Erzion. Seeing bloodshed was never entertainment, especially between brothers.

Sweat soaked his headscarf making it stick to his forehead. He absentmindedly lifted it with his little finger and scratched his itching skin. The air in the arena was sweltering, hotter even than the desert. Normally Erzion loved how heat fed his red magic; right now, though, he could not allow his magic any freedom, and it was stifling him.

Think! he told himself sternly. *What would an assassin find in this heat to use as a weapon? Where would she wait for her prey?*

Vendors sold their wares all around this level of the arena. This close, the smells of cooking and spices overpowered the stench of so many bodies, sending his starved belly into a frenzy. It had been a full day since he had last eaten—he was starving, even his legs were shaking. He frowned. He would eat and walk. Allowing his energy to wane was not sensible.

Stepping up to a vendor, he purchased a flatbread full of spiced lamb.

Swallowing the mouthful of saliva that rushed his tongue, he took his first bite—and groaned as the flavours burst across his tongue.

Not wanting to waste any time, he continued to chew, but snapped his attention back to the arena.

At the far side stood large wooden doors where the wizard heirs would enter the arena. Erzion glanced over the guards standing in front of the doors. They looked stoic and completely unruffled by the noise around them.

Pushing his way through the crowd, he ignored other people's curses and angry grumbles and made his way down the stone tiers before he came to halt. Guards lined the lower railings, making it difficult for Erzion to look down upon the arena floor.

He snarled in frustration. It would be so much easier if he could spread his wings and hover over the crowd, but flying of any kind in Ion Kugat was banned. And looking at the army of wizard warriors who manned the stadium, it would be a quick end for any who tried.

Curbing his irritation at the forced limitation, Erzion continued to scrutinise the arena, his eyes scanning everything visible.

His brow furrowed. *If I were a young girl wanting to see my love, where would I go to make sure he knew I was here?*

Erzion swallowed the last of his food and turned full circle as he wiped his hands down his tunic. Ignoring the muttering crowd, he leaped back up to the main walk way. Disregarding the people banging into him, he spun on his heel.

The gates.

Tanelle would be where the heir could see her, either in the stands near the gates or on the lower level, perhaps immediately behind the barrier where she could be seen.

He had to get down there.

A head of pure white hair came into his eyeline as he twisted. There was an "oomph!" as he knocked the ancient old crone down to her hands and knees.

"I'm so sorry," Erzion muttered in rusty Ionian. He bent down but didn't look at the old lady's face as he grasped her under her arms and hauled her back to her feet; he was too intent on getting down to the gates and searching the crowd down there.

Cold breath fanned his hand for a fraction of a second before she brushed him off with a muttered, heavily accented curse and disappeared into the crowd.

Erzion did not spare the old lady another thought; instead, he began pushing people out of his way as he headed for the lower tier of the arena.

∼

Leaning his shoulders over the railings, Erzion peered down to the arena floor just as a fanfare sounded and the gates cracked open. The crowd roared, shouting and cheering, though it didn't escape his notice some spectators jeered at the two young men who emerged.

Both were dressed in loose pants similar to Erzion's but both had naked torsos, oiled and gleaming against the vicious touch of the sun. One had jet black hair and looked stoic and tight-lipped, the other was white-haired and grinning widely.

Erzion frowned as the younger man strode forward, playing to the crowd.

Kalib, Erzion presumed. He disliked the young man already. His arrogance was astounding.

Kalib lifted his arms as though already victor of the fight then paraded around bowing to his audience. The jeering reached a crescendo. Clearly the crowd did not love him as much as he loved himself.

Curious, Erzion looked back to see how the brother was handling this show. The heir seemed older, more mature. Dark eyebrows pulled together across a handsome face. Startling blue eyes narrowed as he watched his brother's antics. Both men were tall and lithe and moved with grace, but the older was slightly heavier in the shoulders. His fingers curled into fists.

Erzion didn't blame him; he wanted to punch Kalib too.

The heir strode forward and gave his younger brother a dark look.

Kalib pointedly ignored him and continued to rile the crowd.

The heir scowled, lifting his gaze to look into the stand opposite Erzion. He nodded at a tough-looking warrior, who in turn nodded back.

A clap of thunder made everyone in the arena screech and jump in surprise. Erzion tensed, reaching for his magic.

The older warrior wizard had both arms raised. His voice carried clearly across the arena, augmented by magic of some kind. "As is the law of this land, the passing of our revered High Wizard has left his title open to challenge. He has named Prince Parran as heir. Today is the thirtieth day of mourning. The day of challenge. Challenger and heir come forward. Kneel before me and your supreme rulers, the guardians."

Kalib halted his antics with the crowd. A look of utter hatred darkened his face as he glared at the warrior.

Ignoring each other, both young men stepped forward.

The warrior wizard stood on a dais, flanked by the horned and scaled stone dragons. Their fierce amber-stoned eyes glared down malevolently at the heirs.

Parran kneeled.

Kalib hesitated, glaring up at the wizard on the dais.

Tension rippled through the crowd when the challenger did not kneel but continued to hold the wizard's icy regard.

Noticing the crowd's murmuring, the heir looked up, his eyes flitting from the wizard to his brother. He seemed to hiss some words and, grabbing his brother's wrist, yanked him to his knees.

Kalib jerked his arm away, his eyes going back to the wizard who had begun to speak.

Erzion's whole body tensed. That was no normal amount of dislike in those eyes; it was cold, murderous intent.

"I am General Chix, advisor and protector to the High Wizard," the general announced to the restless crowd. He glared down. The hate in Kalib's eyes was clearly reciprocated. "Prince Kalib, do you challenge the named heir, your brother, and first born son of Haron for title of High Wizard; or do you pledge to serve him with honour and valour until the guardians guide your soul to the next life?"

Kalib bounded to his feet. He pointed a pale finger at his brother. "Yes, I challenge him, for this throne and for his life! I will not bow down to someone so weak!" he roared to the crowd, earning a tumult of responses.

General Chix glared at the younger brother, not bothering to hide his hatred. "Then I hereby ban you and Prince Parran from the use of spells and enchantments for the duration of this challenge." His next words almost seemed to get stuck in General

Chix's throat, but he forced them out. "As is the law of this land, I shall protect you both from harm and you shall fight as mortal men—until one of you lies dead and an heir is decided."

The crowd roared and screamed and stamped their feet, rattling the air until Erzion was convinced the arena might collapse from the vibration alone. The yells of support and hatred mixed together until it was impossible to distinguish one from the other.

Kalib slapped his bare chest with his the flat of his hands, the sound lost in the cacophony.

General Chix uttered the spell that would stifle Kalib's wizardry.

The man ignored him, instead he turned to the crowd. "Me!" he bellowed. "It is me who will prove myself strong enough to lead you! My brother is weak. He wishes to mix our blood *and* our lands with that of a new, unestablished kingdom. A kingdom of traitors and misfits! A weak kingdom! Against our laws, he has become betrothed to the reclusive princess of the Fire Mountains!!"

The crowd roared their disapproval.

The malevolent atmosphere raised goose bumps on Erzion's skin. He melted back against the wall, alert and watchful. Scuffles began breaking out as supporters of the heir defended their prince against those who were horrified by the news he had entered into a betrothal without the knowledge of the people.

Fury darkened Parran's face, though he remained on his knees in the face of his brother's onslaught.

Erzion strained his ears against the noise of the crowd, managing to pick up their conversation.

"Brother, stop this. Father worked for peace all his life. Don't destroy everything he built."

"Me, destroy it? Ha! Father never could see clearly where you were concerned," he sneered. "You're the one willing to sully our bloodline with that of a traitor! You would even bring her to our lands, and put our people at risk from attack by a foreign ruler! There will be no trade agreements with those kingdoms not willing to suffer the wrath of the Avalonian queen and her army. *You*, Parran, will plunge us into a war which will empty our coffers and destroy any hope of prosperity for our lands. You do not deserve to be heir!"

"My betrothal to Princess Tanelle is about love, not power or money," spat Parran. "But you are wrong. Our union *will* make our lands powerful, possibly even invincible to attack from the other kingdoms. Think, Kalib! The Fire Mountains have a queen who is a guardian. That alone will ensure peace for all of us."

"Peace!" spat Kalib. "I do not want peace in my lands. Not yet. And neither does any self-respecting wizard who follows me. My wants are very simple. I want total power, and riches beyond anything we have now. And when I kill you, *brother,* I will have it. I will *make* the Ionians treat me, and every other wizard, with the respect we deserve. They need to learn they are inferior in everything, to us. They should serve us and worship us. You just can't see it and neither could Father. No wonder he chose you to succeed him, you're just like him—weak-willed and a coward who will not fight for what is rightfully his," he jeered.

Parran flushed with anger at Kalib's words. "Father always told me that you were mad, that one day I would have to kill you. I never really believed him until now."

Kalib grinned evilly. "Oh, you should have. Now you will lose more than your own life."

"What do you mean?" Parran blanched, his head whipping around to search the arena with frantic eyes. "What did you do?"

Kalib laughed madly. "Nothing—yet. I just made sure your love got word of this challenge. I expect she will show herself once I make you scream." With a vicious smile, he nodded to the guards who stood at the back of a furious-looking General Chix.

Realisation flickered in the general's eyes. Too late, he whirled. He was dead before he stopped moving. A spear protruded through his neck, blood gushing from his mouth as he toppled forward.

"No!" Parran yelled, shock and grief distorting his features.

Kalib laughed out loud at his brother's expression just as he sent the sand from the arena floor snaking around his brother's legs.

The crowd went wild.

∼

Erzion moved.

Around him the guards and wizard warriors looked at each other in shock. It was clear they had no idea who they should be fighting for or protecting now that General Chix was gone. Most of the guards gripped their weapons, watching their fellow guards and the crowd with confusion.

Pushing through the throng, Erzion forced his way to the wooden rails. Below him the gates to the arena were tightly closed.

An explosion of power and the sound of shattering glass filled the arena. Erzion looked down at the battling brothers. Kalib had thrown a glass prison around Parran, who in turn had shattered it. Blood dripped from cuts to both their faces and hands.

The crowd roared. This was the spectacle, the bloodshed, they wanted. What they hadn't counted on was the magical attacks now exploding across the arena as the brothers battled.

Spells and magic frightened those without it, as much here as anywhere else in the Eight Kingdoms. Hundreds began running for the exits. It was pandemonium.

Erzion took a steadying breath and concentrated on the figures who were not running. Tanelle would not run. The assassin would not run.

Parran ran for the arena wall and leaped. Sure-footed, he

landed on the smooth stone before lithely bounding up the tiers to the general's fallen body.

Erzion frowned, hoping the young man was not about to flee.

The remaining crowd jeered until the heir bent down and yanked the spear from the general's neck.

A weapon! He wanted a physical weapon.

Erzion felt his respect for the heir climb.

The crowd noticed the heir's actions and cheered, their attention wavering from one potential leader to the other, as if they had no idea which they would rather follow.

Erzion snarled at their fickleness, disgust rippling through him at their lack of loyalty.

Kalib watched his brother through narrowed eyes. His lips worked quickly, forming spells. But he was vulnerable whilst he cast. He had no other magic with which to protect himself.

Erzion tensed. Parran needed to take advantage of that delay and kill Kalib quickly. The spear would do. It would be far quicker than trying to cast a spell.

But Parran did not launch the spear from his hand; instead, he climbed the plinth of the nearest stone dragon.

"Tanelle!" he roared, his eyes desperately searching the crowds from his elevated position. "I don't know where you are—but run!" he urged.

Erzion swore at the heir's stupidity. That delay to strike might just have cost his life—and alerted everyone to Tanelle's presence.

Idiot!

A blast of wind surged forward, bringing with it a storm of projectiles. Shoes, cooking pots, food, even knives—plucked from the belts of the nearby guards, all hurtled toward Parran. They hit him full force, knocking him off the plinth and cutting off his scream as a knife slashed deeply across his bicep.

Below, a young woman screamed.

Erzion's head whipped toward that heart-wrenching sound.

On the opposite side of the gates, on the lowest tier, a girl flung off her cloak. Her long silver hair hung loosely down her back, shining like silk in the bright sunlight. Her tunic and pants were of the finest pale blue silk, edged in fine gold thread. Soft goatskin boots reached halfway up her legs, and a necklace of black metal and crystal glinted from the shadow between her breasts.

Erzion's stomach lurched.

My queen!

His eyes darted to Kalib, who was already running toward Tanelle.

Heart hammering, Erzion threw himself over the wall and dropped, desperate to reach her first. He snapped out his wings to slow his descent, but he was not high enough. He crashed into the ground feet-first, jarring his body from his feet up through his spine. He grunted, ignoring the pain and immediately rolling, softened his fall as best he could. Back on his feet, he pushed magic out between his feathers, armouring his wings. Glorious and red, they spread; his markings glowed, the swirls illuminated like rivers of red fire.

Releasing his glamour, he threw red magic at Kalib. The time for pretence was gone. Saving his queen was far more important than preserving his own life. He knew Commander Edison was watching somewhere, and Erzion didn't care. He would deal with the commander later.

Kalib, dived to the side. Magic exploded around him in a cloud of dust and debris, missing the young prince by inches. The energy of the explosion sent him barrelling into the arena wall.

"My queen! Run toward me!" Erzion bellowed.

Tanelle glanced over her shoulder at him. She frowned, suspicion narrowing her sapphire eyes. Ignoring him, she vaulted up to the next tier—then the next. Her grunts of effort reached him as he launched skyward again, determined to get to her before the assassin struck.

Tanelle jumped off the last stone tier and landed by Parran.

In the shadow of the stone guardian she dropped to her knees at his side, placing a trembling hand on his chest.

A second later, Erzion slammed his feet into the stone by her side. Magic swirled in a red haze around his arms. "Please, we need to leave," he told her, urgently.

She glanced at him coldly. "I don't know who you are. I will go nowhere with you." She turned back to Parran, dropping the golden spear she had been clutching. It clattered against the stone.

Erzion's heart missed a beat. He stared at it.

Lunaria's spear!

A frown creased his brow. Its etched markings did not glow as they had done when Lunaria held it.

"Parran wake up!" Tanelle urged, shaking his shoulders.

Erzion's attention went back to his queen.

The young man opened his eyes. "Tanelle? No, you shouldn't be here. You have to run," he croaked. "Kalib challenged me to lure you out. You know better than to leave the safety of your palace."

Tears shone in Tanelle's eyes. "I don't care. I can't let him kill you."

Parran pushed himself up, grunting. Large purple bruises peppered his skin, small cuts oozing blood, and a deep knife wound in his arm bled heavily. "Please have more faith in me, my love. I am a better wizard than Kalib ever will be." Parran gave Tanelle a watery smile.

"That's not what I mean," she answered. "He doesn't care about hurting others. He likes it. And he wants what your father gave you. He always has."

Erzion twisted, looking for Kalib, for the assassin, even for Commander Edison. "We do not have time for this conversation. We need to get away from here," he growled.

Tanelle threw him a baleful state.

"You cannot stop this fight, Tanelle," panted Parran, sparing

Erzion only a questioning glance. "Your magic has not manifested. You have no defence against anyone here."

"I'm not completely helpless," Tanelle bit back. "I can still fight better than you with a spear and a sword."

Parran huffed a pained laugh. "I know," he agreed.

Erzion sucked in a sharp breath. *No magic.* His heart banged against his ribs, sudden anxiety drying out his mouth. Tanelle was more vulnerable than he had thought. She would be easy prey for the assassin now that she was outside the protection and enchantments of her home. No wonder Lexon did not allow her to leave. Erzion doubted even the Queen knew this bit of information.

"Come. We must leave," he barked at her. With no time for debate, he pushed one big hand under her arm and yanked her to her feet. He would beg forgiveness later.

"No!"

An elbow struck hard under his chin, snapping his teeth together with a painful jolt. Surprised by the force of the blow, he staggered back; only one pace but it was enough for Parran to yank Tanelle from Erzion's grasp.

"Who are you?" growled Parran, his eyes flitting to Kalib, who was dragging himself up from the dust of the arena floor.

"I cannot give you my name, but you must trust me." Not knowing what else to do he dropped to one knee. "Please, my allegiance is to you, Tanelle Arjuno. You are my queen. I mean you no harm. Let me take you away from here. Kalib is working with the Avalonian queen to kill you. There is an assassin here. We must go," he entreated.

Tanelle looked uncertainly at Parran, at the blood flowing freely down his arm.

Erzion stood, then without warning sent a small ribbon of heated magic to cauterise Parran's arm.

The prince hissed and swore but it took mere seconds for the light in his eyes to change. Realisation. And no small measure of relief. "Thank you," he breathed.

"What did you do?" demanded Tanelle.

Parran put his arm reassuringly around Tanelle's shoulders and kissed the top of her head.

He opened his mouth to speak, but an almighty screech echoed across the arena, drowning out his words. People slapped their hands over their ears for protection.

Pain exploded in Erzion's head, dropping him to his knees. *An Ice Mage!* Fighting the agony, he twisted his head to find the source.

In the top tier of the arena, an old woman stood. The screech stopped, the ensuing silence almost as painful.

Erzion stumbled to his feet.

The old hag's pale face crinkled into a map of amusement as she watched him struggle. Then she cackled loudly, her almost colourless eyes fixated on Tanelle. A predator honing in on its prey.

Erzion did not hesitate. He leaned down, grabbed Tanelle around the waist, shoved Parran away and snapped out his wings, armouring as he moved.

Parran vaulted back to his feet and, with a snarl, clutched Tanelle's boots.

Erzion tried to kick him off, but the young fool did not let go.

"She's the assassin!" bellowed Erzion. "Let us go!"

The old crone dropped her cloak. Her naked body was a twisted mess of growths and deformed bones. But it was her pale skin that caught Erzion's eye. It sparkled as though covered in ice crystals.

More nimble than he would have thought possible, the old crone launched into a run. She leaped mid-air and screeched.

Prepared this time, Erzion wrapped magic over his ears, protecting himself as that awful sound incapacitated others.

In a flash of light, the witch disappeared and a huge ice

serpent crashed down through the arena tiers, sending rubble flying in every direction. Its smooth, wet body began to slither forward even as dust and debris hit them all in a cloud.

Erzion coughed and choked. He blinked rapidly, his vision clearing enough to see the rippling body of the serpent heading right for them. Two large fangs of ice protruded from its mouth. White scales, smooth as glass, gleamed along the length of its shining body. Colourless eyes flickered with malice.

Shit! How in Chaos do I fight anything that big?

Parran's hold loosened on Tanelle's boot. Clearly the young wizard was in shock too. His arms dropped loosely to his sides, his mouth agape.

Below, Kalib laughed madly at his brother's response, though his own face was still pale and blood ran from his nose.

Erzion moved, the hot air rushing by them, whipping his long red hair back from his face. His heart pounded in his throat, agony flooding his back and shoulders as he drove his wings, desperately trying to lift higher than the serpent's reach. With his free hand, he sent a wave of burning red magic into the serpent's side, uncovering the flesh and blood beneath its icy exterior.

It screamed with rage.

Parran shook himself, gaping up at Tanelle in horror.

Tanelle wriggled and kicked, then slammed an elbow into Erzion's belly. Her attack landed in his stomach muscles, tense in anticipation of her reaction, with no effect. Screaming for Parran, she looked down, tearing at Erzion's forearms with her fingernails. Pain burned his skin where she gouged out long lines, but he would not let her go.

Erzion saw the words Parran uttered as the serpent whipped its head around and arched its tail.

"I love you too," sobbed Tanelle.

The serpent had spied where his prey focused her attention. Its triumphant screech sent Erzion's blood cold.

Tanelle looked over her shoulder at Erzion, panic in her eyes.

"Take me back! Now! I command you to! She will kill him!" she screamed.

Erzion hated to defy his queen, but he had to get her out. Steeling his nerve, he ignored her.

They were now above the level of the serpent's head and climbing. Way below, the remaining crowds ran from the arena, screaming and tripping over each other in their haste. Like ants, they scurried for cover.

It was anyone's guess whether the guards would help the heir or turn and run like cowards.

Erzion's mouth pressed to a thin line. He could not let himself care about Parran. He had to go. Now.

Warm air glided under his wings as he banked left. He wobbled, trying desperately to balance himself and Tanelle's weight. Her legs flapped around in an ungainly way as she struggled, still trying to break free. She swore loudly at him. A clenched jaw was his only response.

Distracted by his queen, Erzion did not see the devious serpent curl its body like a coiled spring.

There was a shout of warning from Parran.

Then burning pain.

Erzion cried out. Huge jaws had clamped down on his thighs, one razor sharp fang piercing his flesh.

Squeezing his arms tightly around Tanelle, Erzion felt himself flung sideways. A yell ripped from his throat as his flesh tore apart.

The world spun. There was no hope of using his wings. Knowing they would likely be snapped beyond repair if he tried, he gritted his teeth and pulled them into his back as he plunged toward the ground.

From the corner of his eye he saw the arena floor rushing toward them. All he could do was brace himself and yank Tanelle to his left.

He had to protect her.

His right shoulder and side slammed into the ground, followed by his legs.

Bone snapped.

He screamed, his body bouncing and sliding along the loose sand.

Tanelle's head jolted back, knocking into his jaw. The blow snapped his teeth shut, stunning him. His own head ricocheted against the ground, rattling his brain, darkness hovered at the edge of his vision. There was no hope of stopping Tanelle as her body rolled from his arms.

Through a haze of agony, he saw her stagger to her feet and run. For a moment his heart lifted, then in almost the same heartbeat, it plummeted. Her shadowy figure had to swerve, diving sideways.

The serpent had seen her prey run. Its colourless eyes found Tanelle's movement. A storm of ice shards and freezing breath rained down upon his queen from the beast's open maw.

Helplessly, Erzion watched.

One shard thrust straight through Tanelle's left calf, one into her thigh, the others smashing into the ground behind her. Even with no magic, the half-Goddess was swift enough to avoid most of the murderous shards.

Tanelle cried out, stumbling and sprawling on her stomach in the dirt.

Saliva dropped from the beast's fangs, cold enough that it froze into solid ice where it hit the ground.

Behind Erzion, Parran had used the beast's distraction to cast his own magic. Columns of blue sand arose. Ten of them spiralled around the arena. Frantically, the young wizard used them to try and distract the Ice Mage from his betrothed.

Erzion shook his head, trying to clear the pain from his skull. It didn't work, instead it pounded harder, threatening to pull him into unconsciousness. Erzion spat the blood from his mouth and stumbled to his feet.

Parran's efforts were working.

The serpent writhed, trying to get away from the barrage of dust. Systematically, the heir sent columns of sand blasting into the serpent's eyes, whilst yelling at Tanelle. "Get out! Run!" he begged her.

Erzion began half-staggering, half-limping towards Tanelle, who now dragged herself over the stone tiers, leaving a trail of blood behind.

Erzion's heart almost stopped at the sight, the smell of it.

No. He would not fail. His whole existence was built around this young woman. She was meant to come back, to reclaim her kingdom; to save it—and him. He had to stop that creature from harming her or all was lost. Every horrendous act he had committed would be for nothing.

Erzion pulled on his magic, ready to help Parran. He did not anticipate the attack that came next. His arms were suddenly glued to his sides, disappearing into his skin. Frightened beyond belief, he thrashed around. Then his mouth sealed over.

Kalib howled with laughter. "You look like a fish caught on a hook," he taunted, mirth in his eyes. "Wriggle little fishy. I'll gut you soon!"

Erzion stilled the panic in his mind. He did not try and breathe, instead he controlled his fear and reached for his own magic. It was still there—hot and writhing, desperate for release. It gave him no small measure of comfort. If he had to, he would burn through his own skin to break free.

"Brother! Let him go! What in the name of the guardians are you doing!?" screamed Parran. "Help me! Help me fight this creature!"

Kalib spun toward his brother. Then laughed.

Sweating freely, beads of moisture running into his eyes, Parran shook his head in disbelief. Realising his brother would be no help, he ignored the younger wizard; instead, his body swayed, mirroring the movement of his hands as he controlled the columns of sand, sending them crashing into the eyes of the beast.

But exhaustion etched his young face.

Thankfully, his efforts were working; the beast screeched with frustration and rage, but with each new casting, Parran's power weakened. The sand columns were thinner, easier to see through, though he managed to dance around the serpent's tail as it swung blindly in an attempt to stop him.

It took all Erzion's willpower to fall against the arena wall and quiet his mind and body.

Breathe in. Breathe out. Grim-faced, he closed his eyes and concentrated on pulling air in through his nostrils. Words were not necessary for his magic to augment the spell he formed in his mind.

Heat and the tingle of wizardry swelled inside him.

He shut down his senses, blocking out the agony of his broken body and torn leg—even the destruction happening nearby.

Kalib didn't notice Erzion's change; his attention had returned to his brother. An evil smile curled his lips, his eyes flashing with hatred and glee as he stared intently at Parran, then up at the creature. "Why would I help you? When you are dead, I will rule this land." His lips curled derisively. "No, brother. I think I will watch you die first, then I'll take great pleasure watching your princess scream her last breath."

Parran glared at Kalib, his pale face shining with the effort of casting. Knowing his brother was a lost cause, the heir screamed at Tanelle, "Get up and move!"

Erzion closed his eyes as he prepared to cast a spell.

Kalib's eyes narrow upon him. "What are you doing? Are you *casting?*" he hissed.

Erzion fell as Kalib kicked him off balance.

"Open your eyes, warrior. Watch the show. Your princess and my brother will soon be together forever—in Eternity. Will the goddess welcome her daughter's spirit into the land of the dead, do you think? Or will Lunaria be angry at her daughter's failure to survive?" He huffed a laugh, turning his attention back to the serpent and his brother.

Parran's magic was running out. The columns were merely clouds of dust now.

The creature's eyes narrowed. It opened its maw and shot jets of saliva toward Parran. Parran's eyes widened and he dived sideways.

Erzion's heart lurched as the liquid hit the ground where the heir had been standing, and froze.

The serpent slithered across the arena, heading for Parran, who was running for Tanelle.

Erzion worked quickly at his spell, pushing it through his body. He felt it—the moment his skin began to respond. His arms emerged once again.

The serpent lunged for the heir.

Tanelle screamed her anger and grief as it swept Parran into its jaws. It raised its snake-like body high into the air and glared down balefully at the princess, who had somehow dragged herself up to where the stone guardians stood.

"Kill him!" screamed Kalib, completely unaware of Erzion's success.

Erzion moved.

His wings snapped out, armour clattering across them. Grinding his teeth against the agony of his ravaged body, he hurled himself upward over the vast expanse of the creature. At the same time he propelled a violent wave of red magic downward, knocking Kalib off his feet and slamming him into the arena wall.

Kalib collapsed in a heap on his belly.

Erzion somersaulted in mid-air, vaguely registering the roar of another creature nearby.

"Let him go!!" screamed Tanelle at the Ice Mage.

It hissed and the old woman's cackle filled the air. The serpent lowered its head with Parran still in its jaws, until its baleful eyes fixed upon Tanelle.

Erzion could do nothing as the beast's lips drew back in a hideous parody of a smile before it snapped them shut.

Parran's spine shattered.

Tanelle's scream filled the arena.

Despite all the death he had seen, the sound of those bones cracking, the scream of that young, innocent heart breaking was something that would stay with Erzion for the rest of his days.

He dived, throwing out waves of burning magic against the shell of ice that encased the serpent's flesh.

Tanelle swiped something from the ground at her feet. Gold metal glinted as she straightened. But the serpent's attention had flicked to Erzion and it did not see her movements.

It tossed Parran's slack body away and lurched, slamming its head into Erzion's side.

Erzion slammed up a shield of magic a second before that big head hit him. The impact still sent him crashing into the top tier of the arena. Pain exploded through his body, made far worse by his already broken bones. Vomit rushed his mouth, his world spinning as he tried to feel something other than agony.

His fingers curled against the smooth stone, breaking his fingernails, but it was enough to ground him. Groaning, he pushed his torso upright. Unable to tear his horrified gaze from the jagged bone sticking out of his thigh, he watched blood pulse onto the stone beneath him.

Waves of dizziness crashed through him, his ears beginning to ring. Determined not to faint, he growled through clenched teeth and yanked up his power.

Red hot blasts hit the serpent's body. Over and over Erzion hurled his power forward until his well of magic was empty. Sensing its end, his body reached for Lunaria's gift. Immortality.

And he began again, blasting away that serpent's skin, even as his own life's blood seeped onto the stone.

Scales of ice melted from its body, leaving raw, bleeding flesh behind. It screeched, spitting huge globules of icy saliva his way. Yelling his agony and fighting unconsciousness, he rolled away. More. He needed more power if he was to hurt this thing.

Spells began to fall from his bloodless lips. He cast faster than he ever had before, praying his wizardry would be enough. Sweat flowed down his waxen skin as he threw magic-laced spell after spell from his failing body. Flesh exploded from the serpent's side, spraying him in ice cold blood when, at last, he found his mark.

Across the arena, Tanelle stood cursing and sobbing—and faced down her assassin. "You killed him!" she screamed.

The creature swung its head back towards her.

Erzion gasped as Tanelle's body came fully into view, Lunaria's spear clutched in her fist.

Before she could launch it, a resounding roar cut the air. The downdraft of massive wings sent sand into his eyes and mouth, but his heart lurched.

Vaalor? Alethia?

They were the only two known dragons in existence.

Tanelle's focus did not falter. Her silver hair whipped around her head, her sapphire blue eyes flashing with murderous intent. It hurt his heart though to see the fear shining from them.

She pulled her arm back and launched her mother's spear with all her might.

A crack of lightning shot from her arm way up into the sky above. But Erzion did not see his queen collapse on the ground, his eyes were honed in on the spear. He scooped up every particle of his waning magic—and cast, hurling every bit of power he had left toward that golden spear.

For a moment nothing happened, then in a blur of speed the

spear shot forward and buried itself in a raw patch of skin in the serpent's neck.

The Ice Mage's screech made his head swim—or maybe it was his blood loss.

Hissing, it lunged toward him, sending a rush of freezing saliva his way. That ice-laced slime slammed into him, encasing him from the chest down and stealing his breath. He could only watch helplessly as the injured serpent approached.

For the red wizard it was not fear but sadness that filled his heart as he faced death. He had failed to save his queen, and failed to fulfil his promise to the goddess. He wondered who would protect the fae of Valentina once he was gone.

A shadow glided across him. But it was not from the serpent who was poised to strike.

A huge silver dragon roared and slammed its barbed tail into the side of the serpent. Again and again it struck, until blood splattered the arena.

The serpent fought back, its jaws snapping at the dragon's tail. But lithe and quick, the dragon dipped sideways, almost inviting the serpent to follow it.

The Ice Mage screeched and whipped its head back to Tanelle's unconscious form. It did not want to be lured away.

"No!" whispered Erzion, at the intent look in its eyes. It was going to kill her.

The silver dragon immediately swooped again. Fire burst from its maw, raining down upon the Ice Mage.

The pained screeches of the serpent turned into the agonised screams of an old woman.

Erzion watched in disgust as the serpent shrank until only the Ice Mage remained. But the guardian did not stop. Mercilessly, its flame burned and burned. Not once did it waver. Skin and bone melted until all that remained of the old crone was a pile of grey ash.

Erzion's relief was short lived. Waves of agony swamped his

dying body. Immortality did not mean invincibility. The ice encasing his legs had turned red as blood pumped from his wounded limbs.

He did not notice.

His eyes were drawn to the figure of a man who knelt beside that pile of ash. Dark fingers reached out grasping Lunaria's golden spear.

Erzion, though barely conscious, wanted to storm over and yank it from the man's hand. He tried to yell but only an angry growl erupted from his lungs, no words.

The man turned. Blue metal gleamed across his forehead and jaw. He smiled reassuringly and nodded at Erzion before standing tall and hiding the spear inside his robes.

Another figure walked up and clapped him on the shoulder. They exchanged words before the sun-marked man turned and strode towards Tanelle.

The other sprinted up the tiers, his easy, fluid movements making a mockery of his bulk. He leaped up the last step and dropped to his haunches.

Erzion blinked furiously, tears burning his eyes.

A dream, surely?

Lexon's sapphire eyes regarded him anxiously, his slightly pointed ears visible from under his shoulder length hair. All Erzion could do was stare into that familiar face, unable to form any coherent words as both joy and devastation hit him.

Lexon peered down at Erzion's ruined leg—and swore viciously. "Alethia!! Quickly. Set my friend free!" he bellowed.

"No! Tanelle..." Erzion protested weakly.

Stone crumbled under the dragon's talons, its huge body rippling with muscle when it landed. Standing only feet from Erzion, it lowered its great head and regarded him solemnly.

Even through the haze of blood loss, Erzion's heart and mind became calm. He was not afraid.

The Goddess of Truth.

Alethia's eyes were a thing of beauty—silver, never-ending beauty. He smiled, wanting to touch her silver-scaled snout. But his arm was too heavy. He couldn't lift it.

No, he tried to tell them, *you should be saving my queen.* But no words would form.

Alethia huffed a worried breath. Its warmth washed over Erzion, his muscles became fluid and the agony from his leg disappeared completely.

He stared droopy-eyed at his friend, his skin icy cold. His head was too heavy. It lolled back, thumping against the stone.

Lexon stepped forward, but Alethia stopped him. Gently, she exhaled again. This time hot, steaming breath erupted from her lungs and melted away Erzion's prison of ice.

He groaned, his eyes flying open as his leg gushed bright red blood and fresh waves of pain assaulted him. He could not protest as his friend sent red magic burning into his skin, snapping the bone back into alignment and cauterising the severed blood vessels and flesh. Darkness was clutching at his mind, wanting to pull him into its soft, safe embrace. He didn't fight it this time.

Hands grabbed him, hauling him onto Alethia's back. Grim-faced, Lexon settled himself behind Erzion, grabbing onto Erzion's slumped body.

D'thy climbed on to Alethia's back behind Lexon, and two Fire Priests carefully lifted Tanelle's limp body into his arms.

"Keep her safe," whispered the king of the Fire Mountains in a broken voice.

"Of course, my friend. But diplomacy and negotiation may be the only deterrent for war between our kingdoms. Perhaps you should stay and speak with the new High Wizard."

"Diplomacy be damned! If he ever sets foot in my kingdom, I will burn him alive!" Lexon hissed. "He tried to kill my family."

A dark chuckle. "Indeed he did. He has also managed to

secure his brother's death. Even if it was not by his hand, the wizards will declare him their leader."

"Don't think you have got away with this! Any of you!" screeched Kalib, staggering to his feet.

Alethia lowered her silver head to better see the murderous glint in the young wizard's eyes. She thrust her jaws up against him and snarled. *Do not threaten any of us.*

Kalib paled, despite his anger.

"Do not think to enter our lands, wizard. If the guardian senses any threat to us from this kingdom, it will burn. Nothing will remain but ash—no one will escape—especially not you," warned Lexon.

Alethia let out a barrage of flame. It crackled across the arena, its heat soothing Erzion, even as the panicked screams of other people rang out.

He cracked open his eyelids.

Parran's body burned.

"May the gods and goddesses protect your soul and the guardians guide you on your final journey," Lexon rumbled as the heir's remains snaked up into the sky.

Wings unfurled then thumped at the air.

Gravity pulled at Erzion. He had just enough awareness to feel the solid strength of Lexon's arms holding him and the agony of his broken body. But the blackness didn't release him for long. Praying that Tanelle was alive, he tumbled into oblivion.

CHAPTER 22

LEXON

Lexon brushed his fingers down Tanelle's pale cheek. Her skin was soft and warm under his gentle touch.

Is this my fault? he wondered. "She always was so headstrong," he murmured, sadness thickening his voice.

The last two weeks had been a blur of anxiety and guilt.

His heart squeezed painfully in his chest. He was Tanelle's father in every way but being her sire. He had cared for her as a helpless babe and seen her grow and change from a gregarious child to a headstrong young woman. He had witnessed her fight to find her place in this harsh world once she learned that there were those who wished harm upon her.

Lexon had tried to keep her from that cruel world. Guilt at not realising she would want to save Parran crippled him. He relived that bolt of lightning over and over, every time he closed his eyes.

"Alethia warned her not to use the spear. It never was meant for her hands," he choked out, his voice breaking.

"What do you mean? Is it meant for your heirs instead?" asked Erzion, quietly enough it seemed as though he didn't want to disturb the warm, still air in the cave.

The stone around them glittered. Lexon had ordered this cave, deep in the volcano, made bigger when he had first started construction of the palace. On either side of the space, two huge, stone dragons guarded the room. The large statues reached almost to the roof, forty feet above. Their bodies glittered in the eternal torches Alethia had ignited.

Lexon had intended this place to be a sacred room, a sanctuary of peace and tranquillity in which his descendants could worship the guardians. He swallowed the bile burning his throat. He had not intended it to become a tomb for his daughter.

Lexon turned to face his friend, his lips forming a tight line. He shrugged his big shoulders. "I don't know. It seems the High Ruler has looked into the future and seen who will wield it. But he will not share that knowledge—and Alethia was sworn to secrecy."

For a moment the friends stood in silence.

It was incredible to Lexon that he was standing side by side with the friend he loved and missed so much.

He had wavered between fear and joy when Firan had sent word that Erzion was intending to foil the Queen's latest assassination attempt. Fear for his daughter, but joy at the chance to see his old friend.

It had been a dangerous thing for Erzion to do. Not only could he have been killed by the Ice Mage but any spy of the Queen's might have recognised him.

Lexon was thankful Erzion had been awake enough to tell him of Commander Edison. It hadn't taken D'thy long to locate the man, or to persuade him returning to Avalonia was not an option. It seemed the commander was more than happy to remain under D'thy's care.

Lexon had not taken his friend to task on his decision to put himself at risk for Tanelle; Lexon was far too happy to have Erzion here, even for a short time, and he knew Mariel was over the moon.

It was hard not to show how much he *hated* that Erzion's time here was ending. But together with Erzion's immortal blood, the healer Lexon had assigned to his friend had done a good job in healing him. Erzion's thigh wound had all but disappeared, along with his other injuries.

Lexon's gut tightened. He didn't want to think about his friend leaving, not at all, but neither of them could avoid it forever.

Erzion had told Lexon how his pledge to the goddess weighed heavily on his soul—as did his vow to the High Ruler. It seemed both amounted to the same thing. Erzion was to protect the Avalonian people and Valentia by any means necessary, until such time as its destined king or queen returned.

Part of Lexon felt guilty for being thankful that pledge was Erzion's; Avalonia had once been his home, after all. But he loved his new land and his people with every shred of his soul. He had no wish to return to the ghosts that would surely haunt him in Valentia.

Erzion glanced sideways as Alethia stepped up beside Lexon and leaned into him. Lexon kissed the top of her head, draping a supportive arm around her shoulders and pulling her close to his side. It was overwhelming to feel such love and such loss at the same time.

For a moment Lexon's heart ached for Erzion. His friend had already confided he would never allow himself to experience such a love as existed between Lexon and Alethia. For Erzion, the agony of losing a mate to the inevitable ravages of time would tear him apart.

Lexon's strong-jawed face, though tight with grief, softened as he glanced at Alethia. Every day he gave thanks to her father for sending her to him all those years ago.

"I have to leave today. I must get back to the war in the north."

"I know," sighed Lexon, his disappointment hard to hide, even as he smiled at the small stone Erzion held in the palm of his hand.

"Firan will come running when I call," smirked Erzion, though his expression soon sobered. "You know your father and Noan would be so proud of the kingdom you have managed to carve out of this volcanic landscape. It is amazing indeed," Erzion said. But his next words were careful, considering. "You have more than fulfilled your pledge to Lunaria too, now that your army is so strong. Though perhaps when that army is needed to reclaim Avalonia's throne, it will only follow your heir." His red gaze drifted back to Tanelle. "Not Lunaria's."

It was a question phrased as a statement. Lexon couldn't blame his friend for asking. The army he had built for Tanelle was a long way from Avalonia, and now she was nothing more than a beautiful shell. Not even Alethia had any idea when the young demi-goddess would awaken—or even if she ever would. Lexon couldn't begin to understand how that must make Erzion feel, stuck as he was serving the false queen.

"The future is unknown. All we can both do is cling onto our pledge and protect our homes and our people," Lexon answered carefully. "But I promise you, my friend. Even when I am nothing but ash and memory, I will ensure my descendants honour my part of the pledge we made. They will fight for the rightful ruler of Avalonia's throne, and if you ever think the time has come and call upon me or them, we will fight alongside you."

Silver lined both of their eyes as Lexon let go of Alethia and embraced his friend.

"Thank you," Erzion choked out, his voice thick.

At that contact Lexon's emotions came crashing down around him. He gripped his friend's tunic, the smooth silk almost ripping. "I failed Tanelle. I failed my daughter," he choked out, unable to hold his words inside any longer.

"You did not fail her," denied Erzion immediately. "You and Alethia have given her a home and kept her safe. You have raised her and loved her as your own. She *chose* to leave the safety of your kingdom and risk everything for her young heart. She took her mother's spear, even after you told her it was not meant for her. That wasn't your fault, either of you," he said, looking at Alethia.

A single tear ran down Alethia's cheek. The beautiful goddess leaned forward and placed a gentle kiss upon Tanelle's forehead. "No, it's not our fault," she echoed, her grief-stricken eyes searching Lexon's face as if willing him to believe her. "And I would have done exactly the same thing for the one I love, if I were her," she whispered, cupping Lexon's face.

Lexon's nostrils flared delicately, his eyes darkening in response to his mate's touch.

Beside him, Erzion shifted his weight, his attention dropping to Tanelle's throat where a small black dragon held an unpolished crystal in its talons.

The crystal often pulsed with soft light when Alethia was near to it. Its gentle glow had caught Erzion's attention.

Lexon didn't know where the necklace had come from, only that it had appeared around Tanelle's neck in the darkness of the night on the eve of her thirteenth birthday. She wouldn't take it off—ever. He had often heard her talking to the tiny dragon as if it were alive. He had thought it quite amusing, for a time, but had begun to chastise her for it the older she became. Her behaviour had worried him. Now he would give anything to hear her sweet voice chattering to that damned miniature guardian.

Lexon's boots grated against the rough rock floor as he turned to Erzion. His heart ached at their inevitable parting. "I know you have to go, but it feels so gods damn wrong. I wish you could stay here. We would keep you safe from her," Lexon bit out.

Erzion clamped a hand down on Lexon's shoulder and squeezed, holding his friend's gaze. "I know you would, but who would protect Valentia and the fae from her? Who would build an army fit to serve the rightful heir, if I were here?"

Lexon gritted his teeth, his jaw muscles popping, then he raised his palms to Erzion's shoulders and sighed in defeat.

Their pledges weighed heavily on their souls.

Just as he would ensure Tanelle was protected, no matter how long she slept, Erzion would not abandon his responsibility to watch over Avalonia.

"No one," he answered reluctantly, trying not to sound like a petulant child.

"That's right. It has to be me. I will not grow old and lose interest—and I will never forget who the First Legion is intended to serve. I will work tirelessly to build our army, no matter how long it takes for my true queen to awaken."

Lexon bent and kissed Tanelle's forehead. He murmured a soft goodbye in her ear, then turned to Erzion, a rueful smile stretching his lips.

"You are such an honourable bastard, you know that? It's a good job Firan will be around to make sure you are dragged into having fun at least once every hundred years. He's about as honourable as you are deceitful," he scoffed.

Erzion raised a brow, clearly wondering if Lexon had thought that statement through.

Lexon grinned at Erzion's assessing look. "Yes, I know exactly what I'm saying. You lie to thousands of your own people every day. And I'm glad Firan will be there for you when I can't be," he finished.

Lexon grunted as Erzion grabbed and hugged him again, squeezing the breath from his lungs. It seemed his friend was as reluctant to leave as Lexon was to see him go.

"You will always be there for me. In here," Erzion told him, tapping a finger over his own heart.

Lexon rolled his eyes to hide the tears that welled in them.

Alethia laughed softly. "He's embarrassed by your words, Erzion, but I can feel the truth in them. I'm glad the love you hold for my mate warms your heart. I fear it will be a long time until the army you are building will be needed."

"What makes you say that?" asked Erzion, his voice coloured with dread.

"A feeling—in here," she said tapping her own heart. "Only the stars and the fates that rule us truly know if what we did that day to Erebos was the right thing, or so my father once said. All he would tell me was to complete the scroll and return home to Eternity when I was ready."

"Did he say anything about when the heir would return to Valentia's throne?"

"No, I'm afraid he didn't. He only said that until Chaos looms and their destinies align, there was nothing to do but follow our own paths." She glanced down at Tanelle before hooking her arm through Lexon's and turning them towards the cave door where two guards waited patiently.

"Whose destinies?" asked Erzion, a visible shudder running through his body. "I do not wish to live forever, serving that monster."

A frown creased Alethia's brow but her tone remained empathetic. "Nothing lasts forever, Erzion. All I know is that the fate of both Eternity and the Eight Kingdoms is in the hands of people not yet born. It was never going to be Tanelle's destiny to rule Avalonia, but that doesn't mean she is not important to the future of this world."

∼

They emerged into the daylight.

Alethia bade Erzion farewell. Despite the heat of the sun, Lexon knew her guardian needed to replenish its fire from the flowing river below the volcano's surface.

He watched her walk farther across the courtyard. She smiled playfully and blew him a kiss. In an instant his mood lifted. A flash of light and the glittering bulk of a dragon loomed before them.

Lexon's heart soared, his blood heating at the sight of the beautiful silver guardian. He watched his eternal mate, his queen, soaring into the blue skies, heading for the entrance to the old lair.

Erzion grinned at Lexon's intent gaze. "You may not have wings anymore, but you are still a red blooded fae, aren't you?" Erzion quipped.

Lexon growled for effect, then grinning widely, he followed his friend over to a large bay gelding that was tethered nearby. A small boy was busy securing supplies to the saddle. Lexon tried not to laugh or do the task himself. Lishan was Lexon's youngest son. At ten years old he was still skinny and short, only reaching as high as Lexon's thigh, but he was a hard worker and so stubborn as to be an ungodly handful at times.

A slightly taller boy with deep brown hair and eyes came into view behind the horse's rear flank.

Lexon grinned widely. He knew Varil and Lara's youngest son wouldn't be far away. The two were much like he and Erzion had always been.

Inseparable.

"No, you idiot, you don't do it like that, you do it like this," the boy instructed imperiously.

Lexon and Erzion exchanged an amused glance as Lishan growled with frustration when the buckle came undone yet again. Clenching his jaw with determination, Lishan just began his task again.

"Remind you of anyone?" questioned Erzion through the side of his mouth.

Lexon laughed. "Yeah, you. I would never have had the confidence to try again."

"Maybe not once upon a time, but you do now, King Arjuno," Erzion re-joined, bowing low.

"Indeed," Lexon agreed, unable to say more as his friend marched toward the pair.

"Here, let me show you how," he said to the boys, who gazed up at the red wizard with awe on their young faces.

Erzion winked at Lexon and began giving instruction to his willing students. It didn't take long for his supplies to be secured to the expensive but comfortable saddle.

A small group of guards clattered noisily into the cobbled courtyard.

Erzion frowned and looked questioningly at Lexon.

"I will not let you go unescorted into Gar Anon. It is a place of slavery and war. When you are close enough to fly to the coast, the guards will return your horse."

Erzion nodded his understanding.

For a moment the two friends stared at each other, both at a loss for words. This was it, the moment Lexon had been dreading for the past two weeks. "I am glad you came to save her," he managed to say, his throat aching with unshed tears.

Erzion huffed. A derisory sound. "Not that it did much good," he answered.

"Yes, it did. You gave her a chance. Her fate is in the hands of the guardians now. And I am more grateful than I can say that your actions have given us these last weeks together." He stepped forward and embraced his friend.

The two young boys nearby watched solemnly, as if they knew how much this goodbye would hurt both warriors.

Erzion gripped the back of Lexon's tunic for a moment, then pulled away. "I will miss you too, you soppy bastard." He flung himself up into the saddle in one smooth move. The gelding danced a little at the new weight on its back. "I'll meet you in Eternity when my pledge is complete, my friend. Just make sure you're there to meet me—or I'll come back and drag you there," Erzion told him.

"Oh, I don't think you will be there before me, red wizard.

You have far too much work to do first, and you're not efficient enough to do it before I die."

Erzion snorted, though nothing could hide the sadness in his eyes. "My king," he drawled, bowing his head and shoulders. When he raised his face, his hair was no longer a bright vibrant red but a deep chestnut brown, his eyes golden. A long cloak covered his wings but Lexon suspected they too were now gold, not red.

Grinning at Lexon, Erzion flipped up his middle finger whilst urging his horse into a gallop. Lexon bellowed a laugh at his friend's obscene goodbye.

In a cacophony of sound, the group of guards whirled their horses around and followed the Red Wizard.

Lexon quickly strode to the gates, the two boys close on his heels. A cloud of dust followed Erzion's progress down the dirt road. Lexon's heart cracked, unashamed tears running down his cheeks as he watched his soul brother and best friend disappear from his life forever.

CHAPTER 23

ERZION

One thousand years later

"Hogs balls, Erzion, you're a heavy bastard to drag around!" Firan complained, panting loudly. He gripped Erzion's arm across his shoulders and half-carried his friend onto the ship.

Erzion could only grunt in reply. His head was swimming. The unfortunate wound to his stomach would have killed a mortal male, but he had merely shoved his guts back inside his abdomen and forced magic into the layers of sliced flesh before burning it closed. It had been festering ever since.

Gods damned idiot! he cursed himself silently. It had been his own fault. He had been distracted, thinking about returning to Catava—to his home, when the Ometon had attacked. The huge northern snow beast had struck swiftly and with a surprising amount of cunning. It had been waiting in the darkness for a lone warrior to leave the safety of the camp. He rolled his eyes at his stupidity. He hadn't even heard it stalk around behind him. When he had turned to head back to camp, the beast had taken an almighty swipe. Its claws had ripped open Erzion's belly.

He had killed it swiftly, feeling neither anger nor sorrow toward the beast—only irritation at being caught unawares.

It had taken another week to reach Farndisport—the main trading town on the northern coast, during which time his belly wound had burst open twice whilst flying.

Not wanting to appear weak, he had dismissed all but his personal guard and flown straight to the ocean where he had lowered the smooth calling stone Firan had given him, into the water.

Firan had arrived within two days.

Erzion didn't understand why he wasn't healing, why his magic couldn't heal him. He had never felt so unwell, so weak. It was as if his magic had been used up trying to fight this infection. His glamoured red-winged warriors had not left his side during those two days. Thankfully, his commanders were capable of overseeing all issues with running the legion. He had asked them to ensure his legion of the Queen's warriors did not begin their journey back to Valentia within the next week. That would give him at least four weeks to recover from whatever this problem was, and to spend some time in the secret city he had built in the cave system under the Rift Valley before he returned to Valentia.

It had taken hundreds of years to construct Catava, to develop it into a thriving community. In that time, Erzion had seen so many friends live and die that he very rarely allowed himself to become close with anyone anymore. Glamouring Catava and protecting it with spells had kept his home—his city—safe. It was still a secure haven for fae who wanted, or needed, to hide from the Queen and her cruelty. The First Legion had grown under his care and command, to such a size many glamoured red-winged warriors were now integrated into the Queen's own ranks.

Maybe one day the true heir would appear and the First Legion would prove its might—until then Erzion would continue to rule them in secret. He had never forgotten his purpose—or his pledge to his goddess. Catava and the First Legion would always await its true queen.

He grunted as Firan hitched him up.

At least the spells he cast upon those who entered Catava prevented any living soul from divulging its existence —even Firan.

Erzion had never been so relieved to see his friend as he had been when a blue-clad figure walked confidently, if somewhat urgently, down the gangplank of this ship.

He had wanted to see Firan for months. Erzion knew his constant low mood had contributed to his current predicament, and Firan was the only one he knew who would truly understand his inner weariness, the reason he had been so distracted. It was not a physical fatigue but the absolute lethargy of his soul. Firan was always a balm for his aching heart, if only because he knew the Lord of the Wetlands understood and forced Erzion to remember who he was, not to mention what his purpose was. Somehow, the blue-skinned lord always managed to lift him from his melancholy.

Erzion huffed a smile, knowing he would return the favour for Firan when it was needed.

"I'm not heavy, you're just old and weak," Erzion replied, but his voice was hoarse, his throat dry and burning almost as hot as his skin. Rivulets of sweat trickled down from his hairline, soaking the collar of the tunic he wore underneath his armour.

"Piss off—I'm not old," Firan grumbled, but continued to help Erzion board the ship then guide him down the steps to the lower deck. Still taking most of Erzion's considerable weight, Firan kicked open the door to his own cabin then pulled him across the room before dumping him on the seldom-used bed. The bed frame creaked in protest.

Erzion swore loudly and viciously as agony shot through his belly. Waves of nausea hit him. Heaving and retching pulled on his wound—then a rivulet of warm fluid trickled down his belly into his waist band. Lights flash behind his eyes, his vision fading. "Shit shit shit!" he breathed clutching at his stomach.

Firan eyed Erzion anxiously. "What the hell's going on with you? You're immortal; you should be healed by now, not throwing your guts up on my ship."

"I know. That." Erzion panted, swallowing over and over. "I don't know what's wrong—just—get me back—to Catava—to my house. Maybe—the magic there—and the healers—can help."

Firan nodded but didn't leave until he had forced some cool, sweet water between Erzion's dry lips.

"This will be a painful journey for you, my friend, but we will get you back by tomorrow. Lay down. I'll give the order to set off, then I'll return and do what I can with that wound."

Erzion nodded, swallowing the waves of nausea that crashed over him. A moment after Firan left him, the ship lurched. The mers were propelling the ship onward.

∼

Firan and one of the First Legion guards helped Erzion through the stone corridors of Catava. Firan's magic held Erzion's wound together but he knew it wouldn't last.

They half-dragged, half-carried Erzion into his home and up to his sleeping chamber, lowering him into a sitting position on his bed. The soft mattress sank under Erzion's weight.

Gripping the soft throw, Erzion closed his eyes and swore at the pain shooting through his abdomen.

The green-winged healer standing in the doorway raised her brows at his cursing but said nothing.

Firan lifted Erzion's legs onto the bed and stared down. "You are never going for a piss by yourself again if this is what happens," he admonished, but worry etched his brow.

"Never is a damned long time for us," Erzion growled. "And if anyone—dares try to babysit—me for that—I'll piss all over them!" he grated, each word an effort.

"Well, never had better be a long time. Us immortals have to stick together," Firan quipped. "Now, do what your healer tells you, and be nice to her or I'll come back and kick your grumpy arse."

Erzion huffed a chuckle at Firan, though he nodded. "I'm always nice," he replied, through gritted teeth, though he knew that wasn't true. He had been dead inside for years and these last months he had not been able to force himself to care if he upset or angered his warriors—or anyone else. That was why he needed his friend. He needed to ground himself, to get out of the gloom that was swallowing him. They had both suffered bouts of depression over the years, but they relied on each other to help deal with it, to lift each other out of the darkness and into the light again.

Firan looked at him now. Understanding—and regret—shone in those deep blue eyes. "Good, because I have to leave. I'll be back in a few weeks. And you'd better be recovered by then. I have a feeling I'll need a corn liquor session when I return," he said darkly.

Erzion's eyes flew to his friend, concern now etching his own brow. "Why? What's—going on—with you?" Guilt festered in his chest. He needed to be there for Firan too.

Firan sighed and rubbed his face. His eyes looked troubled. "I am to be a negotiator again," he told Erzion. "Between Queen Kilar of the Fire Mountains and the Gar Anonian king. The king is causing problems for the young queen. He is threatening war again."

Erzion swallowed hard, silently reprimanding himself for selfishly wanting his friend to stay. He forced a sly grin. "I've heard—the young queen is—extremely beautiful," he panted.

Firan cocked a blue brow. "So have I. But she is also married and has a young daughter."

Erzion grinned wider. "Hmm, and since when—did that ever stop you?" he rejoined.

Firan tried to look affronted. It didn't work. "Yes, well, I'm there to stop a war, not start one." He reached out and grasped Erzion's inner forearm in a gesture of farewell.

Erzion mirrored Firan's action. He smiled and nodded at his friend.

The healer stood respectfully at the end of the bed, watching them patiently. Her long brown hair was pulled back in a braid from her elegant features. The simple style seemed to make her beautiful, soft brown eyes even larger.

Erzion pretended not to notice how she studied them with keen interest.

Firan smiled, noticing where Erzion's gaze lingered. "Behave with her, and try not to upset her. You need the best healer in this city, and she is your best."

"Is she?" Erzion replied, staring at the young woman in disbelief. She was too young to be the best! Then he scowled. If his magic hadn't healed him, he doubted this inexperienced greenwing could. He'd get rid of her as soon as Firan left. He had no desire for the ministrations of some flighty girl.

Her chin lifted, defiance flashing in her now narrowed and astute gaze. "Yes, *she* is. And my name is Ophelia," she replied tightly. "Please use it, Lord Riddeon. And," she added, stepping closer and crossing her arms over the curves of her chest, "you will not order me away, as you are planning to do. I took a vow to the goddess to heal the sick in this city—and you, my lord, are sick. This city relies upon you for our safety and secrecy, so no matter how many times you think to dismiss me, I will not listen. Not until *I* decide you are well again."

Erzion stared at her, stunned. No one ever dared speak to him like that.

Firan snorted. He stepped back from the bed, grinning widely.

"Ha! It seems you have met your match, my friend. I have no worries about leaving you in Ophelia's capable hands."

Ophelia missed the suggestive wink Firan gave Erzion.

Erzion opened his mouth to swear at his friend then thought the better of it when Ophelia cocked her head and raised her brows. He snapped his mouth shut, causing Firan to shake his head whilst trying not to laugh.

"I will see you soon," Firan said, his eyes sparkling with amusement. The lord of the Wetlands turned to Ophelia—and bowed low, the way he did for other royalty. "Good luck taming the ill-tempered, old bastard, my lady," he quipped with a smile.

Ophelia's mouth dropped open and her cheeks flushed a beautiful shade of pink at Firan's manner of address, not to mention the meaning behind those words.

"Oh, for gods sakes, Firan, just leave," begged Erzion, feeling the stirrings of embarrassment himself. Firan had just openly suggested that Ophelia might want more than to be just Erzion's healer.

Firan saluted and, still grinning, left.

Silence settled between Erzion and Ophelia.

"Well," she said, a small smile twitching her lips. "He's fun."

Erzion barked a laugh. That wasn't the reaction he had expected at all. "Yes, he is," he agreed. "So, if you're too stubborn to leave, what's your plan?" he asked curiously. "I'm sure my magic will heal me eventually."

"Probably, but it might also leave you permanently disfigured or in pain if we don't find out what the problem is." She stepped forward. Her face and voice now brooked no nonsense. "So let's get you out of these clothes and have a look at your wound."

Erzion felt too sick to argue. He allowed Ophelia to help him discard his stinking armour. With a look of mild disapproval, she dropped it in a heap near the door.

"I hope you aren't attached to that, because it's going to be burned," she told him.

Erzion smiled. "It is pretty foul, isn't it?"

"Indeed," she agreed. "Right, Lord Riddeon, lay back. Are you in pain?" she asked with a frown as she narrowed her attention upon the red and inflamed skin of his abdomen.

Erzion hesitated to answer. Showing weakness—to anyone—well, he just didn't.

Ophelia raised her eyes from his stomach to his face. She exhaled through her nose, her lips pressed together. But there was understanding in her eyes. "I'll be right back," she sighed.

She moved gracefully to a wooden chest of drawers. His eyes followed her every movement as she bent forward and lifted a wicker basket. Her body was slim and elegant. She was not tall, but he guessed her head would reach to the middle of his chest—should she ever get that close. He immediately ignored those thoughts.

Along the top of the drawers she laid out a number of small jars, phials and bowls.

Erzion watched with interest as Ophelia tipped two of the phials into a small glass and added what looked to be corn liquor. He eyed her questioningly when she returned to his side.

Her generous lips curled into a wide smile at his obvious confusion—and suspicion.

"May I?" she asked, indicating the side of the bed.

Erzion nodded and shuffled sideways to give her room. He swallowed hard as she perched upon the edge of his bed. Her gentle, sweet scent ruffled his composure and he found himself gripping the bed sheets, as his whole body tensed.

What the hell?

Ophelia didn't appear to notice his reaction, she merely held out the glass. "Drink," she instructed. "The herbs will help with your pain and the alcohol will disguise its foul taste." She shrugged her elegant shoulders as Erzion smiled.

"Oh, I don't know, corn liquor—can be pretty disgusting at times," he chuckled.

She smiled back at him. "Really? I, of course, have no idea about that," she rejoined and he knew she was joking. Ophelia held the glass out insistently.

Erzion had no idea why he trusted this female, but he did. His magic stopped burning through his gut, trying to heal him. It was as if it sensed she could help.

He took the glass and tipped the contents down his throat. The liquid burned all the way down his gullet and into his belly. It immediately began to warm his limbs and relax his muscles. Ophelia smiled and took the glass back as he groaned at the pleasurable feeling.

It felt good to let himself to relax, to at last allow someone close enough to help him. It had been hard hiding the extent of his pain, especially from Firan. But he hadn't wanted his friend to worry. Aboard ship, Erzion had removed his armour and cleaned the large slash wound daily, but he had never asked for help and had only let Firan use his magic on the last leg of the journey into Catava.

He glanced down. The skin remained healed over the biggest slash wound, but he could see pus gathering below the new silvery, pink scar, ready to burst out. He grimaced.

"Don't worry. We will find out what is doing this to you," Ophelia reassured him, dropping her large brown eyes to the ridges of his stomach.

A strange, alien feeling tightened his throat as those beautiful eyes travelled back up his body, lingering on the dips and cut of muscle across his chest. He swallowed down a growl as her irises shifted from brown to green and desire began to simmer inside his soul.

Despite feeling more relaxed than he had for years, despite the trust he had in this female, Erzion smothered those feelings. She was his healer, nothing more. He eyed her hot cheeks coldly. It didn't matter how beautiful she was, or how much her scent told him she wanted him too, he would not let her in.

He pressed his lips into a thin line as she hastily dropped her gaze from the ice in his. Her voice was hoarse as she asked, "may I touch the wound, my lord?"

Erzion almost refused, shaken by his body's reaction to her. But for some reason he wasn't ready to send her away. "Yes," he responded curtly.

Ophelia swallowed, her own response becoming coldly professional. "Then can you lay flat for me? It will relax your stomach more."

Erzion acquiesced, though it was utter agony to stretch out his abdomen.

Her touch was steady and confident as she probed his flesh with warm fingers. Her wings glowed and her eyes shone with emerald magic.

Erzion gritted his teeth at the pain her touch caused. Minutes later she withdrew her hands and her magic.

"There is something inside the wound, my lord. It needs to be removed," she told him, her voice clipped and to the point.

"Fine. Do it."

"I can't just *do it,* my lord. I need help and supplies. I will also need to put you to sleep."

"Why?" snapped Erzion. "My belly has been bursting open every few days all by itself, and I haven't been asleep for that. Just lance it open and find what's doing this to me," he ordered.

"Really?" she said, ignoring that order. "Well, you may have been awake before, but this time you won't be. This will be extremely painful and I will not have you moving and making things worse because of that pain. I will also not have you trying to order me around because you think you know better. No, Lord Riddeon, this time you *will* be asleep."

They stared challengingly at each other.

Erzion snarled, unsure how to handle the defiance of a female who wasn't one of his warriors. His fingers curled into the bed cover when she still did not drop her eyes. He found he wanted to grab her slim shoulders and shake her.

Ophelia merely raised her brows. Anger flashed in her own gaze. "Snarling will not make me change my mind—or intimidate me. You *will* drink the potion that will allow you to sleep, and I *will* remove whatever is trying to kill you," she declared. "I have a vow to the goddess to keep, my lord."

"Erzion. My name is Erzion," he grated out.

Ophelia stared at him coldly. "I will return very soon with an assistant, Lord Riddeon," she said turning away.

Erzion watched her march from the room. He couldn't believe it. Not only had she dared to ignore him, she had uttered the last words in their conversation, yet again! *Stubborn female!*

By the time Ophelia returned with a green-winged fae in tow, Erzion had finished fuming; instead he was smiling inside, determined to get the better of the bewitching green-winged healer.

CHAPTER 24

ERZION

Erzion stirred at Ophelia's gentle touch on his shoulder. His skin tingled under her slim fingers, goosebumps raising across his body.

"I'm sorry, my lord. I need to check your wound again," she murmured, leaning in. Her soft brown eyes searched his for any sign of pain.

Thankfully, there was none. There hadn't been any since he had awoken for the first time, hours ago. "Of course," he breathed, welcoming the sound of her soft voice almost as much as her touch. It drifted over him just like her scent, making him want to wrap himself around her, to touch her, to protect her—to kiss her.

Erzion did not take his eyes off her, could not, as he allowed her to help him sit up. He was sure she knew he didn't need her assistance, but it seemed both of them wanted that contact.

With simmering red eyes, Erzion watched Ophelia's every move as she efficiently peeled off his dressing and probed his already healed skin.

Grunting with satisfaction she left him, though only long enough to retrieve a large jar off the nearby table.

"This is what stopped your healing, my lord," she said, holding the jar up.

He grimaced. It was a large piece of Ometon claw. "That was lodged in my belly?" She nodded and smiled at the curse that passed his lips. "Don't worry, my lord, you will heal fully now. Soon you will not need me by your side."

He fixed her with an unwavering look. He might be overly relaxed by the potions she had given him but he knew exactly what he was doing when he allowed his gaze to heat. "My name is Erzion, and who says I won't *need* you when I am recovered."

Her face flushed, even as her throat bobbed, but Ophelia held his gaze. "I hope you do—Erzion," she whispered hoarsely.

The sound of his name on her lips brought a low rumble of approval from his throat.

"Now, swallow this. You still need to rest," she told him, though he didn't miss how the brown of her eyes melted away, her magic turning them a stormy green.

Erzion almost refused, wanting to push a little of his dominance on her just to see her spark of defiance, but he decided against it. She was right. He needed to rest.

No small amount of satisfaction warmed his male pride as she held a glass to his lips. Her scent had become sharp with desire. There was no denying it. Erzion deliberately saturated his stare with fire. Her hand trembled as she encouraged him to swallow the cool, sweet liquid.

Drowsiness began to tug at him. Holding her emerald gaze, his lids became heavy. Before sleep claimed him again, he could have sworn he felt her fingers brush down his cheek and her voice whisper, "Sleep well, my lord."

Erzion slept for two full days. A gentle restorative sleep, induced by magic, potions and exhaustion. When he awoke, it took him a while to come back to his senses. He groaned. His bladder bleated with an urgency that had him jumping from the bed and running to the bathing chamber. He chuckled as he relieved himself—copiously. It was perhaps a good thing he was alone this time.

The gurgle of a nearby spring was too enticing. Each bathing area had one, the warm, constantly replenishing water was fed through a series of pipeworks or there were natural springs in many of the cave homes. Carefully removing the dressings from his stomach, Erzion gingerly probed his red scar. There was no pain—and no pus. Erzion smiled in relief. His wound was completely healed.

Eagerly, he dropped his undershorts then stepped down into the steaming water. Its turbulent warmth caressed his skin. He sighed and relaxed back, enjoying his moment of peace. Then his belly growled. *Right. Food.* He scrubbed his skin until it tingled, then ran a sharp blade over his bearded chin. Satisfied, he climbed out of the water and grabbed a towel. Vigorously, he dried his honed warrior's body. Glad to feel his magic stirring, he inhaled the power-infused air. The energy emanating from the archway behind his home would replenish his magic, though it would not completely lift the darkness from his soul. He sighed. It never did. A pair of brown eyes swam in his mind. Perhaps something else could heal that bleak, lonely part of him.

Dressed in a linen shirt, wool leggings and boots, Erzion strapped a dagger to each thigh and headed down the stone steps. He needed to meet with his commanders. He had been absent from Catava for months, and he needed to apprise himself of any current issues. When the Ice Witches had begun to renege on the trade agreements for the raw Silverbore ore they mined and supplied to Avalonia, the Queen had demanded he show some force in the north. She needed that metal to ensure the Avalonian armouries were fully stocked.

Unfortunately, that meant Erzion had to leave his home. He snarled a little, even after all this time, he hated that he was at the bitch's beck and call.

Erzion requested some food brought to his study. He ate

whilst contemplating when he should return to his quarters at Valentia's palace.

His study was quiet enough that he could sit and think. His guards rarely disturbed him in here. The smell of books, old and new, tickled his nose. He loved this peaceful haven he had cultivated. His eyes drifted to the locked and magic reinforced box which sat on the top shelf before drifting over the thousands of books he owned. He had works and tomes from all over the Eight Kingdoms. This was his sanctuary when he needed to hide from the world.

Erzion rubbed his face. Now he had eaten, he felt weary again. Despite wanting to remain in his true home, for a far different reason than usual, he couldn't stay more than a few weeks. The Queen would be expecting him to report back to her. He clenched his jaw. He knew he should go and find Ophelia, that he should thank her. But common sense—and self-preservation—told him to stay away from the healer who had not left his mind, even whilst sleeping. In his dreams her eyes had changed from chocolate brown to vivid green as he kissed her.

A low growl rumbled up from his chest. His behaviour with her had been irresponsible. Not least because he had never felt such a need to go and seek out a female like he did her. It was disconcerting. Confusing. No, he would not act on his—or her—feelings. He had managed for nearly one thousand years to have nothing but fleeting physical relationships. One beautiful, stubborn female could not be allowed to crack the shield around his heart; to burrow her way in to his emotions.

A knock at the door snapped his head up. "Enter!" he barked, instantly alert.

Ophelia pushed open the door. It didn't escape Erzion's notice that she seemed to square her shoulders and lift her chin, as if giving herself enough courage to walk in.

His shirt stretched tightly over his biceps as he crossed his arms over his chest. Deliberately, he kept his face dark and impassive. But her scent assaulted his senses. It was intoxicating. Against his will, his heart banged in his chest. He shifted his wings, allowing them to flare slightly, then pushed some magic into the markings that adorned them. His eyes glowed—just a little. He knew his show of power intimidated many, and he had to keep this confusing female at a distance. He had no idea how to handle the way she made him react. He had to protect himself.

Do not let her into your heart. Do not let her in.

Ophelia glided forward and stood before his desk.

Erzion waited. He expected a nod, or at least a gesture of some kind to show respect. That was what normally happened. Not because he demanded it but because his warriors and the people of Catava had always freely given it. They knew who and what he was—that it was as much his wizard blood as his red magic that protected this city.

His look darkened further as she stared at his face as if frozen to the spot. She clearly had no intention of showing subservience.

That defiance sparked a wave of desire in his soul. He stood up, leaning forward, his palms flat against the desk top. The wood, smoothed over time by his touch, was cool and familiar against his skin.

Ophelia's throat bobbed as she blinked, following his movements. Her attention grazed over his wings, then as if she couldn't help herself, the rest of his body; her eyes widening a little as his muscles tensed and his nostrils flared.

His heart pounded against his ribs, his blood heating. *Ridiculous! I am nearly one thousand years old. I have managed to survive with my heart intact, even if my soul is shredded. I will not allow her to control me like this, to destroy me.*

He clenched his teeth, wanting to order her away from him. But the words wouldn't come out of his mouth; his throat was too tight to speak. He was fighting a war between his heart and his head—and he knew it.

"I came to see how you feel today, Lord Riddeon," she said,

her eyes meeting and holding his, a slight waver in her voice. She studied him with those huge brown eyes narrowed as if hearing his thoughts, his doubts.

He wanted to tell her to leave, that he would be no good for her, that he had to push her away, that he never let anyone in to his heart. But he didn't.

Her scent changed as he leaned toward her, his wings flaring further. Desire and apprehension tainted the air. He inhaled, his gut tightening as she shuffled her feet. Her own wings flared and shivered a little. She was becoming nervous as the silence lingered between them. But he was still trying to decide how to behave with her. She was infuriating, bossy, defiant—and so damned beautiful he couldn't tear his eyes from her. He wanted to vault over the damned desk and wrap himself around her.

His red gaze swept from the tip of her grey boots, up her body to linger on the curves of her waist and breasts, before moving to the tresses of long chestnut brown hair that cascaded around her flushed face.

Erzion gritted his teeth and sighed, his shoulders slumping. He didn't want to fight the attraction he had for Ophelia, not at all; but he knew he had to. He had to remain distant despite the simmering attraction between them. Swallowing hard, he kept his voice steady. "I'm feeling much recovered, thanks to you, Ophelia. I was going to find you later—to thank you," he said, bending the truth. He had thought about finding her—but he knew he would not have done so. He was a gods damned coward where his heart was concerned. He would have avoided her at all costs.

Ophelia huffed and gave a small regretful smile. "No, my lord, you weren't." She clasped her hands together in front of her as if unsure what to do with them. "But I understand why. A lowly, mortal healer is not a fitting lover for a handsome immortal lord."

Erzion's brows knitted together in a dark frown. *What? Does she seriously believe that's why I am pushing her away?* Still, he did not speak. Despite how it angered him, it was better she believed him so shallow.

Ophelia squared her shoulders, her face becoming impassive. "You will need your wound checked again this evening and daily for a few days," she told him, her clipped and efficient healer's tone grating on his nerves. "If you will consent?"

Erzion nodded once. "Of course," he agreed, his voice flat. His fingers dug into the wooden desk as he fought his instincts to thrust it out of his way so that he could hold her and implore her to forgive his coldness and cowardice, to tell her that she was *too* good for him, and that it was this immortal warrior who did not deserve such a talented, beautiful woman by his side. He wanted to beg her to allow him to pursue her—but he bit his tongue and forced his feet to remain stuck to the floor.

He ground his teeth so hard they hurt, even as his fingernails began to smart under the crushing pressure of his grip on the desk top.

Ophelia pressed her lips into a straight line and nodded with a quiet, resigned sigh. "So be it. Send word later today, when you are ready." She hesitated then added, "I know I have just made this situation uncomfortable by making my feelings so obvious. For that I apologise, but I truly am glad you are recovered, my lord," she said softly, straightening her spine.

The tremor in her voice nearly undid his control. Erzion swallowed then inhaled a steadying breath as he considered his next words.

"I will bid you goodbye then," Ophelia almost whispered.

Erzion still bit down on his words, his plea for her to stay.

Tears lined Ophelia's eyes as she turned on her heel and pulled open the door.

Erzion wanted to call her back but could not bring himself to. No matter how much his heart wanted her, fear paralysed his voice.

Ophelia did not look back.

Erzion spent the next few days carrying out his duties. He met his commanders, he checked on his people and he trained with the First Legion. While his body was exhausted, his mind still churned with thoughts of Ophelia. As another day ended and unsure what else to do to ease the ache in his soul, he headed to the archway. The strange stone always had a calming effect on him, and he welcomed its replenishing effects on his magic.

Its runes flared with light at the touch of his hand. Sighing, he leaned his forehead against the warm stone.

His gardens and home had been built around the archway, to both hide it and protect it, and although he was well-guarded, here in this tranquil garden, he was alone.

"What do I do, Mother?" he asked her long-dead ghost.

The archway seemed to pulse in response. He could almost hear his mother's soft voice echo around the garden. *"Loving someone, even if it's for a short time, is such a gift. One worth any amount of pain."* He swallowed and squeezed his burning eyes shut as he remembered her last words. *"Don't let her turn your heart to ice."*

He had promised his mother he would love, but until now, he had not allowed himself to even hope for such a thing. Memories of Garnald and his mother, of Lexon and Alethia flowed through his mind. He smiled. Maybe it was time to honour that promise to Mariel—to take a chance with his heart. Perhaps he could allow himself happiness with such a kind and beautiful woman as Ophelia—even if it was for a short time.

Erzion jumped to his feet. Loving Ophelia would be worth the inevitable heartbreak. Just as his mother had told him, it would be a gift, one he would cherish. "Thank you," he whispered to his mother's ghost, hoping she could see him from Eternity and would be proud of his decision.

Excitement and apprehension tightened his gut, but Erzion did not falter; he strode quickly into his home. He ordered a guard to go to the healer's section and inform Ophelia he needed her to review his wound. He bit his lip as he watched the guard leave, then turned on his heal and headed towards the stairs. He would bathe and change into something suitable. He stumbled on a step. He had never needed to pursue a female before, they always came to him. *What does one wear for such an occasion?* he wondered with a grin, then his grin widened—she *had* called him handsome. That had to be a good start. All he had to do was persuade her to forgive him for his churlish behaviour and convince her she was more than good enough for an immortal lord who was utterly inept in matters of the heart, despite his age.

Erzion sat in his study waiting impatiently for a knock upon his door. When that knock came, making him jump, he practically ran to let her in. He flung open the study door with such gusto that the thin, green-winged male on the other side, jumped back in surprise.

"Where is Ophelia?" Erzion barked down at the startled healer. His hands curled into fists as disappointment and anger warred for supremacy.

"S-she's back in her quarters," the healer stuttered, wide-eyed. His fear stung Erzion's nose.

"Where? Take me to her—now," ordered Erzion.

The healer gulped and nodded nervously. "Y-yes, sir."

Red warriors fell in behind them as the healer guided a furious Erzion from his home and through the city. The warm air eddied around his glowing wings as they flew to a dwelling on the lower level, near the healers' section of the city. They landed quietly in a nearby garden area.

"There." The healer pointed to a door, flanked either side by a small tree bearing beautiful purple and white blooms.

Erzion eyed the brightly lit windows. "You may go," he told the healer. The male's relief would have amused Erzion but for the anger and nerves churning in his belly. *How could she send someone else to see me?* Then he remembered their conversation. He groaned, his feet dragging on the soft green grass as he walked forward. He hesitated. He needed to think.

Not caring what his men thought, he ordered them away. Reluctantly, they left him. He watched them fly away into the night of the cave city.

When she had said *goodbye* to him in his office, he hadn't thought she actually meant she wouldn't see him again. His lips tightened into a determined line. He would not allow her to believe she was not good enough for him. He had been an idiot to let her think he did not want her. Nothing could be further from the truth.

Striding forward, he lifted his fist and banged on the door. The wood and hinges vibrated under the force of his blows, the sound echoing through the quiet neighbourhood. He did not care, not even as curtains twitched.

The door opened, flooding him and the gardens with light and warmth.

Ophelia's mouth dropped open, her eyes immediately becoming as round as saucers. "My lord?" she whispered, blinking as if she didn't believe her own eyes.

Erzion could not hide the growling quality in his voice. "My name is Erzion," he corrected her.

Ophelia watched, her mouth snapping closed as he stepped close enough she had to step back. Once inside her home, he turned and carefully shut the door. Then he faced her, this female who held his ancient, fragile heart in her hands. She swallowed hard, meeting his burning eyes. His wings flared, the swirls that adorned them burning brightly at her regard. His throat was so tight it was difficult to speak. He knew she could still reject him. And he wouldn't blame her, his cowardice, his fear of being hurt had been reprehensible.

"Why didn't you come to me tonight?" he asked, cringing when the words came out more like an accusation than a gentle question. He took a breath as she crossed her arms protectively over her chest. He had to tell her how he felt about her or this was going to end badly, no matter what she had admitted to feeling for him.

"I needed you," he whispered hoarsely, doing his best not to reach for her.

"No, you didn't," she replied, her voice turning cold. "Torren, the healer I sent, is more than capable of checking your wound."

Gods, she thinks me here for my wound.

"Ophelia, you are not listening to me. I needed *you*. No one else." Heart in his mouth he slowly reached out, giving her time to pull away. When his fingers touched her face, she didn't flinch, merely watched him. His heart hammered painfully against his ribs as he trailed his fingers in a featherlight touch over her soft, full lips. When they parted a little, he couldn't stop the possessive growl that rumbled in his chest.

Ophelia's eyes widened and she jerked away. "Why?" She stepped back and Erzion's hand dropped to his side. Nausea at her rejection churned in his gut. "Why would you need me? You can have anyone you please. I am *nothing* compared to you—"

"Ophelia, stop. You are everything," he whispered. "You are a promise I made to the only woman I have ever loved."

Ophelia snarled and pulled away, her eyes flashing a deep, stormy green.

Erzion bit his lip to keep the satisfied smirk off his face. *The green-eyed monster indeed.* "My mother, Ophelia," he told her, holding her furious gaze. "She made me promise to love—to not become cold and heartless like the Queen. Up until now, I have failed to keep that promise." He stepped close enough to feel the warmth from her body seep into his.

Disbelief twisted her features.

"No, you have to believe me," he entreated. "You are the only person I have met, in all my years in this realm, that has begun to melt the ice around my heart." His chest heaved as he took a huge steadying breath. "Ophelia, no one has ever affected me like you do. Please, will you give me a chance to know you—to love you?" he asked, his voice shaking. He had never felt as vulnerable as he did now.

"But you are the Lord of Catava, the immortal Red Wizard. You have lived for a millennia. What can you possibly see in someone like me? I am mortal, I will age, I am nothing but a speck of dust in your long life. I am nowhere near good enough for you," she protested, her eyes shining with distress and unshed tears.

Erzion reached out, gently cupping her face with both of his hands, preventing her from looking away. Her skin was so soft, so warm beneath his calloused touch. He could not hide the growling quality in his voice. "My name is Erzion," he corrected her again. "And you will always be good enough for me," he breathed, knowing in his heart his words were true.

Opheila opened her mouth to speak but Erzion would not hear any more weak protests. Holding her eyes he lowered his head. The feel of her lips against his, her taste... He fell into everything that was her, knowing he would never want to leave. All he needed to do was convince her of his love too. And he would do whatever it took to win her heart.

CHAPTER 25

ERZION

A frigid autumn wind buffeted Erzion. He signalled for his squad of golden-winged fae to bank left. The movement of his arms exacerbated the vicious aching in his back and shoulder muscles. They burned with every beat of his wings. Nevertheless, he pushed against the saline-laced air.

He turned his golden gaze to where Tu Lanah hung like a great pale eye over the ocean. It would be at least two months before it caused the winter storms to rage.

When he had left Avalonia, it had still been a balmy summer; now the air temperature had plummeted.

Still, he reasoned, *it is only just dawn.*

Erzion hated that he had been away from home—his true home, for so long.

The Hourian king had been as arrogant and annoying as always. However, the Queen insisted upon Erzion attending the yearly trade meeting. Not to negotiate, of course; she would never trust him to do such an important task, even after a millennia of leading her armies. He was her warrior dog, obedient and fierce when needed, nothing more. He sometimes thought she forgot he existed; he sometimes thought she didn't remember who he had once been.

Erzion had once loved the duties she gave him away from Avalonia's shores, but now he hated it when she ordered him to personally protect her emissary, whoever that may be.

Erzion's face twisted, looking as if he were trying to swallow a bitter taste. The immortal Hourian king was known for his disdain of females—human, fae or otherwise. It was why the Queen had sent the toad-like councilwoman to negotiate on her behalf. Erzion didn't think it really had anything to do the woman's negotiating skill, but more to do with the fact that she was female, ugly and forthright. All the things the king hated in the opposite sex.

The past three weeks had been long and boring. Babysitting the woman, both behind the negotiating table and in her other activities, had driven Erzion to the point of madness. As had the king's attitude. He had always hated the selfish leader, but as the king was one of the only immortals left in this world, Erzion had to be respectful to him, even when all he really wanted to do was break his supercilious face.

Refusing to take the ship home with the emissary, Erzion had left enough warriors to protect the vessel and flown with the remainder of his men back to Valentia. It was a gruelling journey, with only an occasional rocky island to rest upon, but Erzion had done it many times over the past thousand years. There were plenty of supplies and good shelter on the rest stops. He knew because he had ordered them stocked for fae travellers years ago.

He and his men had rested only for the bare minimum of time. Erzion was desperate to get back to Ophelia and their beautiful son.

Erzion cringed to realise that before Ophelia had melted his heart, he had allowed himself to become nothing more than the Queen's puppet, leading her armies with cold precision and very little mercy. Only Catava had left him with any purpose, a kernel of hope in the recesses of his heart and mind.

He grinned. Ophelia often reminded him of Lexon. Her under-confidence in her role as his lady had been endearing, but it had melted away to leave a kind and self-assured woman in its wake.

Erzion swallowed hard, his memories of Lexon were still secreted away in his heart and soul, along with the memories of his beautiful mother. Sometimes it was like remembering a wonderful dream when he let himself relive his life growing up alongside the red prince.

Tanelle, on the other hand, was a painful memory, even now. Erzion had never forgiven himself for failing her. Despite Alethia's words, he was convinced she would have returned to reclaim the throne and set him free—if she hadn't been thrown into a never-ending sleep by using that spear.

Oh, she had been long forgotten by the Queen, but he had no idea if Tanelle still slept in that cave below the obsidian palace Lexon had constructed.

None of the spies he sent could ever find any information about her other than in legends and songs, which were not helpful. He had tried in the past to get into that room, but Lexon's wards still held strong. Only those with Arjuno blood in their veins could enter her resting place.

Today, though, he just wanted to return to his family. Ophelia and Elexon had given him a different purpose, one of love. For the first time in nearly a millennia he had allowed himself to truly *feel*. His mate and his son were a gift, and though his time with them would be short, he would not waste it.

And being with that spiteful councilwoman these last weeks had definitely wasted it.

A dark scowl furrowed Erzion's brow.

The Queen did not know about his family. She would discover his son's existence at some point, of that he was sure, but not yet.

Erzion's jaw muscles tensed. He would keep Elexon well away from the Queen, even when he grew to maturity and joined the ranks of the fae army. There were other fae in Valentia who shared his last name; one more Riddeon among the ranks would not raise suspicion.

Erzion had already begun Elexon's training. His son would be prepared, and have the skills to play this dangerous game with the Queen. Erzion would make sure of it.

Glamoured and golden-winged, Erzion took a deep breath and propelled himself onward. Once he had visited the training yard to address the new recruits, he would return to Ophelia. His gut squeezed in anticipation. He had missed her tender smile, her scent, and the feel of her soft curves moulding to his.

Against the force of the wind on his face, a smile curled his lips.

Would Elexon have changed much these last weeks? Would his wings have manifested fully?

At ten years old, the son he had named after his soul brother, had begun to change. When Erzion had left, Elexon's wings had begun to expand and glow with the colour of his magic.

Erzion was so proud his son was a red wing. Of course, he would never voice such pride in the hearing of others, but he loved that his son would be a powerful wielder of light and heat. Maybe he would even carry some of Erzion's wizard blood.

Erzion grinned. He would soon begin teaching his son how to glamour and how to cast.

Only two of his guards accompanied him to the barracks after Erzion sent the others to their quarters to rest.

As he flew over the city, other fae manoeuvred out of their way. At the palace walls the palace guards dutifully stopped them and made him repeat the call sign. He nodded his approval and commended them for not trusting their eyes. The warriors relaxed a little, clearly anxious they may have offended their Master Commander.

Erzion dived down over the barracks, then levelled out, surveying those below him. Many paled or stumbled. The sight of their immortal commander instilled fear in many of his troops.

Erzion ignored them. He was here to do just that; besides, it had been too many years for it bother him anymore.

The new recruits needed to respect as well as fear him. And respect was hard to earn if you were only a tale or a name in a book. Erzion didn't acknowledge that he was, in fact, a living legend. He refused to acknowledge it.

Ophelia teased him about it incessantly, though it had taken him months to persuade her many of the stories about him and his cruelty were simply not true.

He grinned.

Ophelia had never been one to truly listen to those tales.

Erzion was thankful she had given him a chance to prove himself worthy of her. He had taken many lovers over the years, but none had even come close to penetrating that icy cage around his heart. Ophelia, however, had cracked it and then completely melted it away in a matter of days.

Erzion kept his face blank and imposing, even as the prospect of holding his love and their son filled him with a giddy sense of joy.

Ranks of new warriors filled the barracks. He had sent word he wanted to address his new troops today. With the exception of very few, their faces turned up to watch him as he hovered above the dusty training yard.

Erzion pushed a little magic into his armoured wings, intentionally making his markings glow brighter. To most of the young warriors below, that sight would be utterly new. Learning to armour and push magic into their wings was only something taught to warriors in the Queen's army. Civilian fae were never taught such skills.

He swallowed a sigh as the stench of fear reached his nostrils. He had never been intentionally cruel to his soldiers but that was the power of carefully crafted lies. It was easy to distort the truth and turn it into the stories people wanted to hear; those stories became legend, especially over hundreds of years.

Hovering, he allowed his gaze to travel over the nearest young warriors, then flew at a leisurely pace over the others, making sure to hold the eye of any who dared catch his gaze.

He tried not to roll his eyes. Young males, even some females, when going through their *urge,* could be spectacularly arrogant and aggressive. Erzion tried to remember what it had been like for him and Lexon, then swallowed his grin as memories flooded his mind. Even after this long, his adolescent antics with his friend were fresh in his mind.

For most fae the *urge* passed after a year or so, but for some it became unmanageable. They
lost themselves to their baser instincts. It was Erzion's job to root out those who were destroyed by the urge to mate. They would be incarcerated until their sanity returned, or if they showed no sign of rationality and self-control, he had no choice but to send them to the Hourian jewel mines or Silverbore mines in the frozen north. He knew the Ice Witches treated the unstable fae far better than the Hourians did, so that was his preference.

It did not sit well with Erzion to send away his countrymen to what amounted to a life of slavery, but keeping unstable fae in the city prison to rot was equally unpleasant.

On the other side of the yard, Erzion noticed the Lord Commander of the Queen's Elite guard bringing in a group of young boys ranging from about six to ten years old. It was hard not to react. Hundreds of years ago the Queen had taken on the practice of procuring her elite guard as babies. Supposedly the poor boys were gifted from their parents, and it was an honour to be chosen.

Erzion snarled, hating that people actually believed those lies, or at least pretended to. His impotence in stopping this practice made his blood boil.

Her elite guards followed her orders without question. He swallowed the bile that burned the back of his throat. They had no choice but to take the tiny males from their homes, either by threatening their parents or just snatching the poor things from their beds. It had always sickened him, but now that he had Elexon, he could not imagine the devastation he would feel at losing his son and never knowing where he had gone. If it wasn't for his pledge to his goddess, not to mention his promise to the High Ruler of the Guardians, Erzion would have killed the Queen a hundred times over for destroying so many lives.

Erzion watched as Lord Commander Ream smacked a brown-haired boy on the side of the head, sending the young one sprawling face down in the dirt. The boy glared up at his commander defiantly, but Erzion could see the way his eyes glistened, the fear he carried under the surface. It sickened Erzion to ignore it.

"You will come to my chambers after training. You need to be taught a lesson in respect, Sarou!" barked Ream, grabbing the scruff of the boy's tunic and dragging him to his feet. Roughly, he shoved the now pale-faced boy back in line.

Ream stalked over to a nearby weapons rack. Choosing a short, wooden training sword, he spun and threw it at the boy, who caught it without hesitation.

"Tallo, keep that filth out of our way!" he yelled across the yard to where Captain Tallo Nosco had entered, flanked by another young boy.

Erzion saw a smaller boy jump as Ream's meaty forefinger pointed directly at him.

"You! Tawne! Take your foul, shifter stench over there too," ordered Ream, before turning his back, effectively dismissing Tallo and the boys.

With pale blue eyes, the young shifter looked over to where Tallo stood, something like relief on his face.

Erzion almost smiled as the boy tried to curb his enthusiasm and half-walked, half-ran away from Ream. Below him, the mass of new recruits began to shuffle. He was well aware they were waiting for his address.

Let them wait, Erzion decided. The dark-haired boy with Tallo had caught the Master Commander's curiosity. The boy seemed to be around eight years old, but that was where the similarity to any other boy in Valentia ended.

Ignoring his duties and the army awaiting him, Erzion slammed his feet into the ground in front of Tallo. To his credit, Tallo did not flinch or show surprise, he merely placed his fist to his chest and bowed his head.

Ream watched from his place across the yard but he did not approach. No, Ream had the sense to stay away from Erzion when possible, especially after Erzion had given him the long, ugly scar which marred his hateful face.

Erzion glanced at the Lord Commander, his own gaze icy. He snarled a warning.

Ream scowled but looked away.

Erzion stepped forward, his boots scraping on the gritty ground.

Tallo gestured for the boys to step up next to him. When the boys complied, they stared wide-eyed at the immortal Master Commander. It took effort not to smile at their awed faces. Both were frightened—he could smell it—but both boys copied Tallo's greeting then met his gaze.

Each was defiant in their own way. It was only when he found himself looking into a sea of sapphire blue flecked with silver that Erzion froze. All thought ceased and grief hit him with the full force of a winter storm.

He couldn't breathe. Pain seared his heart.

For a moment all he could do was stare back at the child.

Lexon!

This boy had Lexon's eyes.

Erzion almost gave into the weight of his grief. Tears blurred his vision and his knees actually wobbled. He swallowed against the painful lump in his throat. It was like being shoved back in time to when he and Lexon were boys, facing each other on the training field.

He was so wrapped up in his memories and grief that Erzion didn't see Tallo's brow furrow or his eyes dart between the Master Commander and the dark-haired boy. He didn't notice anything—until Tallo coughed—loudly.

Erzion immediately tried to pull himself together. He looked away from the boy's intense stare. In the background, Ream's squad had started to spar. The sound of wooden swords battering against each other filled the air.

Sweat lightly beaded his brow as he studied the boy. *Amazing! Blue wings.* Already stunning, they had begun to grow from the child's back. As yet, they were undersized, but covered in a glossy new growth of feathers that shone like liquid silk in the autumn sunlight.

An image of Firan's unique robes came to mind.

Erzion frowned. *How has this child survived the Queen's need to consume magic? How has he survived at all in a city where fae with wings other than gold or pearlescent are persecuted?*

Erzion had hunted down many red and green-winged fae over the years. Some he managed to get to before the Queen, others he did not. Now they were so rare, the Queen had to hunt outside Avalonia to find them. He knew she needed to consume their magic to sustain her own. And no matter how rare they had become, she *always* managed to find one.

His throat bobbed.

Erzion had never seen blue wings—ever. They were utterly unique.

"Master Commander? Sir? Is everything alright?" asked Tallo slowly, suspiciously.

Was it? Erzion had no idea. *Is this who I have been waiting for? Not a queen, but a king?*

Inhaling slowly, deliberately, then exhaling in the same manner, Erzion composed himself. In control once again, he turned to the captain.

Tallo was a tall and powerful warrior, and although he had been allocated to work with the Elite Guard recruits, Erzion had never seen him be cruel; harsh—demanding even, but never cruel.

Erzion looked directly into Tallo's face.

"Of course. I was just—interested in your new recruits," he explained softly.

Tallo raised his brows, then smiled, looking meaningfully at the boy. "It's understandable, sir. Most people are."

Erzion almost smiled back until he heard the boy growl. Long, low and resentful.

Slowly, deliberately, Erzion turned and met that stunning sapphire stare. Anger and resentment burned back at him.

Swift as the wind, Erzion spun. When he stopped, a dagger lay against the boy's throat. But the boy did not flinch, he only lifted his chin defiantly. Silky strands of sable and blue hair slid over Erzion's arm.

"Do not dare to growl at your superiors, boy. You are different, and as such will always be an object of curiosity for others. Deal with it!" he advised loudly, then he lowered his voice and tapped the boy's chest with his free hand. "Inside here. Do not allow anyone to destroy what is in here. Cage your heart. Protect the courage that burns inside here from the evil that surrounds you," he whispered, so quietly even Tallo would not hear him.

The boy's eyes shot to Erzion's, wide with shock, but he recovered quickly and nodded once. "Yes, sir," he said, loudly enough it seemed as if he were answering Erzion's command to show respect.

"Good," Erzion said, raising his voice to a normal level. He straightened, thankful for the cold breeze fanning his hot face. The leather of his flying armour creaked slightly as he moved to face the boy. He placed his hands on the boy's solid shoulders. "What is your name?"

The boy held his gaze. If he was confused by Erzion's reaction to him, he did not let it show. "Hugo Casimir, sir," he answered, strong and unafraid.

Erzion inhaled through his nose. "Well, Hugo Casimir," he replied sternly. "Do not think to show such insolence to a superior again." With that, he nodded to Tallo and flung his wings out, armouring them more slowly than normal for the benefit of the boys. Inwardly he grinned as Hugo's eyes widened. Feeling simultaneously high with hope and sick with fear for the boy, Erzion bent his knees and tensed the already stiff muscles of his back.

Both boys watched as Erzion raised himself into the air. With controlled movements, Erzion continued his perusal of his new troops. He went through the usual speech, landed and spoke with the squadron captains and commanders. He even assessed a few of the new recruits' fighting skills. All the while, all he could think of was how he was going to ensure the safety of the boy with the sapphire eyes, until it was time for him to fulfil his destiny.

∼

Far across time and space the High Ruler fixed his multi-faceted eyes upon the events unfolding in the mortal world.

His attention shifted through the lands of the Eight Kingdoms to a young silver-haired girl who played with her father, oblivious to the power that simmered in her blood.

Soon the events that he had foreseen would unfold. He could only hope destiny would see fit to grant both the Eight Kingdoms and his own world a chance at survival.

The High Ruler raised his magnificent horned head. Around him the Guardians of Eternity regarded him, their eyes shining with inner fire. He had no heart to tell his brothers and sisters of the death and war he had foreseen.

It would serve no purpose.

He still had hope.

Instead, he raised his head, opened his huge jaws and released a roar that shook the foundations of every realm.

Even destiny listened.

EPILOGUE

Twelve years later

Sulphurious slammed his talons into the ground, screeching with rage. He had been given one stinking taste of freedom! One! The Lord of Souls had reclaimed him, pulling him back to the coldness and the dark of Chaos with a suddenness that made his great horned head spin. He snarled. The icy air hurt his lungs, but that agony seemed tenfold after breathing the warmth of the mortal world.

His mother's key had almost been in his grasp. Its power had called to him. It was his to reclaim—and he had been thwarted—by his own lord!

The girl's new and untamed magic had been astonishing, especially with the might of another's magic abetting it, but he was certain he had been close to breaking down her shield. In fact, he was sure of it!

His stinking breath saturated the air as he snarled.

"Oh, do quiet yourself, guardian. Your key will be easily found again. That young mortal prince is too stupid to know what he holds. And I have my sights set on more than just that one key," his master said.

Sulphurious huffed but quieted down. He had no choice. Erebos was the one who commanded his allegiance and his obedience.

He lowered his horned head. His mirror-black scales gleamed and rippled in the soft light the goddess emanated. He stared balefully at the emaciated woman. It pleased him to stomp closer, knowing how her cage of souls would react.

Those trapped souls writhed, held in their columns by the magic of his lord. Screaming filled the air.

The goddess cringed, wincing as the high pitched wails hurt her sensitive ears.

Sulphurious snarled his satisfaction at her pain even as Erebos chuckled darkly.

"How are you, sister?" the Lord of Souls crooned, brushing his long, dark hair from his colourless face. His attention fixed upon her face, nothing but a void of darkness where his eyes should be.

Lunaria shot him a steady glare, but did not bother to speak. Only her eyes were bright, conveying her hate; the rest of her was faded, utterly depleted by captivity in Chaos.

"No? Still no words for your loving brother?"

She looked away.

Sulphurious narrowed his red eyes. Maybe it was the light of the mortal world which had affected his sight, but those blue eyes seemed brighter, more alert.

Erebos sighed dramatically, seeming not to notice. "But Sulphurious and I have such good news," he continued. He lowered his skeletal body, squatting down to watch his sister's face through the writhing bars of her cell. "Your true heir has awoken, sister dearest. My way into your precious, mortal world of souls is coming. Soon, all of them, all of that power will be mine—along with the keys." Smirking, he ran a blackened fingernail down a column of the captured souls, then inhaled the ones who broke free from their torture, consuming them.

Sulphurious ignored the screaming of those still trapped; instead, he watched a light flicker in the goddess's eyes. He snarled, baring his black teeth.

Hope.

Anger erupted from him in a huge roar. She had no right to hope.

"Do not fret, guardian. Her heir will not survive long enough to stop us. You will soon be returned to the mortal world to find your precious key. I, on the other hand, have much to plan for before I can join you."

Sulphurious stretched his newly healed wings. For the past millennia they had remained shredded—until Erebos had felt the magic of Eternity stir in the mortal realm. With a flick of his wrist he had healed them and sent him to hunt. Sulphurious went gladly. He would serve this god eternally to repay him for such a gift, but ultimately he knew they wanted the same thing—war and revenge; and the Lord of Souls needed him to get it.

Once Sulphurious had his mother's key in his grasp, he would take great pleasure in hunting down and destroying his brother. Vaalor was in that mortal world somewhere, hiding like the coward he was—from grief—from responsibility. It was time he paid for sending Sulphurious to this realm of darkness and ice.

Erebos shimmered into shadow and mist before disappearing.

Knowing it would cause her pain, Sulphurious dropped his bulk onto the ice-covered ground next to the goddess's cage. Maliciously, he ran his talons over those screaming, trapped souls —again and again.

As the black dragon revelled in the goddess's pain, as he waited impatiently for his lord to return him to that mortal realm, he grinned. He would no longer have to suffer the ice that coated his belly. He would drink from the Fire Mountains, then he would wreak destruction across all the Eight Kingdoms. Finally, he would see Eternity and his brother, burn.

∼

The End
Please can you spare a moment to review my book? Reviews are so important for visibility for indie authors and to help other readers find new books. Thank you!

(Read on for Chapter One of A Bond of Venom and Magic: Book One in The Goddess and the Guardians series)

The Goddess and the Guardians series continues here:
https://karentomlinson.com/goddess-guardians-series/

KAREN TOMLINSON
USA TODAY BESTSELLING AUTHOR
A BOND OF
VENOM
AND MAGIC
THE GODDESS AND THE GUARDIANS
BOOK ONE

KAREN TOMLINSON

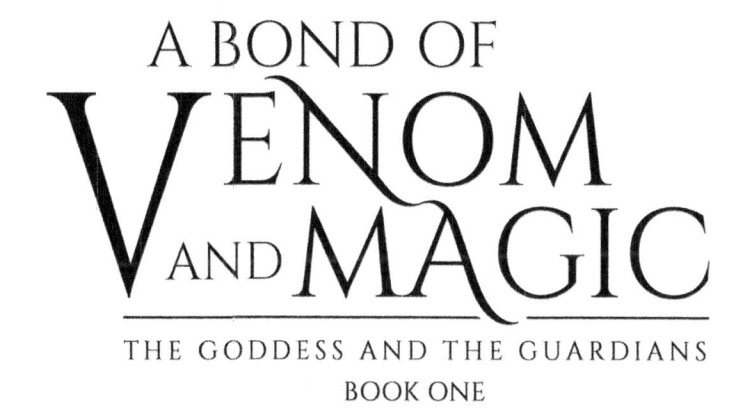

A BOND OF VENOM AND MAGIC

THE GODDESS AND THE GUARDIANS
BOOK ONE

CHAPTER 1

Silence swept through the forest, deafening to Arades Gillon's fae ears. In the act of shoving a freshly felled tree further onto the ancient cart, he froze, his gut twisting with fear. The fresh scent of pine sap tickled his nose as he ignored the woodcutters bantering across the small clearing.

He pushed his bulk upright. Sweat beaded between his shoulder blades and trickled down his spine. Arades sucked in a deep breath, desperately reaching for the cold, calculating calm that had kept him alive for so many years.

It wasn't there. His heart raced, pounding against his ribs; for the first time in his life, Arades readied himself to flee from his enemy. His breath became shallow and fast, his keen eyes searching out the nightmarish shadow that lurked in the gloom of the old forest. It wouldn't be alone.

A guttural growl rippled through the trees, sinking deep into his bones. A violent shudder racked his body. For seventeen years that sound had been blissfully absent from his life; there was no mistaking it. The creature fixed its yellow, predatory gaze on one of the other woodcutters.

Arades had to run. Now.

Spinning on his heel, he burst into motion.

The Seeker snarled. Drool ran from its gaping jaws as it leaped from the dark shadows.

Yelling a warning to his friends would achieve nothing. They were as good as dead. Wild snarling filled the air as more Seekers burst from the forest. Petrified screams were cut short as human throats were slashed open by razor sharp claws.

Arades did not look back. Experience told him what he would see, and he did not wish to see his friends die such violent deaths. Terror squeezed his heart as yet more screams were abruptly silenced.

He would not—could not—fail. Panicked, Arades increased his effort and sprinted toward the town, its people and his beloved daughter.

~

The Seekers tore at the warm flesh and blood of the dead men, splintering and gnawing on their bones. Cranach gorged himself quickly and efficiently. He growled long and low; that small amount of warm human flesh did not sate his blood lust. If anything, he craved more. His pack had travelled for weeks without stopping to hunt, bypassing settlements where fresh fae and human flesh lived. On and on they had run, focused only on surviving and reaching their prey.

Relenting for one moment Cranach watched his brothers feast with an almost paternal relish, giving his starving pack time to drink the blood that would make them strong again. Minutes later, when only blood and ragged remains soiled the ground, Cranach snarled. The pack reacted instantly.

Their prey was so close; he could almost taste her filthy, mixed blood. She would not escape now. Besides failure would mean having his body broken slowly and painfully into pieces by his lord. His clawed fingers curled tightly around a small scrap of cloth. Snarling in distaste, he raised it to his nostrils, inhaling the sickly sweet scent that clung to it. This girl was more than the usual mix of human and fae, she was something he had never encountered before. The ancient power in her stench burned his sensitive nose, causing him to snort mucus into the air in an effort to expel it.

Revolted, he bared his teeth, stretched his body to its full height and howled. The pack instantly followed Cranach's order. The muscles of their back legs bunched and rippled under their thick, greenish-brown hair as they burst into movement. Sweat glistened across their filthy, humanoid torsos, and their gore-covered jaws snapped menacingly at each other.

With shoulders hunched and heads thrust forward, the Seekers ducked between the branches of the dense trees.

Cranach growled, snapping a tree branch out of his way with one gigantic claw. Running upright was impossible in this forest. He howled once. His brothers immediately complied with his order. Without breaking stride, the Seekers fell on to all four limbs and increased their speed. Their black claws churned up the forest floor as they charged towards their prey and the unsuspecting trade town nearby.

~

Arades pumped his arms and legs until they burned, crashing through the forest, forgoing stealth. Wind rushed by his ears as he forced himself to go faster. Vaulting a rotten, moss covered tree trunk, his hands slipped and he stumbled over exposed slimy tree roots as he landed. Years of training and instinct kicked in and he righted himself immediately.

The forest was so thick around the northern trade town of Berriesford that taking to the sky was impossible. Arades needed at least ten feet of clear space around him to spread his wings and fly. His lungs burned, sweat running down his forehead into his eyes. Feral snarling and crashing permeated the dark damp shadows behind him as the beasts gave chase, but he dare not look back lest he stumble and fall.

Brambles clutched at his boots, branches catching his clothes and legs—but he pushed on resolutely, his long legs devouring the uneven ground.

He broke from the forest into the arable land surrounding the town. Arades roared as he launched himself upwards into the sky. He snapped out his wings and beat against the air, faster and with more vigour than he had used for years. Thousands of tiny feathers covered the strong membranes, catching the invisible strength of the breeze.

Gods, he had been so stupid! As a warrior he should have flown more, armoured more... "Complacent idiot!" he berated himself.

His wings were weak from underuse. Arades clenched his jaw, forcing the armoured particles out from between his feathers, shifting them with his fae magic until they completely covered the whole of his wing span. Within seconds a burnished, golden metal coated his wings, tattooed with his own unique pattern of glowing markings.

The stone town of Berriesford nestled in gently rolling farmland two miles in the distance. Even from here he could see the busy trade roads leading into the town. Arades swallowed his fear for all those people, feeling the malevolent presence of the Seekers behind him. With all his strength, he drove himself onward using the wind to help him soar towards his daughter.

Curious faces looked up. Berriesford folk were unaccustomed to seeing armoured fae warriors in their skies. Trouble was scarce in these parts since the treaty with the Ice Witches nearly one hundred years earlier.

Arades ignored their surprised exclamations and gazed anxiously toward the roof of his own small house. Landing solidly on the dirt track outside his home, Arades sprinted to his front door. He nearly knocked the door off its hinges. The shelves he had put up the month before rattled enough to knock down the small statue of Lunaria, the goddess of creation. It smashed into pieces on the floor. Arades grimaced, hoping that was not a bad omen.

"Diamond! *Diamond! Where are you!*" he bellowed.

He belatedly remembered she was working in the school house. He had promised Tanelle, Diamond's mother, he would educate their daughter and that is what he had done. Now she was on the other side of town, the side nearest to the beasts that hunted her. Growling with frustration at his stupid mistake, he grabbed his two Silverbore swords from beside the fireplace, turned and ran back outside.

The stooped form of General Edo came limping around the corner of the house. To the people of Berriesford this man had only ever been seen as a scruffy forest dweller—a loner, who lived in a small hut in the forest and spent his time gathering and selling the sweet yellow berries that grew among its vast emerald depths.

"Arades! What's going on?" General Edo shouted, narrowing his steely grey eyes and scrutinising Arades' armoured wings and urgent movements.

"They're here! They're here for her. We have to get her away from this town. *Now!*" shouted Arades, his brown eyes full of anxiety.

His friend nodded and immediately shook off his tattered cloak. General Edo straightened his shoulders and spine to expand his wings, transforming into a fae as tall and broad as Arades. Metal shimmered across the general's wings. Grim-faced and determined, both fae warriors bent their knees, spread their golden wings and launched in to the sky.

Continued in Book One. Available on Amazon, iBooks, Kobo, Nook, Smashwords.

Find your next book here: ***https://karentomlinson.com/goddess-guardians-series/***

Book Two: ***A Bond of Blood and Fire*** available now on Amazon and FREE in Kindle Unlimited.

Book Three: ***A Bond of Sovereigns and Souls*** coming spring 2018

NEWSLETTER

Newsletter sign up:
http://karentomlinson.com/newsletter-landing-page/

ABOUT THE AUTHOR

Karen Tomlinson is the author of The Goddess and the Guardians YA fantasy books.

Karen adores books and will read any genre that catches her eye, but she likes nothing better than an epic fantasy, heavy on the romance, which is set in a new and magical world.

Karen lives in Derbyshire, England, (think Mr Darcy territory) with her husband, twin girls and her dalmatian, Poppy. When she is not busy writing, reading (or eating cake and drinking coffee) Karen likes to keep active. She has been practicing Shotokan karate since being fifteen, loves running, mountain biking and walking in the hills with her family.

Karen loves to connect with her readers. Join her mailing list and Facebook group for the latest on her books and giveaways or just to chat.

Follow Karen:
Twitter @kytomlinson
Facebook group:
Karentomlinson'sSilverGuardians
https://www.facebook.com/groups/1531458143821861/
Facebook Page:
https://www.facebook.com/ktomlinson.author/
Instagram:
@karentomlinsonauthor

ACKNOWLEDGMENTS

First of all I have to thank you, wonderful reader, for taking the time to read ABODAD. I hope Erzion's and Lexon's journey has taken you to a new and fantastical world which you have enjoyed reading as much as I have writing. This book is for all the readers of The Goddess and the Guardians series to show the events that have led up to the beginning of Hugo and Diamond's story. There is more to tell and I can't wait to share their epic journey with you all.

There are a few people I'd like to say *thanks* to. I'm sure you know, writing can be very solitary process, but producing a book is not. I could not have done this without the feedback of my wonderful beta readers. I have to say a huge *thank you*, once again, to Lauren Rebecca Hassan whose honesty made me work hard to make this book and Lexon's character, better. *Thank you* to my lovely friend Jenny Baker. Your continued support and encouragement, not to mention giving me an ear to bend, and a shoulder to cry on keeps me sane (Well, relatively)!

And I can't miss out my gorgeous family. Aaron, Annie and Abbie, thank you for putting up with my obsession with writing, for all the evenings you have entertained each other whilst I have retreated to my fantasy world to write. I love you all.

Printed in Great Britain
by Amazon